Istanbul Love Bus

a novel

Tom Brosnahan

Travel Info Exchange, Inc.

Published by Travel Info Exchange, Inc.
Concord, Massachusetts USA
infoexchange.com
books@infoexchange.com
tom@tombrosnahan.com
Ver. IS 80426

ISBN 10: 0-9767531-4-6

ISBN 13: 978-0-9767531-4-8

CONTENTS

For all my friends in Turkey.
Müteşekkirim.

Answers to all the questions of our lives,
and our very destiny,
can be read in the sacred letters
the Almighty has written on our faces.

—Nur Baba

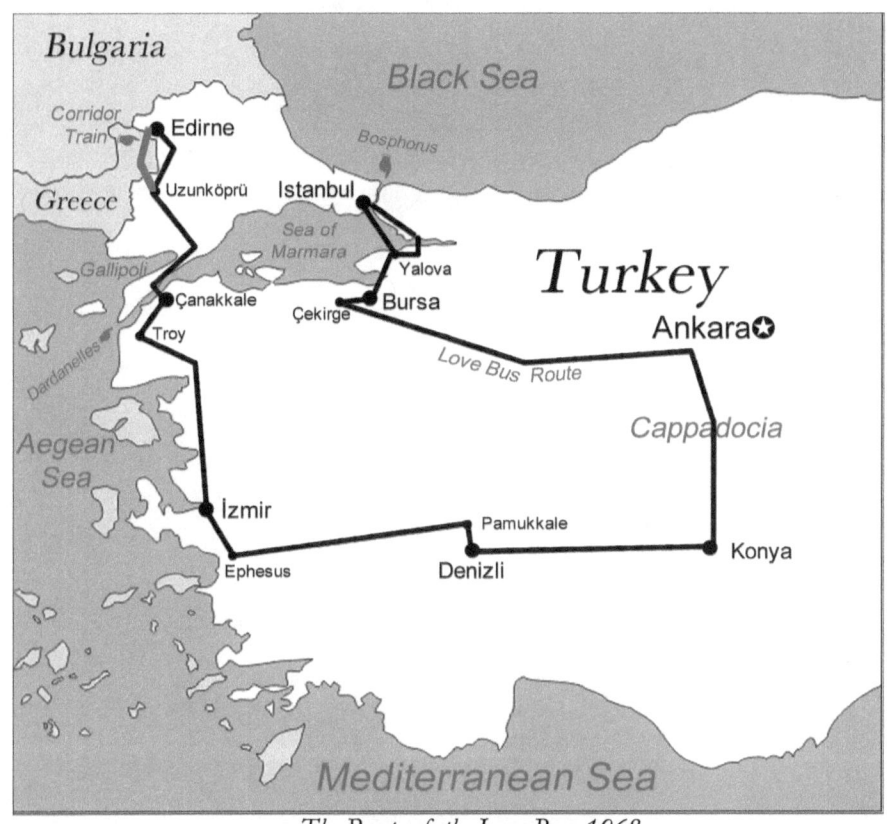

The Route of the Love Bus, 1968.

Turkish Spelling

The Turkish alphabet uses several letters not used in English, including the soft-g (ğ), s-cedilla (ş) and undotted-i (ı). For pronunciation rules, see *100TravelWords.com*.

Prologue

"Aman!" Ahmet Kamanbay gasped.

He pushed a button on the armrest of his car door, it swung open, and he scrambled from his limousine to stare at the cataclysm.

People close to the explosion ran from it in terror, those farther away gaped in shock.

Kamanbay's face was stung by the heat of the inferno sweeping down from the Selimiye Mosque, the greatest masterpiece of Ottoman architecture.

Two hundred meters away, as the driver of a Mercedes sedan stared in amazement at the fireball, a tall blonde woman sitting in the back lunged forward and grabbed with both hands for the pistol on the front seat. The driver whipped his head around toward her and she jerked her left elbow violently into his face. When he opened his throbbing eyes he was staring into the muzzle of the gun.

"Let me out!" she screamed.

The driver pushed a button. Click. The woman swung open the left rear door and leapt out. Pistol in both hands still pointing at his head, she shrieked "GO!"

Tires screeched. The car sped away.

She stood on the street corner and stared up the hill at the inferno, staggering backward as an even bigger explosion shot a gigantic mass of smoke and flame into the sky.

* * *

In the Soviet Russian Consulate-General in Istanbul, 240 kilometers to the southeast, GRU Lieutenant Colonel Boryana Zimanskieva glanced at the clock on her office wall, took a long pull on her cigarette, and smiled. November 14, 1968, she thought. A good day. A day to remember.

A day of victory!

PART ONE

SEPTEMBER

1

1968

The hippy Summer of Love was last year. This year, the world was on fire.

By New Year's Day 1968, the US military's Operation Rolling Thunder had dropped 864,000 tons of bombs on North Vietnam.

In January, with Russian and Chinese aid, North Vietnamese troops flooded into South Vietnam for the Tet offensive.

By February, with over a half-million Americans in Vietnam, the United States reported the highest number of American casualties of the war so far: 543 killed and 2,547 injured in just one week.

(By the end of the war, the number of Vietnamese soldiers and civilians killed would be over 3.4 million—more than 8% of the country's entire population.)

In March, his leadership weakened by the war, President Lyndon B Johnson announced that he would not run for re-election.

On April 4th, Rev. Dr. Martin Luther King, Jr. was assassinated in Memphis, Tennessee. Riots broke out in more than 100 US cities.

In May, students and union workers protested in France, leading to bloody police riots and a nationwide general strike. President Charles de Gaulle fled to a French military base in Germany.

In June, university students in Istanbul demonstrated and the police response led to more protests and riots.

In Los Angeles, a candidate in the election for the presidency of the United States, Senator Robert F Kennedy, was assassinated.

In *August, Soviet Russian, Polish, East German, Bulgarian, and Hungarian troops invaded Czechoslovakia and put an end to the liberal reformist "Prague Spring" government of Alexander Dubček.*

At the Democratic Party's National Convention in Chicago, 10,000 demonstrators clashed with 23,000 police and National Guard troops.

2

Bruce

"How much?" Bruce asked.

"Cinq francs," the *bouquiniste* answered.

Bruce nodded, and the bookseller carefully wrapped the small blue hardcover book in a square of newspaper. Bruce handed him five francs, took the book and walked past the other bouquinistes perched on the stone wall of the Quai de Montebello. Across the Seine on the Île de la Cité, the Cathédrale Notre-Dame de Paris loomed in his peripheral vision on a hot mid-August day. He turned left, walked through the Place Saint-Michel and saw an empty seat in a café on the Place Saint-André-des-Arts. He sat and ordered *une bière.*

Hachette World Guides - Turkey, 1960 edition. He opened the book to the Istanbul section and began to read.

The next morning he dressed in his usual travel garb: white shirt, slender tie, blue blazer and grey slacks, and took the Métro to the Gare de Lyon.

"Orient Express à Istamboul," he said to the ticket-seller. "One person, one way."

"First class, yes?" the agent asked.

"Second class, please."

The agent stared at him for a few seconds, then counseled him strongly to go first class.

"It may not be necessary in Europe, but you will be *plus content* in the Balkans, I assure you," he said. "A first-class ticket costs 386 francs."

"Okay," Bruce said.

"And you would be even more comfortable in a sleeping compartment," the ticket-seller added, "for 600 francs more."

"No," Bruce answered. "Out of my budget."

Bruce was six feet tall and, in his own opinion, ten pounds heavier than he should have been, but not fat. He wore his blue blazer, white shirt and grey slacks while traveling. If you're dressed well, he thought, you get more respect and cooperation.

He had bought the used, eight-year-old guidebook on a whim, but a half hour's reading in the café had convinced him that this was his next stop: Istanbul.

What struck him was the variety of religions: Greek and Armenian Orthodox, Sephardic Jewish, Catholic, Protestant, Syriac, and among the Muslims Sunni, Shi'a, Alawite, Sufi and more. For a graduate student in Religious Studies, this was religion in the real world, not in a Berkeley classroom. The great cathedrals of France were astonishing, but France was traditionally Roman Catholic, a faith familiar from his growing up in Stockton, California, with its Cathedral of the Annunciation. He also knew about Baptists—or at least some of them. His father was a Baptist pastor.

What about all the other religions in the wider world? Why did people believe such different things? Why did these beliefs, based on love and generosity, cause people to despise and even to harm one another?

He walked from his hotel on the Rue Saint-André-des-Arts to Notre-Dame for a last look. The first person in his family to travel to Europe, Bruce was awed by the cathedral's size, grandeur and workmanship—much more impressive than the one in Stockton—and that it took nearly two centuries to build.

For thousands of years, from the great temples along the Nile to the Parthenon and the Hagia Sophia, people had built triumphal temples to the Sacred. This medieval Paris masterpiece, grey beneath the dust of centuries, was one of the finest.

After a simple, late dinner of *steak-frites* and a beer at a bistrot on the Rue de Buci he walked along the Seine carrying his suitcase and shoulder bag to the Gare de Lyon. Searching the station platforms he found the Orient Express. He walked along past the plush *wagons-lits* sleeping cars, peering in the velvet-curtained windows at the compact hotel-rooms-on-wheels. Too bad he couldn't be here at the back of the train far from the noisy locomotive. "Even more comfortable," the ticket agent had said.

Past the sleeping cars, the compartment coaches bore the national railroad insignia of France, Switzerland, Italy, Yugoslavia, Bulgaria, Greece and Turkey. He boarded the Turkish coach, walked along the narrow corridor to the first-class section and found his compartment and seat. After putting his shoulder bag in the overhead rack and his suitcase on the seat to his right, he took an International Aerogramme and a ballpoint pen from his jacket pocket, unfolded the flimsy paper, and began to write a letter to his parents back in Stockton.

At 10 minutes to midnight he heard the shrill blast of the stationmaster's whistle and the crunch of coach doors closing as the train pulled slowly out to begin its 3034-kilometer, 2-1/2-day journey across Europe and through the Balkans to the ancient city on the Bosphorus.

Bruce finished his letter, folded and addressed it, switched off the lights in his compartment, and closed his eyes.

Covered by a white robe, he was standing in cold water up to his waist. Two figures stood beside him in the water, looking at him.

One spoke.

"I baptize you in the name of the Father, and of the Son, and of the Holy Spirit," the figure said, and gently pressed Bruce's chest with one hand as his other hand supported Bruce's back.

"Know ye not, that so many of us as were baptized into Jesus Christ were baptized into his death? Therefore we are buried with him by baptism into death."

Bruce felt himself being forced backwards slowly into the water and it closed over him. It was cold. He closed his eyes and blocked his nostrils from the water. It penetrated his ears and muffled the sound. The cold was a shock.

Time stopped. He couldn't breathe. He waited.

It seemed an eternity.

Then the strong hand on his back pushed upward and Bruce's torso came slowly out of the water. He could hear again. He heard splashing and dripping.

He gasped. His hands went up and wiped the water from his face.

". ..that like as Christ was raised up from the dead by the glory of the Father, even so we also should walk in newness of life."

Bruce blinked the remaining water from his eyes and looked toward the shore. Several hundred people stood or sat on the riverbank looking at him in his soaked white robe and dripping face and hair as they smiled and sang a hymn.

Bruce looked to his left and right at the two figures next to him standing in the water. They smiled at him and nodded.

Baptized into death? Walk in newness of life? What does it really mean?

Bruce walked away from the two figures slowly, pushing his legs against the weight of the water, pushing toward the shore. The white robe dragged at his legs and held him back. Pushing through the cold water was like the dream when you have to escape something dangerous but you can't run fast, something is holding you back, your legs are heavy, they won't move quickly as they must do for you to escape. You push them, you want to force them to go faster, you know they can... but they won't! The danger is always there, gaining on you, and you know you must go faster to escape it—but you can't.

The people on the shore were smiling and singing. They watched him as he walked, pushing toward the shore. They smiled and sang.

"As I went down to the river to pray, studyin' about that good ol' way, when you shall wear that starry crown—Good Lord, show me the way..."

Bruce reached the shore and clambered up on the grass, the heavy wet robe clutching and confusing his legs and dragging under his feet. He stepped on the hem, tripped, and fell on the grass. The pastor's son! People near him jumped up to help. He regained his footing, and smiled at them. They continued to sing.

Bruce wanted to sing with them. He knew he was supposed to be happy and sing. He was reborn! He had been born a sinner, but they told him the cold water of the river had washed away all the sins he had committed since birth, and the sins inherent in him just for being human, just for being born, and now he was reborn, without sin! He should sing!

Bruce opened his mouth to sing, but he could make no sound. He filled his lungs with air, raised his chin and forced out a sound, but it was nothing, an indistinct moan. The smiling people looked at him, puzzled. He must sing! He gulped air again, and again he forced out a sound, but the people couldn't hear him. Sing! The people's smiles faded as they looked at him. What's wrong? Why can't the pastor's son sing?

Bruce gave it everything he had. Dragging up the heavy, sodden white robe as he raised his arms, he took an enormous breath, clenched his stomach muscles and tried to shout.

With a jerk he woke from the dream, his arms in the air, the muffled cry ringing in his ears, his head and neck damp with sweat.

Bruce blinked, exhaled deeply, and looked around. Train compartment. Outside the window a station sign: Lausanne.

He took a deep breath and exhaled again.

The motionless train suddenly lurched and shuddered as the Swiss car was detached and the remaining cars were recoupled.

A whistle.

The train jerked forward, couplings clanking, as it accelerated toward the Alps.

As the train gained momentum, Bruce heard the faint tinkle of a small hand bell which grew louder as the dining car steward walked along the corridor outside his compartment and past it, announcing the opening of the dining car for breakfast.

Wiping his eyes, Bruce roused himself and stood, steadying himself in the swaying train coach. He picked up his toilet kit and towel and made his way carefully along the narrow hallway to the toilet at the end of the coach.

As I went down to the river to pray, Bruce hummed as he washed his face, wiped it with a towel, lathered it with shaving cream, and scraped it with the razor.

...studyin' about that good ol' way... he hummed, brushing his teeth.

Face washed and shaved, teeth brushed, hair combed, he re-knotted his tie, wrestled into his jacket, stopped at his compartment to pick up Huston Smith's *The Religions of Man* and, consciously cleansing his memory of the dream and the song, he walked back against the forward motion of the train, through the multi-national coaches to the dining car.

The smiling steward, in a spotless white jacket, black bow tie and black trousers, welcomed him and seated him by the window at an empty table for four. Outside, flashes of morning light glanced off the little waves in Lake Geneva as the train rolled along its northern shore.

Bruce ordered breakfast.

"Café ou thé, monsieur?"

"Café, s'il vous plaît." Coffee, please.

The dining car had nearly filled by the time the waiter returned with his breakfast: two croissants, butter, jam, a boiled egg in a tiny white cup, coffee and milk in two small white porcelain pitchers, and a big cup to mix them in.

Two young women entered from the sleeping car end of the train. The waiter led them to Bruce's table. One, short and petite, with straight black hair, wore a pink blouse and dark slacks. The other, taller, was in a deep blue dress with white trim in contrast to her head of short blonde curls. They looked at Bruce as the waiter spoke to him. Bruce nodded, and they sat down on the other side of the table.

* * *

"Good morning," the short woman said. "The waiter told us you were American. We are too."

"Where're you from?"

"We're from New York," the taller one said. "And you?"

"California. My name's Bruce."

"I'm Portia," the tall one said.

"I'm Samantha," the short one said.

"Are you going to Venice?"

"Istanbul."

"All the way to Istanbul? Wow! We're just going to Venice. We're supposed to get there late this afternoon."

"Where do you live in California?" Samantha asked.

"Berkeley."

"You don't look like a hippy."

"I'm not. Not everyone in California is a hippy. I'm a graduate student."

The waiter stood ready. They gave their breakfast orders in passable French.

"What's it like with all those hippies in Berkeley? 'Summer of Love' and all that. We read about it in *Time* magazine."

Yeah, *Time*, July 7, 1967, just over a year ago, Bruce thought. That cover article sent a tidal wave of hippy wannabes crowding into Berkeley's Haight-Ashbury district for last year's Summer of Love. To Bruce, the "mindfulness" of the Summer of Love looked more like mindlessness, the naive newcomers finding not Nirvana but rough life on the street, not enough to eat, ripoffs, petty crime, and occasional violence.

"They're why I left," Bruce told them. "Them and Vietnam."

"You don't like hippies?"

"No."

"Did you go to Vietnam?" Portia asked.

"Not yet, but I may have to."

"Why? Can't you get a deferment? All the boys we know get deferments."

"Not all," Samantha said. "Some *want* to go."

"Some enlist in the Navy because they think it's safer, some go to

Canada, some become Conscientious Objectors, some drop out and become hippies. If you're a drug abuser, the Army won't take you," Bruce said. "If I'm drafted, I don't know what I'll do. For now, I'm going to Istanbul. What about you girls?"

"We were studying French in Paris. The course is over, so now we're on our way to Venice. My parents have friends who have a house there."

"Sounds great," Bruce said, looking down at his plate.

He sipped his coffee.

His parents—Baptist pastor, wife and mother—didn't have friends with houses in Venice. His parents had rarely been out of California. They drank no alcohol, never mentioned sex, avoided "trivial" activities like playing cards or board games and spent a lot of time in church. When they read a book it was the Bible, or something about the Bible, or a novel based on a Bible story. They were good people. They wanted Bruce to go to the University of the Pacific right there in Stockton. It taught everything. You could live at home, they said, but Bruce knew he had to get away.

When Bruce got to Berkeley as an undergraduate, he discovered a different world. Fierce intellectual discussions instead of doctrine. Drinking, drugs, girls who liked sex and used diaphragms or took The Pill.

Sophomore year he overdid it, got drunk, got gonorrhea, got bad grades, almost got badly hurt once while bicycling through Berkeley high on weed. He crashed, then shaped up, made the Dean's List, and graduated near the top of his class.

'What are you studying?" Portia asked.

"Religion."

"Are you gonna be a priest or minister or something?" She looked uncertain, like she should watch what she says.

"No, not at all. I'm just interested in religions. I want to understand why people believe what they believe, why they do what they do. Kind of like philosophy or psychology."

"So what are you gonna do if you're not a priest?" Samantha asked. At least a priest was a professional, like a doctor, lawyer or banker.

"I don't know," Bruce answered. "We'll see. I just know I have to learn about religions."

The women looked down at their plates, put jam on their croissants, sipped their coffee and looked out the window at Switzerland.

The train slowed to a halt at Brig for Swiss passport control before entering the 20-kilometer-long Simplon Tunnel, longest in the world. Emerging from beneath the Alps, it stopped at Domodossola for passport control entering Italy.

Milan, then Venice's Santa Lucia station. From his window, Bruce saw Portia and Samantha walking along the platform toward the station exit followed by a uniformed porter pushing their pile of luggage on a cart.

Trieste. The Italian coach decoupled. Bruce showed his passport to the Italian immigration officers, and a few minutes later to Yugoslav Immigration officers at Sežana, then he settled in for another night's fitful sleep in his first-class train seat.

Belgrade. The train wasn't scheduled to move for an hour and a half. Bruce took his Blue Guide and went to the dining car for a breakfast without the coffee sloshing in his cup.

The dining car was nearly empty. He sipped his coffee and read about Edirne, the first Turkish town he'd enter. According to the guidebook, the Selimiye Mosque, rated at three stars ("of exceptional interest"), was "the masterpiece of the celebrated architect Sinan and the result of a lifetime's work in the service of Ottoman architecture."

Bruce had only seen mosques in photographs, and the Sikh Temple in Stockton wasn't really a mosque at all and Sikhs weren't Muslims even though they wore turbans.

Yugoslav Customs and Immigration at Dimitrovgrad, then into Bulgaria at Dragoman, then Sofia.

At dinner, he asked a waiter what time the train would reach Edirne in Turkey.

"About an hour after midnight, sir."

Oh well. Come back to Edirne later, then.

3

Astrid

"Carrot muffins!" the boys said, grinning up at Astrid from their seats. She knew they were undressing her with their eyes as she looked down to scribble on her little Kongsberg Kaffe order pad.

"Big, plump muffins!"

"Coffee?" she asked with a haughty frown, not looking up.

"Yes…and we like it hot!" one said, winking. They all laughed.

Carrot muffins, Astrid thought as she walked toward the kitchen to put in the order. Their dirty little minds!

Her mother watched from the cash register. They taunt her because they want her but are afraid of her.

In her mind she saw her happy little tomboy of a girl, always in motion, her blonde curls tossing in confusion as she ran, jumped, rolled in the grass. In winter, an aggressive skier, more vigorous than any of the boys. They resented her energy, and the way her energy and beauty made them long for her.

How would she ever marry?

"Teach me hunting," Astrid ordered her father in her teens. He taught her, his only child, about his guns, the forests and fields, the prey, the dinners afterward: grouse, rabbit, deer. Once, he took her out for moose. They built a shooting blind and waited behind it until one of the huge beasts came in sight. Astrid aimed, squeezed the trigger, and was knocked backwards from the recoil of the big .30-06 Springfield rifle.

It bruised her shoulder.

She missed.

"Don't worry," he said. "Next time you'll hit. You're a good shot…even though you're not a boy."

Astrid set down the muffins and coffee without looking at the boys, then strode to the cash register and handed her mother the order slip.

"You're a pretty girl and a good girl, but you're a big girl," her mother whispered. "Boys don't like girls who are too tall or strong. They want to feel bigger. If you want the boys to like you, let them be in control."

Astrid stared hard at her mother, turned and walked briskly to a table where an older couple had just taken their seats. She smiled at them and stood ready with her order pad and pen.

Norway was still farming country. The year's greatest excitement was still the annual Nobel Peace Prize ceremony held in Oslo's *rådhus,* the city hall, but the limitless petroleum deposits beneath its North Sea waters were being discovered, and Oslo was attracting important foreign visitors.

After graduation from upper secondary school, Astrid's aunt and uncle called to congratulate her. They invited her to visit them in Oslo.

She loved the big city with all its people and possibilities. During her visit, she combed through the newspaper classified ads looking for work.

A new fine-dining restaurant was hiring waiters.

"We'll try you for a month," the owner said. "Then we'll see."

She was prompt, serious and hard-working. No longer in Kongsberg where she knew everyone and they knew her, she learned hospitality at a higher level, the Oslo level, welcoming the restaurant's customers, making them feel at home, assuring they enjoyed their evening.

A few years in Oslo meeting and serving well-traveled people gave Astrid a vision wider than Norway. She wanted to see the world. When a friend told her that Scandinavian Airlines System was expanding and hiring new staff, she applied and easily passed the interview and training. They offered her a job as a stewardess.

On her first flight, two of the wealthy businessmen who filled the plane pinched her bottom and one touched her ample breasts.

The anger boiled up inside her, and after the fourth incident she turned on the man in anger. Bodil, the pursar, chief of the cabin crew, saw what was about to happen and intervened. She took Astrid aside to the galley.

"Those of us who fly this route regularly know where most of the 'problems' are," Bodil whispered, handing her a slip of paper with seat numbers. "Be formal, be careful. Never be angry. You could lose your job."

"Besides," Bodil winked, "one of them might be your future husband."

Astrid stifled her anger. It was not fair, but she decided to accept the rules of the game. The rewards, the exciting travel, the potential for advancement, were too great to give up.

One night in April 1968 her return flight from Amsterdam to Copenhagen was cancelled due to bad weather. She and the crew went to a hotel and dined together.

The captain invited her to join him for a drink afterwards, which put her on guard. It was important to have good relations with other crew members, particularly the captain, but she feared an awkward moment.

They sat down in easy chairs in the hotel bar. Astrid wore her most formal expression.

"Miss Hugstad, you've proved yourself a good crew member on the shorter routes. You are experienced, excellent at your work, and you get along well with the passengers and crew. *Skål!*"

The captain raised his glass of whiskey. She put her fingers on her glass of mineral water, but did not lift it and did not smile.

The captain took a sip of whiskey, set his glass down on the little table between them and looked at her.

"The airline is initiating nonstop flights several times weekly between Copenhagen and Istanbul using DC-9 jetliners. I'm now training on that aircraft. When the route starts we will need crew. I believe you would fit in well. If you're interested, I will recommend you for the route."

Astrid paused, then smiled and lifted her glass.

"*Skål!*"

* * *

In May the Copenhagen-Istanbul flights began. The captain had recommended Astrid for the first-class cabin because of her excellent rapport with passengers and, her crewmates suspected, because of her beauty.

The first-class passengers—almost all men—looked different from those she had encountered on other European flights: more dark hair, dark eyes and complexions. All wore beautifully-tailored suits, expensive ties, shoes and jewelry.

The first flight, in May, went well. After arriving in Istanbul in the evening, a van took the crew to the Istanbul Hilton for the night.

Istanbul! It was in Europe, with much that was familiar, but also in Asia, and exotic.

After they had changed from their crew uniforms to dresses, Bodil suggested they take a walk.

They strolled along the Hilton's curving driveway to Cumhuriyet Caddesi, Istanbul's status boulevard.

They wandered along the avenue past other hotels, airline offices, travel agencies, restaurants and nightclubs to Taksim Square. After a few minutes there, they walked along busy İstiklal Caddesi, the main strolling and shopping street.

Istanbul was dingy compared to Copenhagen or Oslo, but its sounds, sights and smells were fascinating.

Most of the other strollers on the street were men, with the occasional couple. Some of the men leered at the two blonde women. They made furtive gestures and strange noises. They bumped against them.

Bodil and Astrid turned around.

Back past Taksim Square, on Cumhuriyet Caddesi, the men were better-dressed, and none of them bumped, gestured or made noises. They nodded respectfully, or offered a polite, friendly smile. The staff and other guests at the hotel treated them the same way, with refined respect, politeness and European courtesy. So this was Istanbul….

In June, on a flight from Copenhagen to Istanbul, one of the passengers struck up a conversation with Astrid. In his mid-thirties, quite handsome in a Mediterranean way, he was polite and well-spoken with excellent command of English.

"A glass of champagne, please—your very best," he said, smiling.

When she brought it to him, he looked at her slyly. "Are you sure this is your very best?"

"Yes, sir."

"Did you make it yourself?" he joked.

"Of course! That's how I know it's the best!"

They both had to stifle their laughter—it would not be appropriate in first class.

"Bodil, may I please see the passenger manifest?"

Bodil handed the clipboard to Astrid. First class seat 2C: Halepli, Devin Mr; Turkish.

As Astrid went about her work, she would stop briefly by Mr Halepli's seat to exchange a few words about food, drinks, and favorite restaurants in Oslo and Istanbul. He was insightful and witty, and he soon learned how to make her laugh with almost any comment. She suppressed her laughter, but it was difficult, and he knew it.

On the second flight when she served Mr Halepli, he was even more gracious without taking her time or requiring extra attention which might interfere with her work. He was just as funny, but he knew exactly how much to amuse her without getting her in trouble.

After the meal service Astrid was in the galley straightening up. Mr Halepli approached.

"I own a supper club in Istanbul. We serve a quality clientele with a fine kitchen and the best musical entertainment."

He paused and winked at her.

"I made it myself!"

She turned her head so no one would see, and stifled a laugh.

"The club is quite successful, but my other business interests take me away from the city often, so I can no longer give it the time it deserves."

He looked at her. She returned his gaze.

"I've been observing your work on these flights. I see you know about graceful and efficient service. I need to employ an assistant to manage the club. The pay and benefits will be ample. We can arrange the required residence and work permits."

He took a business card from his jacket pocket and held it out to her.

"If you are interested, please contact me and we can discuss details."

"Thank you, Mr Halepli. I'll consider your offer."

When she telephoned his office a secretary told her Mr Halepli was out of the country, but that he had left instructions in case she called. The secretary recited the job details: hours, time off, salary, housing and benefits.

Astrid was astonished.

This, she thought, was her step up. She knew about hospitality. Instead of being a waitress in a restaurant or a glorified waitress on an airplane, she would be a manager with responsibility, an apartment in sunny, exotic Istanbul, and a very generous salary.

In August, she took the job.

4

Istanbul

Istanbul. Constantinople. Byzantium. For two thousand years, the Queen of Cities, the capital of empires, fount of art and culture, wealthy beyond imagination.

With the proclamation of the Turkish Republic in 1923, the Queen of Cities was dethroned. The new Turkish capital was Ankara, 450 kilometers inland to the east, far from the seas that brought enemy warships to the Bosphorus, their great guns trained on the sultan's palace.

The disaster of the Ottoman Empire's World War I defeat and the privations of the Turkish Republic's World War II neutrality left the once-glittering Ottoman capital an aged relic, a dingy provincial backwater of just over two million souls.

Ankara, in the heartland of the new republic, Kemal Atatürk's headquarters during the War of Independence, was now the seat of power, the city of the future in a young country of 33 million.

Turkey's closed economy and carefully-controlled currency made it difficult for international commerce to flourish. Turks made do with what they had. The streets of Istanbul were thronged with ancient American cars: ten, twenty, even thirty years old, kept humming by resourceful Turkish mechanics. Traditional porters called hamal *did the work of small trucks, carrying huge, heavy bundles of goods on their backs through the city's narrow streets. Central heating in buildings was rare, charcoal braziers, coal, kerosene and wood stoves common. The waiting time to have a telephone installed in your home was seven years.*

Intercity telephone calls were made with the help of an operator and could take hours to connect. International calls cost a fortune. Send a telegram instead.

Foreign visitors to Turkey were few—there was no tourism worthy of the name—and except for diplomats, the very wealthy, and Turkish gastarbeiter *("guest workers") in West Germany, it was nearly impossible for Turks to travel abroad. The expense was simply too great.*

The rest of the world penetrated the Turkish consciousness via newspapers and books, the radio, movies and vinyl records: the Beatles, Pink Panther, the Vietnam War, social unrest in France. Television sets would not be common in homes until the late 1970s.

The minarets of Istanbul's five hundred mosques still pointed hopefully to heaven, the waters of the Bosphorus and the Sea of Marmara still teemed with fish, providing the city's poor with affordable protein, but Istanbul's golden age was long gone. A mist of melancholy shrouded every dilapidated street.

Yet the Istanbullular, the people of Istanbul, loved their city: the dark waters of the Bosphorus rushing south from the Black Sea to the Sea of Marmara; the Golden Horn estuary dividing the European side of the city into old and new, Turkish and European quarters; the bedroom suburbs of Üsküdar and Kadıköy on the Asian shore; the sweeping green Belgrade Forest to the north.

Istanbullular sat in simple coffee houses and tea gardens sipping Turkish coffee or sugared tea, reading newspapers, playing endless rounds of backgammon, dominoes or cards, talking politics, sports, and good food—an easy topic in a country so rich in agriculture. For vacation, they boarded ferryboats and steamed to nearby beaches on the Black Sea, the Marmara, or the nearby Princes Islands. They rarely went farther.

Life in Istanbul was simple, but good.

5

Bruce Arrives

The Orient Express stopped at Svilengrad, on the Bulgarian-Turkish border, just after midnight on September 23rd, and after a half-hour of Bulgarian Customs and Immigration procedures the train pulled ahead to the Turkish Customs and Immigration border post at Kapıkule.

It was nearly lunchtime when the train finally penetrated Istanbul's medieval city walls and rumbled slowly along the Sea of Marmara shore and around Seraglio Point to Sirkeci Station on the Golden Horn. On the hill behind the 19th-century Orientalist train station, the towers and domes of Topkapı Palace rose above the treetops.

As soon as the train came to a halt, the station platform below Bruce's compartment window was a chaos of passengers, relatives and friends, porters, taxi drivers, shills, pickpockets and piles of luggage. He waited in his compartment, reading his guidebook for hotel recommendations, until the crowd had thinned.

First on the list under *Stamboul* was the Ipek Palas Oteli, Orhaniye Caddesi, Sirkeci. He took down his suitcase and shoulder bag, stepped off the train and, with his little Langenscheidt Turkish-English dictionary in hand, walked to the window marked *Müracaat - Information* to ask directions.

On a map, the man at the window showed him the route to the hotel, only a few blocks away.

Bruce walked from the station to Orhaniye Caddesi and the hotel, the "Silk Palace."

It was a drab Art Nouveau building not much different from the cheap hotel he had used in Paris, its façade stained with soot, its floor tiles cracked, its light bulbs dim. The moustachioed man behind the reception desk showed him to a small, simple room, somewhat dingy but clean and cheap. Adequate, especially at the surprisingly low price. Bruce's savings would last.

He settled in, took a shower, then went out and walked back toward Sirkeci Station. Passing a bank, he saw a sign by the door: *Change. Exchange. Wechsel. Kambiyo.* He went in and exchanged some dollars for Turkish liras.

He strolled down to the Golden Horn with its maelstrom of white ship-like ferryboats arriving and departing, churning the sea with their powerful engines as they docked or departed, chased by clouds of seagulls. To his left was the Yeni Valide Camii—the "New Mosque"—and the Galata Bridge crossing the Golden Horn to connect historic Old Istanbul with the new quarters developed during the 19th century.

At the mouth of the Golden Horn, near the New Mosque at the southern end of the bridge he saw two men in a rowboat bobbing in the jellyfish-infested water. The boat was moored to a railing on the quai. He saw flames in the bottom of the rowboat. He walked closer and saw that one of the men was flipping fish fillets on a grill. The other was using a giant knife to slit loaves of bread. The bread man would hold a slit loaf toward the man at the grill, who would slide a fish fillet into it. The bread man would add a handful of greens and hand the sandwich over the railing to a customer on the shore. The customer handed the bread man a coin, grabbed a pinch of salt from a cardboard box tied to the railing, and sprinkled it on his fish.

Bruce walked up to the boat and held out his hand. The man put a fish sandwich into it and held up one finger. One. A lira. Bruce gave him a coin.

He bit into the fish still sizzling from the fire. He didn't stop biting until it was gone. It was the freshest fish he had ever tasted.

As he ate, his gaze swept over the Galata Bridge. There were two levels to it. On the upper level, cars, buses, trucks, horse carts and pedestrians crossed and re-crossed. On the lower level, by the water, were dingy tea houses, a few simple restaurants, and tiny shops selling fishing tackle.

The bridge seemed to be moving up and down slightly as waves from the ferry wakes swept up to it. It *was* moving—floating on large pontoons.

Men were sitting at small tables in front of the tea shops. Bruce walked up to one, took a seat, and within a minute a waiter placed a small glass of ruby-red tea in front of him. The glass, shaped like a tulip with a gold rim, was on a small saucer with a tiny spoon. The waiter plunked a bowl of sugar cubes on the table.

Bruce sipped the strong tea and watched the white ferryboats jockey for position in the mouth of the Golden Horn, sidling up to the dock with a bump, discharging passengers, taking on passengers, and roaring away in a swash of seawater and jellyfish and a shriek of seagulls.

Istanbul!

At breakfast the next morning, Bruce read his guidebook, studied the maps and planned his day. It was going to be hot. Better get out and explore the city before the worst of the heat.

He walked up the hill from the Ipek Palas to Sultan Ahmet Square, the historic center of the Roman, Byzantine and Ottoman city. The Byzantine Hippodrome, once the site of sports events and chariot races, was now a long park stretching in front of the Sultan Ahmet Camii, called the Blue Mosque by foreigners, with its six minarets. He went to the front door, removed his shoes, and entered. His first mosque. All that study of Islam, and now he had finally stepped inside a Muslim place of worship.

It was not prayer time, so it was quiet. The sun streamed through the high windows in the domes throwing blazes of golden light onto the rich carpets. A few men sat on the floor, finishing their late prayers. Bruce had learned that Muslims were supposed to pray at the assigned times, but if this was difficult they could make up the prayers later.

Off to one side, a bearded old man was reading from a big book on a little wooden stand.

This is what I came here for, Bruce thought. To see this. To try and understand this.

He left the mosque and strolled along the Hippodrome park past the Kaiser Wilhelm II Fountain, the Egyptian obelisk, a strange circular hole with a twisted metal column in it, and another obelisk of rough stone.

Old cars and small vans, mostly VW microbuses, were parked along the sides of the Hippodrome, some with laundry hanging on the antennas and roof racks. Music—Beatles, Beach Boys, Joan Baez, the Association, the Mamas and the Papas—blared from 8-track tape decks. Hippies in colorful clothes, sandals, long hair, beards and beads stood in small groups or sat on the curb or on little stools in the shade of the vans, smoking, drinking, dozing, talking. Someone was playing a guitar. Hippies walked to and from the northeast end of the park, to the famous Pudding Shop restaurant or to the public toilets next to the tourist office.

Turks in business suits walked to and from an Ottoman-era building facing the Blue Mosque across the Hippodrome. Some of the men glanced at the hippies, some frowned, most ignored them. Two uniformed officers strolled casually through the Hippodrome, chatting and keeping an eye on everything.

At the far end of the Hippodrome Bruce turned left and walked down the hill along Nakilbent Sokak, heading for the blue of the sea. He glanced up to his right and saw the huge curved stone wall that held up the southwestern end of the Hippodrome.

He stopped to read his guidebook.

The Sphendoneh: to gain the monumental size necessary for the Hippodrome, the Byzantines had to extend the level ground over the slope to the southwest. This end of the Hippodrome is thus an artificial platform held up by an elaborate system of huge, thick walls and arches. The system is called the Sphendoneh. It was an engineering marvel for its time. Behind the curving stone wall there were thought to be stone ramps sloping up to ground level. In Byzantine times, horses and charioteers prepared for the races in the depths of the Sphendoneh, then made their entrance by racing up the ramps to the surface and bursting into view in the Hippodrome as if out of nowhere.

Now, 2000 years later, the Sphendoneh seemed nothing more than a pile of old stones that kept the southwest end of the Hippodrome from collapsing into the Sea of Marmara.

Bruce walked on, downhill to the ancient city walls and the sea. A cool breeze blew down the Bosphorus toward the Sea of Marmara, but the sun was getting hot.

Istanbul.

6

Bruce at Home

The American Library of the United States Information Service was in Beyoğlu, across the Golden Horn on its north side, in 'new' Istanbul, right next to the US Consulate-General and across the street from the Pera Palas Oteli, the grand 19th-century hotel built to receive the posh passengers arriving on the Orient Express. Consular staff, expatriate Americans, Peace Corps Volunteers, and the occasional American vagabond came to the USIS library to sit in clean, well-lit, orderly surroundings, soften homesickness by spending an hour or two with American newspapers and magazines, and borrow American books. Most of the local visitors were Turkish students and young professionals eager to improve their English.

Bruce entered, went up to the reception desk and asked the librarian, a middle-aged Turkish woman, if she knew anyone who might want English lessons.

"No, I do not, but you may place a notice on the bulletin board if you wish," she smiled. "Many people inspect it. You may find a prospective pupil. Do you live here?"

"I just arrived. I'm looking for a place to live."

"Inspect the bulletin board for rental notices. Turkish landlords approve of Americans as tenants, though they favor women over men."

She gave him a knowing look. Her English was perfect, almost too perfect, in the way of punctilious speakers who fear making a grammatical error in a second language.

"Why don't they like men?"

"They believe women are less liable to cause problems. Men may make noise, have parties, have fights, that sort of thing. They believe that is how men are. Actually, what they really approve of is quiet tenants who pay their rent on time, and foreign tenants usually pay higher rents."

She gave him an arch look, only half in jest. Bruce looked like a nice young man, she thought. Probably no trouble, but you can never tell.

"If you wish, you may put your name on the consular list of American citizens living in Istanbul. The Consul-General likes to know of Americans living in his district, in case of trouble."

"Good idea."

"Here is a book you might find useful," the librarian said, taking a book from beneath the desk and putting it in front of him.

Bruce picked it up: *Teach Yourself Turkish.*

"Thanks. Yes, this'll be useful."

"Please write your name here and I will assure that you are included on the consular list."

She put a pen and pad of paper in front of him.

"When you find an apartment, please inform me and I will add your address to the list."

Bruce wandered over to the bulletin board and soon found a notice for an apartment near Taksim Square.

"May I use your telephone?" he asked the librarian.

"Yes, if it is a local call, within the city."

Bruce dialed the number.

"Efendim?" a voice said.

"Uh, do you speak English?"

"Yes. How may I help you?"

"I'd like to look at the apartment you have for rent. I'd like to see it as soon as possible."

"Certainly."

They agreed on Friday, two days later.

The apartment building was on Saray Arkası Sokak, "The Street

Behind the Palace," just down the hill from Taksim Square. When he translated the name using his dictionary, Bruce guessed that the "palace" was the palatial West German Consulate-General building on the way from Taksim Square to Dolmabahçe Palace. The palace-sized consulate had been built in the 1870s as the embassy of the German Empire to the Ottoman Empire.

He pressed the bell button by the building's main door. Nothing. He pressed it again and heard *"Geliyorum! Geliyorum!"*

The door opened and a tall, white-haired, grey-bearded man in an old black suit looked at him.

"I'm here to see Hasan Bey about renting the apartment."

The old man nodded, motioned for him to enter, indicated the stairs and held up two fingers.

"İki," he said. *"İki."* Two.

Bruce climbed two flights of stairs and knocked on the door. It opened and a stately grey-haired woman in a bright flowered dress smiled at him.

"You would be Bruce," she said in British-accented English, and smiled again. "My name is Aylin. Please do come in. Hasan is not here just now but I can show you the flat and then we can have a chat. Would you like tea then? I'll put the kettle on."

When she returned from the kitchen, she led Bruce from her apartment up many stairs.

The apartment was a *çatı katı* ("roof level"), a small, not-strictly-legal assemblage of tiny rooms on the roof of the building. Landlords had them built after the official five-floor construction was finished. If a building inspector asked, the answer was that these little rooms were for "having tea and enjoying the view." The inspector would warn the landlord that the rooms were not designed or constructed according to the building code, and were not to be used as living space. The inspector would depart, and the landlord would furnish the tiny rooms and look for a tenant.

The rooms were small and packed with old furniture and boxes, but the rooftop terrace was large, the view of the Bosphorus panoramic.

"We'll get all of these things and boxes out of here for you," Aylin said.

"Can I keep some of the furniture? I don't have any."

"Of course! Actually, there should be enough to make yourself fairly comfortable. There's probably at least two of everything!" she laughed. "Choose what you want and we'll dispose of the rest."

They went back downstairs, sat down to tea and discussed the rent.

"I'll take it," Bruce said.

Climbing six flights was worth it for the privacy, the view, and the low price—laughably low compared to rents in Berkeley.

The next morning Bruce came to the apartment building, paid the first month's rent and security deposit to Hasan, and helped the building's *kapıcı,* the porter, carry out the unwanted items. The porter's wife agreed to give the apartment a thorough cleaning, including all the windows, for 15 liras. By late afternoon, it was tidy enough, and there was enough furniture in place, for Bruce to move in.

"You will need to have a new mattress made," Aylin told him. "Do *not* buy a used one! It could have bedbugs. I will give you a note for the mattress-maker so he will make you a brand-new one filled with virgin cotton. You will have no bugs."

Aylin was taking a liking to Bruce. She could see that he was a nice young man, cultured, of good family.

"I will lend you linens and towels until you have time to buy your own in the Mahmutpaşa bazaar. I can recommend a good shop there."

"When you hear the *Ode to Joy* from Beethoven's Ninth Symphony coming from the street," she went on, "you will know that the Aygaz truck is coming. The *Ode to Joy* is the tune the truck plays to alert customers. Run down and buy a tank of propane gas from the driver. You will have to pay a deposit on the first tank, and later you will exchange the empty first tank for full ones without a deposit."

"But...doesn't your building have a gas pipe coming in?"

"Yes, of course, but the city gas is worthless! Mostly air! You can't even boil water for tea with it! Trust me, you need a tank of propane."

"What do I do for a refrigerator?"

Aylin smiled at him.

"Ah, Americans. Few apartments in Turkey have refrigerators. In a few years, perhaps—the butcher shops are starting to get them now. You don't really need one. Buy what you need daily from the *bakkal*

—that's the grocer's shop down the street. The grocer's boy can deliver items like fresh bread daily if you wish. You should also get to know the *Balık Pazarı,* the Fish Market, in Galatasaray. It's a complete market now, not just for fish."

The day was wearing on, and growing hot. There was nothing more Bruce could do at his new apartment today. He would return tomorrow with his suitcase and shoulder bag, but for now he wanted lunch: a cold beer and something to eat.

He thanked Aylin, the porter and his wife for their help, and took the T1 bus to Sultan Ahmet Square, nearer the Ipek Palas. He had seen several cafés popular with the hippies. They would be cheap.

7

Astrid Deluxe

It was strange being a passenger and not a stewardess on the SAS flight from Copenhagen to Istanbul. Astrid found herself analyzing the work of the flight crew critically, especially the stewardesses.

She didn't like the word *stewardess*. In the early days of air travel, flights had stewards, just as on ocean liners. When they hired women for the airlines, they came up with the term "stewardess." It was a common female adaptation of the word in English, but she still didn't like it. "Actress," "governess," and all the other "-esses"—she found them demeaning to those doing the work. A female pilot was a pilot, not a "pilotess" or "captainess," so why should a female steward be called anything but a steward? Was what they did somehow less valuable than what male stewards did? She came from an egalitarian country. She thought that if men and women did the same job, they should have the same title, responsibilities, pay, and opportunities for advancement.

But that was all over now. She was no longer a stewardess. She was on her way to a new career as a manager in a country very different from Norway.

At Atatürk Airport in Istanbul, Mr Halepli and another man met her at the arrivals gate. The other man took Astrid's flight bag and baggage receipts while Mr Halepli accompanied Astrid through Immigration and Customs control. It went quickly. The officers treated Mr Halepli with respect.

They exited the terminal into a maelstrom of porters, passengers, relatives, chauffeurs, taxi drivers and touts, but Astrid was accustomed to the crowds from her time flying to Istanbul with SAS. It was only a few moments before Mr Halepli's man drove up in a late-model black Mercedes sedan.

"I'll take you to the apartment. If you like it, it's yours. If not, we'll find somewhere else."

The apartment was in Beyoğlu, in Europeanized "new" Istanbul north of the Golden Horn. When they arrived at the building and got out of the car, Halepli said "By the way, this is Bulut, your driver. He and the car are available anytime you may want them. Just tell the *kapıcı*, the porter, when you would like the car and Bulut will come."

They entered the large luxury apartment building.

"This is Halim, the porter. He or the other porter, Ali, is always sitting here in the lobby, or nearby. If you need anything at all, they're the men to ask."

They took a private elevator to the penthouse.

Halepli opened the door to the apartment and stood aside for Astrid to enter.

The apartment was large and luxurious, covering most of the roof of the building. A wide terrace surrounded the glass walls, offering spectacular views of the Bosphorus and the domes and minarets of Old Istanbul.

She wandered around, trying with difficulty to control her awe.

Beyond the spacious glass-walled salon was a dining area, and next to it a modern American-style kitchen with a wine cabinet. The master suite had a king bed, walk-in closets, a sauna and a small Turkish bath. A smaller room that might have been meant as a second bedroom was furnished as a library with books in Turkish, English, German and French, and a desk and chair.

"How do you like it?"

"It's beautiful," she said finally, keeping her wonder within bounds. "It will do nicely."

"The refrigerator is stocked with food, so you don't have to go anywhere right away. You can relax. The neighborhood here in Beyoğlu has many restaurants. Just ask Halim. He can have any sort of food delivered."

"I'll have this entered as your address in the application for your residence visa and work permit," Halepli continued. "I'll need your passport for the application."

Astrid took her passport from her purse and handed it to him.

"I'll let you settle in and get used to the place. Take a little time, look over the neighborhood. I'll be away on business for a few days. When I return, I'll take you to the club, introduce you to the people there and we'll talk about your work."

He shook her hand.

"Thank you for everything, Mr Halepli. I'm happy to be here, and I look forward to working with you."

He left.

She went to the east-facing floor-to-ceiling windows and gazed out past the terrace to the lights twinkling on in Asia on the far side of the Bosphorus. She felt a long way from Kongsberg in Norway, but she had worked hard and made good decisions. Now, she had arrived.

A week later, things were going well at the club. Halepli introduced Astrid to the staff. The club manager, a man named Ender, had outlined the workings of the operation for her: food and beverage ordering, delivery and preparation, kitchen and storage facilities, accounting, legal requirements. She was learning a lot.

"Until you're familiar with the way things run, I think you should be in the dining room with the hostesses," Halepli said. "You can see how everything goes."

After her first evening in the dining room, Astrid asked the hostesses for shopping advice.

"I need proper outfits. Which are the best shops?"

They wrote down several addresses for her.

Bulut drove her to each of the shops where she chose fashionable evening dresses and had them fitted. When the time came to pay, Bulut took over, counting out large Turkish lira notes to the cashier.

Several weeks went by and she was still in the dining room, supposedly supervising the front-of-house staff, but in fact just helping them out whenever an extra person was needed.

She could see that the male patrons of the club admired her, but all were polite and courtly when they greeted her.

Halepli was out of town again. When he returned, she saw him in the club.

"Mr Halepli…"

"Call me Devin."

"Mr Halepli, I have some ideas on improvements we might consider. Some efficiencies in preparation and service," she said. "Also, I've been looking over the accounts…"

"Yes, of course," Halepli answered. "Meet me in the manager's office in ten minutes."

When she got to the office, Bulut was waiting outside the door. He smiled and opened the door for her.

Halepli was sitting behind the desk. He gestured to a sofa across the room. When she had seated herself there, he sat beside her.

"Please tell me your ideas, briefly."

She took a note from her handbag and read from it.

He listened intently, looking at her. From time to time he nodded in agreement.

When she had finished, he was silent, looking at her.

"Are you enjoying Istanbul?" he smiled.

"Yes, I like it here very much, and I like the club. I thought I might…"

"Good! I'm glad you're happy. I want to tell you that your happiness is of the greatest importance. You are a real asset to the club…and to me."

"Now, about the suggestions, I think we…"

"They're excellent! I fully agree! Please talk with Ender Bey tomorrow about them."

There was a pause.

"Astrid, let's leave that for now, shall we? I'll have to leave Istanbul again soon. I'll only be in the city for a few more days. I'm so busy, and yet I want to be sure and make time for you."

They were silent, looking at one another. She sensed a change in the atmosphere, a change in direction, in feeling.

His eyes were ardent. His smile was no longer one of humor, but of anticipation.

She stood up from the couch. He rose as well.

"Astrid, do you remember how we used to chat on those flights between Copenhagen and Istanbul? That was so enjoyable! I miss our funny chats."

Now he was the charming, handsome traveler again. Astrid smiled at the memory.

"Yes."

"Can we continue them? What if I were to come to your

apartment after the club closes. We could relax, have a drink and a few minutes of our old chatting. I'd really enjoy that. I think we both would."

Astrid paused.

Did she have a choice? Did she *want* a choice? It would be fun to chat in the old way, if they still could. He had such a good sense of humor. Would there be more than that? What else could happen?

She knew what else. What she didn't know was whether she wanted it to happen or not.

It was a simple question: May I stay?

Bulut had driven them both to her apartment after the club closed. They took the private elevator up.

She asked him what he would like to drink, then stopped and said, "Oh, I should know! Why am I asking? What you always order at the club: *Kulüp Rakı*, ice, a little water. Yes?"

He smiled at her.

"Don't forget something for yourself."

She returned with his rakı, a glass of white Çankaya wine, and a bowl of pistachios.

They reminisced about the Copenhagen-Istanbul flights. He asked about her work with the airline, about growing up in Norway. She did most of the talking, but he interjected his jokes from time to time and always made her laugh, just like on the plane—except that now she could laugh out loud without worry.

It felt good to laugh!

She was tired. The wine relaxed her. Talking about the flights made her realize how far she had come from her parents' little café in Kongsberg.

She was happy.

Then he asked the question.

She could say "No," and she knew that he would leave. Is that what she wanted? If he left, would things change? If he stayed....

She smothered that nagging little voice in the back of her head warning her, always warning her.

The next morning he rose before she did, dressed, smiled at her, kissed her tenderly, and left.

She watched him go, then arose to the morning after the night when she had discovered a heat of passion she scarcely knew existed.

At the club, Ender listened attentively to her suggestions. He called members of his staff into the office and explained her ideas to them in Turkish. The staff nodded and went back to work.

There were a few small changes, but Ender was still the manager and Astrid was still in the dining room nightly "supervising" the staff.

Devin was out of town a lot. When he returned, he would come to the club and, after closing, Bulut would drive them to her apartment.

It came to her one day that her passport had not been returned. She asked Devin for it.

"It takes awhile to get the residence and work permits," he said. "Turkish bureaucracy! I'll let you know when everything's ready."

Later, she asked him again. He said the same thing.

Sometimes after work they would have a drink and a chat, sometimes Devin would say he had a long day, he was tired, and could they just go to bed. For a tired traveler, in bed he certainly had enough energy.

In the morning, a kiss, a smile, and the closing of the door.

Unlike Devin, Bulut was always with her. If she went out shopping, or for a walk, he followed her closely "for protection," he said. No other man approached or molested her with Bulut close behind. He was her bodyguard. It was reassuring, but also somewhat spooky.

One day she asked Bulut how long it took to get a residence permit and a work permit. He smiled at her and gave her a quizzical look.

8

Mustafa's Café

Bruce heard "BOOY-roon koom EEN koom EEN SEET HEER *VOT VOOT yu LAYK.*"

Ah. "Please! Come in, come in! Sit here! What would you like?"

He sat where the Turk pointed: one of ten rickety chairs in the ramshackle café. Barely room for three and a half tables, though the terrace in front of the café held a half-dozen more. Inside, fluorescent light, lurid green. A long trench cut in a narrow stone counter glowed with charcoal. Set over the trench and above the coals, three big pots simmered.

"I have soup, stew, pilav!"

"Stew and some of the rice, please. Put the stew on top of the rice," he pantomimed.

The café owner, a short, balding Turk with a prominent nose, dark brown eyes beneath bushy brows, five o'clock-shadow beard, thick black brush-like moustache and rugs of black hair on his arms, took a plate noisily, scooped a mountain of steaming, glistening rice, then a ladle of pungent mutton, onions, carrots, tomatoes, potatoes.

"*Buyrun!*" he repeated and put it on the table. "DREENK?"

"Do you have beer?"

"*Evet,* yes, yes, Tekel beer! You like cold? Hot?"

"Cold, please."

The café man brought the beer, huge grin, pouring it slowly into a tall glass. Three inches of head. Not all that cold. He wiped his hands on his long, once-white apron.

Bruce ate. The Turkish stew was good. The beer was okay.

The café man—cook, waiter, owner, dishwasher—approached and put a large bound notebook on the table in front of him.

"*Buyrun!*" he said again, waving toward it. Help yourself. "*Defter!*" Notebook.

The notebook was the size of a large ledger, two inches thick. Its brown cardboard cover, once shiny and smooth, was now a mess of scratches, marks, stains, its corners frayed and broken, its covers festooned with ring-marks from drinks. Bruce spooned a mouthful of stew and rice, took a pull on the beer, and turned back the battered cover.

The unlined, dog-eared pages were covered in doodles, stains, drawings, scratchy writing. A Greek 10-lepta coin stuck down with tape. A Thai postage stamp. A wilted flower once glued to a page but now loose. Notes written in English, French, Turkish, German, Japanese. Arabic script. Cyrillic. Greek. Mostly English.

Block letters: "Driving to Kathmandu 2 August '65. VW van. Riders wanted to share gas. Tony at Petrol Hotel."

"Mustafa is the best!" in a feminine hand. "We love your *orman kabob!* Peace + love! Susan. "

"Buen provecho, precios economicos, gracias Mustafa!"

Bruce turned the page.

A drawing in ballpoint pen of the Blue Mosque filled half the page, the loudspeakers on its minarets hugely out of scale, clouds of sound billowing out. "WAKE UP!"

Below a scribble: "Istanbul is amazing! The Turks are so friendly (well, maybe not the police...) but I love the Hippodrome and that big church and the big mosque. We took a boat on the Bosphorus, one lira. Now we're off to Iran by bus. We'll be back!"

"29 Haziran shop in the bazaar has leather hippy coats, cheap, good quality, but haggle!"

"You want baklava? I have baklava!" The café man: ey hev BAK-lah-VAH!

"Sure. How much?"

"One lira! Iz goot!"

The owner—Mustafa—brought three rectangles of baklava on a small white plate.

"*Çay!* From me! No price! T'ank you!"

Mustafa set down a tiny tulip-shaped glass of ruby-red tea on a saucer with two cubes of sugar.

Bruce turned the pages of the notebook. More of the same, and all different. Colors of ink, all the world's handwriting. Drawings, stars, hearts, flowers, Turks in fezzes, VW microbuses putt-putting along roads, a good likeness of smiling Mustafa drawn in charcoal (from the cookstove?) Page after page.

The next morning Bruce packed his suitcase and shoulder bag, paid his bill, thanked the staff at the Ipek Palas, and took a taxi through the light Sunday-morning traffic to Saray Arkası Sokak. With his luggage he climbed the six flights of steps slowly. Still, when he got to the top, he was sweating.

Putting down the bags, he went through the small salon, opened the door to the terrace and walked out into the hot sun. The terrace was spacious, at least for a tiny rooftop apartment, big enough for several tables and chairs—if he had any. He went back inside, brought out a chair, and sat at the edge of the terrace.

There was a cooling breeze, and the view was spectacular. Below him was the sparkling blue flood of the Bosphorus, busy with small fishing boats, fast white ferries and large ocean-going vessels transiting between the Black Sea and the Sea of Marmara. In the midst of the flood, on a tiny rock island, a small white building topped by a tall tower and a flagpole—Leander's Tower—stood by itself, a historic Customs post right in the sea lanes. On the far shore in Asia, domed mosques poked their minarets skyward.

He was going to like it here.

Hunger and thirst. The next tasks to tackle were these. He wiped his sweaty face on a towel and descended the stairs to the street in search of supplies.

Saray Arkası Sokak had two *bakkal*s, the grocery shops that supplied everyday needs. He went into one and bought bread, cheese, pasta, tea, coffee, sugar, salt, pepper, tomatoes and cucumbers, olives, margarine, drinking water, beer and wine. That would do for now. He went to pay.

"*Hoş geldiniz!*" the shopkeeper said, smiling. Welcome. "*Nerelisiniz?*"

Bruce did not understand, so the shopkeeper asked "*Siz* where from?"

"America."

"Ah, Amerika! *İyi!* Goot! Goot! Welcome! Now live here?"

"Yes," Bruce said. I suppose I do.

"*Telefon!*" the shopkeeper said proudly, pointing to a black telephone on the counter. Attached to it was a coin box. The shopkeeper took a coin from his cash register and pantomimed lifting the handpiece, putting the coin into the slot in the box, pushing the plunger, and talking on the phone. Ah, Bruce realized, the community pay phone. Good to know. There was no phone in the apartment, and Aylin had told him that getting one installed took years. Hasan and Aylin had a phone which he thought he could use in emergencies, but the grocery shop had the phone he could use anytime.

Bruce took the supplies back to his apartment, opened all the windows to catch the breeze, ate some cheese, bread and a tomato for lunch, then sat in a shady corner on his terrace and opened the *Teach Yourself Turkish* book he had borrowed from the American Library.

After two hours of intense study he looked up at the Bosphorus as though coming out of a dream. The wind had dropped, the sun had moved, the shade had disappeared. He was hot.

He saw the white ferryboats sailing briskly across the dark, cold-looking waters of the Bosphorus.

"That's what I need," he thought. "A little cruise on the Bosphorus to cool off."

9

PCV

It was too hot for coat-and-tie. Bruce didn't feel like he was really in Europe anymore, so he put on a T-shirt, shorts and sneakers, went down the stairs two at a time, then jogged down to the Bosphorus shore road at Kabataş. He hopped on a bus and was soon in Galata, where he boarded the next ferryboat heading for the Asian shore.

He climbed the stairs to the upper deck, made his way to the stern, and sat on one of the open-air benches.

The three young people sitting in front of Bruce, two men and a woman, were speaking English with American accents.

"S'cuse me," Bruce said. "You Americans?"

"Yeah," one of the men answered. "You are too."

"How did you know?" Bruce asked.

"T-shirt and shorts," the tall man said. "Only Americans wear T-shirt, shorts and sneakers. In Europe it's the mark of the American tourist. Here, it's the mark of American military on leave—lower ranks, of course. There aren't many American tourists."

Uh-oh. On this very hot day the two young American men were wearing neat short-sleeved sport shirts and trousers. The woman wore a modest skirt and a blouse with sleeves to the elbows.

Bruce preferred to stay in the background when he traveled, not to stand out much, which is why he usually wore jacket, tie and slacks. Summer was not jacket-and-tie weather, although he saw some Istanbul businessmen fully suited. Even he, a Californian, couldn't understand how they stood the late summer heat.

He saw that he'd have to dress up a bit more, even in summer.

"What brings you to Istanbul?" the short man asked.

"I'm a graduate student in Berkeley, but I've taken a leave of absence. I had to get out of the US for awhile. Couldn't take the Vietnam insanity. I protested and it did no good. Most Americans look upon protesters as traitors when all we want is for people to seriously ask themselves what our country is doing, what it is costing us in lives and money, and what the result might be. All they think is, 'We're fighting. We've got to win.' Yet, if you ask them what 'winning' means, they can't tell you except 'we kill more of them than they kill of us.' God!"

"I'm planning to find some people here who want to learn English," Bruce went on, "and give them private lessons to pay my expenses. What about you?"

"Peace Corps. We teach English at a school in Kadıköy."

"You like it here? How's the teaching?"

"The teaching's fine, the school's great, and we love Istanbul, but you're right about Vietnam. The war and all the bombing make everybody here suspicious of Americans. They can't understand why a superpower is destroying a backward little country thousands of miles away."

"They think we're spies," the tall man said, and they all chuckled. "Like, what do we have to spy on, test papers? Kids' notebooks?"

"Come on," the woman said. "They can't figure us out. They think all Americans are rich, and they can't understand why we'd leave rich America and come to poor Turkey to teach for pennies. It doesn't make sense to them."

"Yeah," the short man said. "And we don't want to say we're trying to stay out of the army. The army's important here. Every male Turk's gotta serve. So they don't understand—and don't like—the idea of men trying to get out of serving."

The ferry carved through the dark waters of the Bosphorus on its way to Asia, passing the huge red-towered bulk of Haydarpaşa Station, the terminus for trains into the Asian Turkish heartland.

"I went to every big anti-war rally and protest," Bruce said. "I left because I got so depressed about it."

"What about the draft? What's your status? Are you a 'draft dodger'?"

The tall man framed 'draft-dodger' with air quotes and smiled.

"My number's not up yet. I don't know what I'll do if or when it comes up," Bruce said. "For now, I'm here."

"Do you live in Kadıköy?" the short man asked Bruce.

"Near Taksim. I just found a little rooftop apartment there. I'm not really settled there yet, but I think it'll be good."

"Cool! But it's expensive, isn't it?"

"It's not too bad. A lot cheaper than Berkeley! And the place has a fantastic view."

"Excellent!" the short man said. "When you get settled, invite us up. PCVs—that's 'Peace Corps Volunteers'—always appreciate a free drink or a meal. Hint hint."

Haydarpaşa Station was behind them and the ferry approached the Kadıköy ferry dock. The captain signalled *Idle Engines* and the ferry drifted silently toward the dock. When it was two lengths away, the engines went to *Full Astern*, the waters of the wake roiled and splashed as the reversed propellers slowed the ferry's momentum. The ferry's broad decks rattled and shook from the vibrations of the engine. With a deft spin of the helm, the captain brought the vessel abeam to the dock. It drifted in with a slight bump, and the mates leapt to the shore to secure the hawsers. The engine rumbled quietly at idle as the mates rolled portable gangways across the gap between the ferry and the dock.

"Speaking of invitations," the woman said, "wanna come have *çay?*"

Bruce and the PCVs left the ferryboat and walked through the Kadıköy market to a simple modern apartment block, then up three flights of stairs. The two men led Bruce into a sparsely-furnished one-bedroom apartment and introduced themselves: Jim and James.

The woman, Sarah, walked to another apartment on the same floor and unlocked the door.

"I'll be there in a minute," she said.

She was of medium height, with long light brown hair pinned up on the back of her head, hazel eyes set in a serious but comely face, and a good figure that could draw men's attention if she wanted it to, but being a teacher in Turkey she dressed with some style but conservatively, which was what she preferred in any case.

"We're both named James, so one of us has to be Jim. That would be me," the tall one said. He had black hair, a thin face, and a slender build.

"Sarah used to have a roommate, Gloria, but she quit and went home. Now Sarah's gotta pay the whole rent herself…out of a Peace Corps salary."

"Why'd she quit, this Gloria?"

Jim laughed. "She thought Peace Corps service was going to be a lark—free travel to an exotic locale full of dark-haired Mediterranean romeos. She thought teaching would just be standing in front of little kids speaking English."

"So, it's not that?" Bruce smiled.

Jim smirked in return. "Well, it is an exotic locale, but on some days we have seven classes, with two hours' prep needed for each class. Ends up being at least a 60- to 70-hour week, especially since Gloria left and we've had to pick up her classes. And if you don't know how to maintain discipline—Gloria sure didn't!—the kids realize it quick and take over, and you have a disaster."

"No wonder she left."

"Good riddance!" Jim said. "The kids are actually wonderful if you let them know who's boss right at the outset. They're used to strict discipline. It's how they expect school to be. They respect teachers who actually *teach* them something. In America, school is just something kids gotta do. They complain about it. Here, they're eager to learn. Education is really respected. When a teacher just wastes their time, like Gloria did and a few of our Turkish colleagues do, they know the difference. They're smart."

James came from the kitchen to the salon carrying a tray with tea in little gold-rimmed glasses. He put a bowl of sugar cubes and some tiny spoons on the table. James was of medium height and body with bright red hair, a freckled face with strong Irish features, a red-striped shortsleeve shirt and blue jeans.

"We had another PCV here the first year—Danny. He quit too, but for a different reason," James said.

"Yeah, to deal drugs!" Jim said.

"Drugs? Really? A Peace Corps Volunteer dealing drugs?"

"He's not a PCV, at least not anymore. He wasn't a very good one before. I think he was just avoiding the draft. He wasn't a good teacher, didn't believe in the Peace Corps mission. New he says he's translating Customs documents for a trucking company, but I don't know.... Another good riddance!" James said.

"Danny says he's working for a trucking company, but we think the company is a front for a drug operation," Jim said.

"Are drugs a big thing here?"

"Well," James said, "there's a town named 'The Black Castle of Opium,' and all the farmers there grow...opium poppies!" He laughed.

"And it's legal?"

"Well... sort of. In any case, you can get opium here pretty easily if you want to. Some older Turks use it in small amounts, but the big users are mostly foreigners."

"But this Peace Corps guy. What if the cops find out? What if he gets caught?"

"Then they throw him in the slammer, and he had it coming," Jim said.

"And if they don't," James said, "he gets rich—or murdered by the mafia. They control the drug trade. I don't think he realizes how much danger he's in."

"Yeah," Jim said. "We see him around sometimes, and he says his 'work' is so easy, and the money unbelievable. You don't make that much money translating Turkish documents into English. He doesn't realize he's just a bug to them. The big guys, the Turkish mafia, run everything. When they want to, they'll squash him."

"Or turn him into the police," James said. "Dead or in a Turkish prison. Tough choice."

Sarah came in, took her seat and a glass of tea. She didn't say much, but she watched Bruce with interest.

10

Danny

She was no hippy. Though she was wearing jeans and a light denim top decorated with appliquéd flowers, her curly blonde hair was tied neatly on top of her head, her makeup was perfect, her hands were manicured, her sandals were casual but expensive. Late-twenties. Tall. Buxom. A knockout.

Seeing her sitting on the terrace in front of Mustafa's café gave Bruce a shock. He felt that rush of adrenaline, that assault on the emotions, that momentary defenselessness a man suffers on seeing an exceptionally beautiful woman.

He sat down at another table, but they were still close to one another on the small terrace.

"Bruce! *Hoş geldiniz! Hoş geldiniz!* How are you? Are you good?" Mustafa emerged from the café and shook hands. "What would you like?"

"Çay, please. Do you have baklava?"

"*Tabii!* Of course! Baklava!"

Bruce forced himself not to glance sideways at the beautiful blonde. It was an effort. Play it nonchalant. Mustafa brought the little glass of tea and the baklava.

"Can I see the notebook?" Bruce asked him.

"*Tabii! Tabii! Defter!*" Mustafa hurried inside, returned with the book and set it on the table. Bruce opened it, trying not to look self-conscious, but that made him look self-conscious.

"Do you live here?" the blonde asked after a minute.

"I do." Bruce answered, his blood rising at being noticed.

"I live here too," she said. Her accent was European, maybe German or Scandinavian, Bruce thought.

"Are you American?" she asked.

"Yes. How did you know?"

"Americans dress a certain way. I know it."

"And you?"

"I'm from Norway, but I live in Turkey now. I like the sun and the warm weather. What do you do here? Are you from the consulate?" she asked. Pretty direct, Bruce thought.

"I'm a teacher. I teach English. And you?"

"I work in a nightclub. I'm a manager."

"Bruce," he said, and stretched out his hand.

"Astrid," she said, nodded, and shook his hand. AHSS-treed. "Have you been here long?"

"Not too long, but I like it. The people are nice. I love the food. It's very different from America, but that's what I'm looking for."

"Where do you teach?"

"I'm planning to give private lessons. To businessmen, I hope."

A manager, she says. Some manager! Most of the world has to work, Bruce thought. A beautiful woman can get paid just to be a beautiful woman. An ornament in a club, or maybe not just an ornament.

They were silent. The silence was awkward.

Bruce picked up the notebook and asked "Have you seen this?"

"What is it?"

"A kind of hippy diary. The hippies write whatever they want in it. It's pretty interesting."

He turned in his chair so he could open the notebook and show it. He was closer to her now.

They looked at the pages. Bruce turned them slowly.

"Is that Norwegian?" he asked, pointing to a paragraph in flowing script.

Astrid glanced at it.

"Danish," she said. "It's like Norwegian, but a little different. We can mostly understand Danish."

"What does it say?"

Her head moved closer to his as she read it. She didn't move, her eyes fixed on the page. She frowned, and said, "Oh, just some comments about Istanbul."

What comments? Bruce thought, but he turned the page. They gazed at the book in silence.

"Do you know how long it takes to get a residence permit and work permit here in Istanbul?" she asked.

"No, I wouldn't know. I have a tourist visa, three months. I'm working under the table—that means 'without the required permits'— the way other English teachers do. At the end of three months you just go to Greece for a night then come back through the border and they give you a new three-month visa. I don't know where I'll be in three months, so I haven't bothered with the permits."

"Is there a Norwegian consulate in Istanbul?"

"I don't know."

Astrid stared into the distance, distracted.

"What club do you work in?" Bruce asked. "What kind of club?"

"It's in Taksim. A bar and restaurant. We have music, and food. You can have dinner and watch the musicians. Rich Turks like it."

"What's the name?"

"Are you going to come?" She gave him a hesitant smile.

"Maybe."

Pause.

"All right. If you come, act like you don't know me. The owner doesn't like friends of the girls to take up their time. He wants us to be nice to the guests. Pretend you're a guest."

"I will be a guest!" Bruce laughed. "I'll buy a drink and listen to the music."

You can be nice to me, he thought.

I wonder what that means.

"Alright, you can come. It's expensive. Everything is expensive."

"I bet I can afford one drink."

"Yes. A drink." She stood up. "I must go. Nice to meet you."

"But what's the name of the club?"

She looked away, then looked back at him steadily.

"Casablanca."

"See you there," Bruce said.

She smiled at him, turned and left.

He watched her go.

Wow!

She crossed the street and entered a pastryshop. A minute later she emerged carrying a box with the shop's name and logo. A black Mercedes sedan was parked in front of the shop. It had been there the whole time Astrid was at Mustafa's. The driver opened the back door for her and she got in. Bruce saw the driver take one last look at Mustafa's terrace and the people sitting there, then drive away.

"That is a nice piece of work!"

Bruce looked to his left and saw a young man walk onto the terrace. He had a big smile as he watched the Mercedes drive off. He took a seat next to Bruce.

"Danny," he said, and stretched out his hand to Bruce.

Danny was short and wiry, with a thin acne-scarred face, longish dark brown hair that covered the tops of his ears, long bushy sideburns, and a cigarette between his fingers. His jeans and sport shirt were fashionable. On the wrist behind his outstretched hand was a glittering Rolex.

"Bruce. So…are you the former Peace Corps Volunteer?"

"That's me," Danny said. "Word gets around in this place. What about you?"

"I was talking with Jim, James and Sarah. They told me you had left the Peace Corps and I was curious. How is living in Istanbul without the US government as a backstop? I just moved here, I'm trying to do that, and I thought you might have some tips."

"It's okay," Danny said. "Good, actually. I work at a trucking company, Gündem Transport, as a translator. They ship stuff to and from Europe. They need help with the Customs paperwork, English to Turkish, Turkish to English. So my Peace Corps training—the language training, at least—came in handy after all," he smiled.

"Don't you need a work permit?"

Danny smiled. He held his index finger in front of his lips.

"Shhh… I still have my Peace Corps residence permit, and I work under the table."

"Do you earn enough to live?"

"Plenty! Much better than a Peace Corps teacher's salary. The company pays pretty well 'cause they need the help. There aren't that many people around who know both English and Turkish. They give me an apartment, and sometimes I can use a company car. The driver takes me where I want to go. Pretty sweet."

Expensive-looking shoes, perfectly shined, but Bruce had noticed that a perfect shoeshine was obligatory for anyone above working class in Turkey. When Danny lifted his tea to sip, Bruce saw the Rolex again. He wears it on his right wrist, Bruce thought, so everyone sees it when he shakes hands or sips tea.

"Tell you what," Danny said. "I'll show you another café, a little different than Mustafa's."

He wrote an address on a slip of paper.

"Show this to a taxi driver. What about Tuesday morning?"

"Sure. Gotta get to know Istanbul."

"See you there."

The next day, Bruce was on a ferryboat going north up the Bosphorus to the Rumeli Hisarı fortress, guidebook in hand.

Beyond Beşiktaş…, he read, *between the avenue and the shore, Çırağan Palace built for Abdülaziz in 1874 by the architect Balian. Murat V (1876) was imprisoned here for 27 years by his brother Abdülhamit II. In 1909 and 1910, the palace was used for the first sittings of the parliament. It was destroyed by fire in 1910.*

He looked at the European shore and saw the burned-out hulk of a large, ornate building. Only the windowless walls remained. Beside the former palace were piles of stone, gravel and what looked like coal. The former imperial residence had become a dumping ground for raw materials.

Beside the piles of stone Bruce noticed a sign: *Gündem Transport*. Hmmm… Wasn't that the trucking company Danny said he worked for?

The ferry steamed onward up the Bosphorus. Bruce got off at Bebek and entered Rumeli Hisarı. The guidebook said the fortress had been built by Sultan Mehmet II in only three months, finished in

1452. A thousand masons and a thousand lime-mixers worked on it. Its cannons controlled the Bosphorus and cut off aid from Europe to the Byzantine emperor. A year later, the sultan's armies conquered Constantinople.

Right beside the fortress Bruce saw a group of buildings that did not look like they belonged in Istanbul. They were different. In fact, they looked exactly like the buildings on some 19th-century New England college campus.

Huh?

At lunch in one of the little seaside restaurants in Bebek, he asked a waiter who spoke some English.

"Robert Kolej," the waiter said. "It is American college. For Turks. If I go dere, I speak English very good!" the waiter grinned.

As Bruce was sipping his after-lunch tea, the ferryboat approached the dock from the north on its southbound journey. Bruce was too far from the dock to make it on before it departed.

Oh well.

He finished his tea, paid, and climbed aboard a southbound bus on the shore road.

"Çırağan" he said to the driver.

He walked from the Çırağan bus stop through the half-ruined walls of the old palace compound. The burnt-out shell of the palace and its grounds were indeed now used for storage: piles of sand, gravel and coal.

Gündem Transport consisted of a small warehouse and a number of two- and three-axle Dodge trucks. Couldn't be for moving big quantities of raw materials like sand, stone and coal, Bruce thought. Those went by train and ship.

What did Gündem Transport ship to Europe? Drugs? Why did they find Danny's help so valuable?

Maybe there were other trucks out on the roads now. Must be, Bruce thought. This doesn't look like much of an import-export operation.

11

Marina

Bruce was in the grocery shop on Saray Arkası Sokak having trouble buying toothpaste. The shopkeeper knew only a few English phrases and Bruce had left his dictionary in the apartment. He pantomimed brushing his teeth. The shopkeeper showed him a toothbrush.

"*Diş macunu,* toothpaste."

This came from an attractive auburn-haired woman in her late thirties, almost as tall as Bruce and, by the look of her, athletic. She had slightly slanted eyes, large facial features, prominent cheekbones, a thrilling contralto voice and a confident manner. She was wearing a nurse's uniform, without the cap.

"Yes, *diş macunu,*" Bruce repeated, and the clerk brought two tubes, different brands. He chose the Ipana.

"Thank you. My name's Bruce, Bruce Harmone. I guess you live around here?"

"Yes," said the woman. "Marina Schiller. I'm a nurse at the German hospital."

"Are you German? You sound perfectly American."

"I'm American. My mother was Russian, my father was German, but I'm American."

"So you speak German."

"And Russian. I was lucky. I learned all three languages growing up. And now I'm adding Turkish."

"How long have you been here?"

"Oh, about a year."

Bruce glanced at her left hand. No wedding ring. As he did so, she glanced at his left hand. So.

"I've just moved in here," Bruce said. "Just! Only a few days ago. I'd love to find out more about this neighborhood. Would you like to have tea sometime?"

"Certainly," Marina said. "I don't suppose you have a telephone."

Bruce grinned and pointed to the black phone on the grocery shop's counter.

"Ah, yes, the neighborhood phone. Well then, let's exchange addresses. We can always drop notes."

"Would you have a moment for tea now?"

"Actually, not right this moment… But *carpe diem!* I like your idea. What about in an hour?"

"Done! Here's my address." Bruce wrote it on a scrap of paper. "Expect some chaos as I'm really not settled yet, but at least I can make tea. I hope you don't mind stairs. It's six flights up, but the view is spectacular."

"In an hour then. Bye!"

Bruce bought some biscuits to go with the tea. Better get some milk and a lemon as well, he thought. You never know. Turks don't seem to put milk or lemon in their tea, but she's not a Turk.

He strode to his apartment quickly and tidied up as best he could. He took a small table and two chairs out on the terrace and got the kitchen ready. Soon there was a knock on the door. He opened it to see Marina breathing deeply from the six flights of stairs, but wearing a bright, if guarded, smile. She had changed out of her nurse's uniform and sturdy shoes into a colored print blouse, jeans and comfortable sandals.

"I brought some *lokum*," she said. "Turkish Delight, you know. From Ali Muhiddin Hacı Bekir. The best. In fact, the original."

They went out onto the terrace.

"Well, I must say, you've done well: a bachelor pad—you are a bachelor, I suppose?—with a panoramic Bosphorus view!"

"I am a bachelor," Bruce answered.

"The apartment isn't much, but I do like the view."

"The apartment's fine!" Marina was definite. "It's adequate for what you need. What matters most are the location and the view, and you've got both."

Bruce brought the tea. They sipped and talked and gazed at the ferries and ships cruising the Bosphorus. At first the talk was of the neighborhood, then of Istanbul and Turkey, then of the world. Marina had lived in a surprising assortment of places: Hong Kong, Moscow, Bonn, London.

"All those places as a nurse?" Bruce was surprised.

"The US has the most advanced nursing in the world," she said. "I've got some specialties that lots of hospitals want, and I have the three languages. It's an unusual combination, and a winning one for me. My job is not just nursing, but teaching the local nursing staff the latest techniques and procedures. It's not enough for Turkish doctors to go to the States or Germany and learn the procedures. When they come back to their hospitals, they need nurses who can back them up in their work."

The sun was low in the sky, flooding the buildings on the Asian shore with golden light. Here and there an apartment window flashed back the sun's full deep-yellow glare like a golden spotlight. The Bosphorus shearwaters soared and wheeled overhead, squawking and crying, alighting on roof peaks to give their full-throated call mimicking the sound of raucous laughter.

"I must go," Marina said. "I've got things to do. This has been fun! Let's do it again, next time at my place...or maybe dinner?"

"Sure. That would be great."

12

Club Casablanca

Kulüp Kasablanka. Üye olmayan giremez. The polished brass sign on the door to the club was small, discreet: "Club Casablanca. Members only."

A doorman opened the door. Bruce walked down a long corridor to another door with a small window. Through the window he saw a beautiful young woman with long black hair looking down at a podium. Beyond her was another, a striking blonde in a close-fitting sleeveless short dark-blue dress with a round neckline enhanced by a string of pearls —Astrid!

He opened the door and approached the podium.

"Good evening, sir. May I help you? Are you a member?"

The hostess smiled at him. She was in her late twenties, with Turkish features tending toward the Asiatic and a clear, pale complexion like fine china. She wore a killer Little Black Dress and four-inch black heels which brought her eyes up to a level with Bruce's.

Member? So this was a members-only club?

Astrid, who had been ignoring them, caught his eye, winked, leaned over, cupped her hand to the hostess's ear, whispered a few words, then ignored them again.

"As you are a foreign visitor to Istanbul, we would like to welcome you this evening as a guest member. Perhaps you will become a member in the future. May I have your name, please?"

The room was ornately, elaborately decorated in pseudo-

Ottoman style: crimson velvet curtains trimmed in gold, baroque chairs at small tables, glittering chandeliers. Most tables were occupied by groups of well-dressed Turkish men or couples, the men's suits perfectly tailored, the women's dresses of fine fabrics in the latest European styles.

"Aslı Hanım will show you to your table, sir."

Astrid approached, said "Please follow me, Mr Harmone," and led him across the room. As they walked, she gave her spiel.

"Have you recently arrived in Istanbul, Mr Harmone? I hope you will be happy here. I think you will enjoy the show tonight. It's Turkish music. May I have the waiter bring you a drink? We have excellent champagne!"

When she said this, she glanced at him, shook her head ever so slightly and whispered "beer or rakı."

"What's rakı?" Bruce asked.

Astrid smiled.

"Try it!" she whispered. "It is not so expensive."

She led him to a small table at the far side of the room next to the curtains.

A waiter brought a menu. The menu offered a limited list of luxury dinner dishes. No drink prices.

"Thanks," Bruce answered without whispering, "I think I'll have rakı."

In a few moments two waiters approached Bruce's table, one with a tall, narrow glass and a bottle of clear liquid, the other with a tray bearing bottled water, an ice bucket, and a dish of nuts. The first waiter put the glass on the table in front of Bruce and began to pour, glancing at Bruce for a signal. Bruce just watched him pour. The waiter slowed his pouring, glanced at Astrid and raised his eyebrows. Astrid came to the table.

"You have to tell him when to stop," she said.

"When's that?" Bruce asked.

"I think you have enough!" Astrid smiled at the half-full glass. 'Rakı is normally mixed with water and ice, a third of each. You already have...quite enough rakı!"

Astrid signalled to the waiter holding the water and ice. He added water, leaving enough room for one piece of ice.

Bruce watched the liquid in the glass go from transparent to milky white.

"See if you like it," Astrid said.

Bruce took a sip. The cloudy liquid was cold and seemed even colder because of the bracing anise flavor, but as it went down it brought up a warmth in his chest and finally in his stomach. Wow, Bruce thought. Powerful!

He smiled at Astrid, who gave him a quick pat on the shoulder and walked away. The waiters followed.

The musicians were already on the small stage with their Turkish instruments: a long-necked guitar-like stringed instrument, a plucked dulcimer, a folk fiddle, a clarinet, and Turkish drums. A dark-haired, full-bodied female vocalist in late middle age wearing a shimmering silver-sequined dress came through the curtains to enthusiastic applause.

The musicians played a long introduction before she added her solo voice. The rhythms were lively but the traditional Turkish minor chords and quarter-tones made the music sound un-joyous and even flat to Bruce's untrained ear. Most of the audience clapped in rhythm, and now and then a few men stood up, raised their arms above their heads, snapped their fingers and danced.

Three young hostesses worked the room: a Teutonic goddess with serious cleavage and waist-length platinum-blonde hair. A petite beauty with almond-shaped eyes, long, shining black hair and a prominent chest. A slender, extremely tall café-crème-skinned African girl with close-cropped hair, flashing eyes and a mesmerizing smile. They jested with the clients in a variety of languages. The jest was understood even if the language was not.

"Tamer Bey! You've finished your champagne! Waiter! Bring Tamer Bey another bottle of champagne at once!" the Teutonic blonde said in mock surprise.

As she said it, she gently bumped her hip against Tamer Bey's shoulder and inclined her smile toward him so he would get the full benefit of her cleavage. The champagne appeared immediately.

At another table, a client signaled to the black-haired girl to come close. He whispered something in her ear, she whispered back, patting his arm. They exchanged knowing smiles.

Minutes passed. The music continued. Bruce sipped his rakı, which was certainly having its effect.

The *chanteuse* finished her song to loud applause, bowed and left the stage with the musicians following. Time for their break.

When the music stopped, Astrid approached a table of four men. One of them, a movie-star handsome, expensively-dressed young man with dark wavy hair and shaded glasses, rose from his seat as she approached. They appeared to be having a serious discussion, glancing around the club at staff and patrons. Something about the club? So Astrid really was a manager?

Bruce's rakı was almost gone. He took a last sip, stood unsteadily, put money on the table and walked toward the door. As he passed Astrid she gave him a little smile, but it was the automatic, professional smile of a host, not the smile of someone happy.

13

Kasımpaşa

Danny had given Bruce the address of a tea house in Kasımpaşa. Bruce took a taxi, found the place, and sat at one of the small tables. The sun was warm and bright, heading for another hot day.

A waiter approached.

"Çay," Bruce said.

After a few minutes, Danny walked around the corner, smiled to Bruce and sat down.

"What's your pleasure?" he asked. "Ever try a nargile? Water pipe?"

"I'm not much of a smoker," Bruce replied.

"Try it! It's not like cigarettes. The water cools the smoke."

"Sure, why not."

"Two nargiles, one light, one strong," Danny said to the waiter in Turkish. "And two teas."

The waiter brought the two glasses of tea and went to prepare the water pipes.

"How's the trucking company?" Bruce asked. Might as well go with the fiction for now. Bruce didn't want Danny to know that he had been told about drugs. Maybe it wasn't even true, just bitching or witch-hunting by his former Peace Corps colleagues because Danny had deserted them.

Danny smirked. "It's great. Business is great! What about your tutoring?"

"I'm hanging around the American Library some, working to meet people who want lessons. The librarian refers people. I found a good little apartment. I think it's going to work out. I decided to start with a high rate for the lessons and see if people would pay."

"The people here with money have *real* money," Danny said. "Price is not important if you give them what they want."

The water pipes came. The waiter attached amber mouthpieces to the long flexible tubes and handed a tube to each of them. He used a pair of tongs to pick up a live coal from a charcoal brazier and put it on top of the tobacco plug on Danny's water pipe. Then he did the same for Bruce's.

"*Çek, çek!*" the waiter ordered. Draw!

Danny and Bruce put the mouthpieces to their lips and sucked in the smoke. The coals glowed. The waiter took a small circular tin from his pocket, opened it, and sprinkled a few grains of a grey substance on the coals, causing little sparks.

They smoked.

They sat in silence, smoked, and thought. Calm. Bruce felt relaxed. As he smoked, he felt happy. Here he was in Istanbul, doing this exotic thing—smoking a water pipe—on a beautiful day. He was out in the real world, making a living. He was away from the mindless hippies and the Vietnam War mess. He was making friends.

"Like it?" Danny asked.

"Pretty nice. Is it always this good?"

"*Özel.*" Danny said. "'Special!' Stick with me."

They sat and smoked.

Bruce soon realized the smoke was having an extraordinary effect on his brain, engendering a confused euphoria. He recognized it from the times he had smoked marijuana in college. So that's what *özel* —'special'—meant. He put down the long tube and ordered another tea. He guessed the little grey pellets were opium. Confused euphoria was fine, but hard drugs were not.

"You should come to our little smoke-and-toke get-together sometime," Danny said.

"Smoke-and-toke?"

"Oh, a bunch of us get together. We smoke, do pot and hash, we can do stronger stuff if we like. It's fun. Not too expensive. Secret place. I run it, so I know it's safe."

Danny runs a drug den? Bruce was shocked and intrigued at the same time.

"Sure," he said. "Maybe sometime."

14

Dinner at Bruce's

"Next time at my place—when I'm settled in," Bruce had said to the PCVs when he left them at Jim and James's apartment in Kadıköy.

Now he was settled, so he mailed them a note with an invitation.

Jim, James and Sarah took the ferry from Kadıköy to Galata, then the T1 bus to the stop in front of the West German Consulate. It was a short walk down the hill to Bruce's apartment on Saray Arkası Sokak.

Bruce had asked Aylin how to entertain in Turkish style.

"You go to Şütte, the best charcuterie in Istanbul," she told him. "It's in the Balık Pazarı, the Galatasaray Fish Market. Buy eveything you need there, except the baklava, which should come from Güllüoğlu in Karaköy."

At another shop in the Fish Market he saw cheap little charcoal braziers. He bought one, and a bag of charcoal.

He had his menu: a half-dozen Turkish hors d'oeuvres and salads, little lamb chops to grill over charcoal on the terrace, *baklava* for dessert, two bottles of red wine, Tekel beer on ice, and a bottle of *Yeni Rakı*. The only thing he had to cook was the lamb.

Bruce installed everyone on the terrace and took drink orders.

"Sarah?"

"Do you have wine?"

"A red to go with the lamb."

"I'll take it."

"Jim?"

"The same."

"James?"

"Rakı, my man, rakı!"

"Me too," Bruce said, and brought the drinks.

They sipped in silence for a minute.

"Why are you here?" Sarah asked, looking at Bruce.

He was not surprised by what she asked, but by how she asked it. It seemed a question out of the blue. She didn't ask, "So, what brings you to Istanbul?" or "Are you studying religions?" She asked *the* existential question: Why Are You Here?

Bruce took up the challenge with a sense of humor.

"Do you mean 'Why am I in Istanbul,' or 'Why do I exist at all'?"

"Both," Sarah said looking straight at him, the hint of a smile playing on her lips.

"Well, as I said, I couldn't stand the deadly stupidity of the Vietnam War. Then the hippies—mindless escapism! 'Make love not war.' If you want war to stop, you don't drop out, you take action against it!"

"As for why I am living on this planet," Bruce went on, "that I don't know yet, but in time I hope I will. I'm studying religion for insights into what *all* of us are doing here, and what it means."

Then Bruce hit the ball right back in her court.

"So why are *you* here?"

"I'm here because I grew up on a farm in Illinois—lots of cornfields but not a lot of people—and I wanted a bigger view of the world. I majored in anthropology—I guess for the same reason that *you* study religion: to figure out who we are and what we're all doing here. I signed up for the Peace Corps because I want to see the world and this is the only way that I could afford to go to a foreign country and start learning about other people in person, not just from books."

"And once you see the world, then what?"

"Then I want to see more of it, maybe as a diplomat."

"Are there lady diplomats?" Bruce asked.

"I don't know if there are *lady* diplomats," Sarah hit back, "but there are—or will be—*women* diplomats. I'll be one of them. I'll be the first if I have to be."

Bruce was silent. Jim decided it was time for a change of topic.

"So Bruce, do you like Zeki Müren?"

"Zeki who?"

"Zeki Müren, Turkey's Liberace, this country's biggest pop star."

"I don't know him."

"You will. He's *huge.*"

"Have you run into James Baldwin in Ayazpaşa?" James asked. "The Negro writer? I heard he visits here sometimes, or used to. Çifte Vav Sokak."

"Çifte Vav Sokak? That's right at the end of Saray Arkası, a half block from here."

"Çifte Vav… That's an odd name for a street," Sarah said. "I wonder what it means. Do you have a Redhouse?"

"A what?" Bruce asked.

"A Redhouse. Turkish-English Dictionary. The essential tool."

"No, I only have one of those little Langenscheidt pocket dictionaries."

"You should get a Redhouse," Sarah said. "Can't live without it."

"No, I haven't seen any black guys," Bruce went on. "I think I'd notice. He'd stand out. He's the one who wrote *The Fire Next Time,* right?"

"Right. I want to meet him!"

"If I see him, I'll let you know," Bruce smiled. "You a writer?"

"I majored in English," James said. "I do write poetry, and I've had a few pieces published in small magazines, but being a poet is probably not a great way to make a living. After my Peace Corps teaching I want to go to graduate school and be an English teacher at a college, if I can manage it—and if I don't get drafted."

"What about you, Jim?"

"Well, I know this sounds silly but I want to work in an art gallery. Maybe run my own gallery some day. My mother owns a gallery and I've helped her out, so I know the business. It's pretty interesting, I love the art, and I like working with creative people."

"You don't want to do what your dad does?" James said, grinning at his roommate.

"God no! He works for an insurance company. He goes to the office every day, works eight hours, brings work home sometimes, plays golf on the weekends. I'm not criticizing him or what he does. I mean, he's provided for our family very well. It's great, I owe him. In fact, I admire him because I just couldn't do it, that routine. I've gotta do something different."

"I like poetry," Bruce said. "Used to write some myself. Looking at it now, it wasn't very good, but it was good for me to write it. I bet yours is better. Do I get to read some of it?"

"Maybe. Introduce me to Baldwin and I'll let you read the poem I dedicated to him. There's an incentive for you!"

"Deal!" Bruce smiled, and got up to put the lamb chops on the grill and refresh the drinks.

"Need some help?" Sarah asked.

Bruce paused. About to say "No, thanks," instead he said "Sure," and smiled at her as she got up from her chair, smiling back at him.

On the street below, invisible from the terrace, a Turkish woman, two Turkish men, and a short black man walked along Saray Arkası Sokak toward Çifte Vav Sokak.

15

Consulate

As Bruce climbed the stairs to his apartment, he heard a door open. On the second floor, Aylin was standing, smiling, with an envelope in her hand.

"This is for you," she said.

"What is it?" Bruce asked.

"I don't know, but the envelope is quite impressive. The porter told me a man in a black car brought it."

She winked at him. "I didn't know you were a diplomat!"

"I'm not!"

The envelope was of heavy paper with his name written calligraphically on the front. On the back was the Great Seal of the United States and the words "US Consulate-General, Istanbul."

The Consul-General of the United States Mr Charles Knowlton
and Mrs Jane Knowlton
request the pleasure of the company of
Mr Bruce Harmone
at a Reception
Sunday, September 29, 1968 from 3:00 to 5:00 pm.
Consulate-General of the United States of America
Meşrutiyet Caddesi, Beyoğlu, Istanbul.
R.S.V.P.
Please present this invitation at the entrance.

* * *

The US Consulate-General was housed in the Palazzo Corpi, a sumptuous Italianate mansion built in the 1870s for Italian shipping magnate Ignazio Corpi at a cost of 99,000 Ottoman gold liras. The finest Carrara marble, Piemonte rosewood and other precious materials were shipped from Italy for its construction, and Italian artisans and artists were employed to build and decorate it.

As he entered, Bruce was stopped by a US Marine in dress uniform and asked for his credentials. He showed his invitation and US passport. The poker-faced Marine pointed to a doorway and said "That way, sir."

As he entered, a dignified gentleman in a dark suit and muted tie turned to look at him, smiled, and extended his hand.

"Charles Knowlton, Consul-General," he said. "Welcome! Are you new in Istanbul?"

"Bruce Harmone. Thank you, sir. Yes, I got here a few weeks ago."

"Business? Pleasure? Study?"

"Wanderlust, I guess. I'm on leave from graduate school, out to see the world."

"How do you find Istanbul so far?"

"So far I like it a lot, sir, especially the food and the history."

"Well, the bar's over there and we'll be serving some hors d'oeuvres just before I give my little speech." He smiled. "We plan it that way. With everybody's mouth full, I'm the only one who can talk!"

He smiled at his little joke, as did Bruce.

The Consul-General glanced across the room at another man who caught his glance and wandered over to them.

"Bruce, this is Dave Coughlin, our DPO. Dave, Bruce…"

"Harmone," Bruce offered. "Bruce Harmone. Nice to meet you."

"Hi Bruce."

As Dave shook Bruce's hand he pulled him gently away from the Consul-General, who turned to the next arriving guest.

"DPO?" Bruce asked Coughlin.

"Deputy Principal Officer, the assistant Consul-General. Mr Knowlton makes the decisions, and I hope I can carry them out.

Let's get you a drink."

Coughlin led Bruce over to the bar. Bruce asked for a beer.

"What brings you to Istanbul?" Dave asked as they drifted away from the bar.

"Leave of absence from graduate school. I wanted to travel. I'm working to find some people here who want to learn English and give them private lessons to pay for my stay here."

"Private English lessons? Good," Dave said. "You can do all right with that here."

Two men strolled up to Bruce and Dave. Dave introduced them.

"Bruce, this is Ralph Graves, and Director Hikmet Yılmaz of Istanbul's security services, the *Emniyet*," Dave said.

Graves was tall and powerfully built, middle-aged, with dark hair, a rugged face and intense, probing grey eyes. Yılmaz looked like many of the other Turkish men Bruce had seen since arriving: medium height, stocky build, black hair and moustache, bushy eyebrows, courtly manners.

Bruce shook hands.

"You're new here, I guess," Graves said. "You're not Peace Corps," he said as though he already knew.

"No, but I *am* a teacher of sorts. Private English lessons."

"Have you met any of the Peace Corps Volunteers? A few of them are here today. Nice kids."

"Yeah, I've met a few in Kadıköy. I like them. I guess some of them have quit."

Ralph's expression darkened.

"It's not the army. PCVs can quit if they want."

He changed the subject.

"Find a place to live? There's an apartment shortage."

"Yeah, I was lucky. I found a pretty good place in Ayazpaşa, behind the West German consulate. Are you a vice-consul, consular officer? I don't know much about embassies or consulates."

"DEA. Drug Enforcement. We help Director Yılmaz stop drugs from moving to the US."

"I guess you're busy. I hear Istanbul has a big drug trade."

Director Yılmaz frowned.

"We do our job. If we got as much help from Congress as we do from Director Yılmaz and the *Emniyet,* we could do our job a lot better."

"Is it dangerous? I hear the drug guys are pretty nasty."

"Part of the job," Ralph said matter-of-factly. "I was a New York cop before. Detective in the drug division. That was a lot more dangerous." He glanced at Director Yılmaz, who nodded.

"I've heard they raise a lot of opium in Turkey. Isn't there even a town named 'opium castle' or something?"

Ralph laughed. "Yeah, Afyonkarahisar, 'the Black Castle of Opium.' Great name! Interesting old town with a stone fort on top of a high rock. Yeah, they've raised opium poppies there for centuries."

"Turkish government is the only buyer of opium crop," Yılmaz said. "Government processes the opium into morphine and other *legal* drugs. For *medicine!*"

"The only *legal* buyer," Ralph added, "but the government doesn't pay as much as the drug guys—they pay a lot more, so some of the crop ends up being sold to the crooks who turn it into heroin. The heroin ends up in the bloodstream of Americans—if we don't stop them."

"Listen," Ralph added, "Not that you would or anything, but don't go near it. Not any of it, ever. Not even the hash or pot. You don't know the territory, and the guys in charge do. To the guys at the top, everybody else is mincemeat, cannon fodder. They'd as soon kill you or rat you to the cops as say 'Hi.' They protect themselves and don't care about anybody else. Stay away."

"Thanks for the warning," Bruce said. "I'm not interested. Beer, wine and rakı are good enough for me."

"Ah, you know *rakı?*" Director Yılmaz asked, smiling.

"Just discovered it. I've had it a few times. I like it."

"Sometime we show you a *gerçek rakı masası,* uh…" He looked at Graves for help in the translation.

"A real rakı table," Graves said.

"Yes! Many *meze* and rakı."

"Turkish hors d'oeuvres," Graves translated. "Good food, drink and conversation. It's an institution in this country."

"I'd love to do it," Bruce said. "Just let me know."

"Hey, speaking of food, here it comes. Grab some and dig in. Keep in touch. Here's my card."

Ralph handed him the card, gave him a firm slap on the back, nodded, and he and Yılmaz wandered away.

"That young man," Yılmaz said to Graves after they had walked away from Bruce, "he is new in Istanbul. He has no connection. He is not military, or diplomat, or Peace Corps, or business. Nobody is telling him what to do. He does not work in office. He is going around Istanbul every day in different ways. He may see or hear things we do not—or cannot."

"Right. Good point," Graves said. "We'll get him on board. Let's see what he comes up with."

Graves made his way over to Dave Coughlin at the bar.

Bruce was standing alone, nibbling a warm cheese *börek* flaky pastry and sipping an Americanly-cold beer.

"Enjoying yourself?" Dave asked.

"Yeah, I was talking to Mr Graves and Director Yılmaz."

"Ralph's a real asset here," Dave told Bruce. "His heart's in it. Works all the time and is very effective." Dave lowered his voice. "In New York, a drug boss put out a hit on his fiancée. They got her. It hit Ralph really hard. He couldn't stand New York anymore. We're lucky to have him here."

Dave was quiet for a minute.

"You know, I may be able to help with your private tutoring. We know a lot of the local VIPs. Some speak English, but I know there are lots who want to learn it better, or learn it at all. And they want the people they work with to learn it. I can give you some names, maybe get you some clients."

"That would be great!"

"There is one thing, though…," lowering his voice, with a conspiratorial smile. "Technically, we're not supposed to do this, to give out names of locals. And I don't know what your work-permit situation is—no, don't tell me!" Dave smiled. "Let's just keep it all… quiet."

"Sure. No one will know. If anyone asks how I got some names, I'll say I was talking with friends."

"Good! Okay, tomorrow afternoon you can pick up an envelope from Emine in the library. You know the American Library next door?"

"Sure. Thanks! Yeah, this is great. I can use the customers."

"Glad to help."

The next day, at the American Library, Emine handed Bruce an envelope.

"Mr Coughlin wanted you to have this brochure of information for Americans living in Turkey," she said, and smiled.

"Thank you."

When Bruce got back to his apartment, he opened the envelope. Folded inside the brochure was the list, typewritten on plain paper with names, office addresses and phone numbers. The first name was Ahmet Kamanbay, Chairman, Beynelmilel Holding, with an office address in Galata.

I'll start with that one, Bruce thought.

He wrote out a short *curriculum vitae* neatly, emphasizing his English skills. He added a note, put it in an envelope and wrote his name and address on it. The next day he left it with the receptionist at Beynelmilel Holding.

16

Armen

Armen Bagratian grew up in Yerevan, Armenian Soviet Socialist Republic, hearing stories of his parents' beautiful home in the old country, in the Ottoman town of Talas. They sighed as they reminisced about their rich Armenian culture, their beautiful church, the Talas American College where Greek and Armenian children could get the best modern education. His parents told these stories to Armen in Turkish, the language they had spoken in Talas except in church, where they spoke Armenian. Armen grew up speaking both.

Talas—whenever things got tough in poor Soviet Armenia, whenever his parents were vexed with communist regulations or having to learn Russian, they would sigh and reminisce about Talas.

To Armen, it sounded like heaven. The anger rose in him when he imagined them being forced out of their beautiful home.

But to Armen, Soviet Armenia was home, and the Soviet Union was the country of the future. In school he learned that Europe and America were decadent and in decline, the people exploited and starving, and that the communist system was overtaking the West in everything—in science, technology, productivity, and military might. Comrade Stalin was the wisest and most beneficent leader in the world.

Then came the Great Patriotic War. In 1942 Armen Bagratian was called to serve the Soviet Union and assigned to the Armenian 89th Rifle Division organized in Yerevan.

After savage battles and heroic fighting in the Caucasus, his crack unit was transferred to Poland, where it joined the mammoth drive toward Germany. The 89th distinguished itself again, with heavy losses, in the conquest of Berlin.

After Hitler's suicide and Germany's surrender, the 89th was assigned to occupation duty in Wittenberg, a city largely undamaged by the war. It was there that Armen realized the truth: Germany and the West were far, far ahead of the Soviet Union in wealth and technological progress. Everything they had drilled into him at home about the decline of the West and the superiority of the Soviet system was untrue.

Drinking with friends one night in Wittenberg, Armen was astonished to meet Dikran, a French soldier who spoke Armenian. Son of a merchant family who had moved from Constantinople to Paris at the turn of the century, Dikran was the French army liaison to the 89th. He told Armen about life in Paris. They became close friends.

Paris must be like Talas, Armen thought. Like paradise.

He made up his mind.

With Dikran's help he obtained false French identity papers, found civilian clothes, slipped away from his unit, and made his way to Paris.

The Paris that Armen Bagratian entered in the summer of 1945 as a 21-year-old deserter from the Soviet Army was largely undamaged by the war, but it was exhausted and depopulated except for American and British soldiers, who were everywhere. The victorious Allies were working to restore the food supply and essential infrastructure of the city. Theirs were the only smiling faces.

Dikran helped Armen locate his relatives in the Marais, a poor district that was home to many Ashkenazi Jewish and other immigrants from the Ottoman Empire—at least it had been before the war, before the Nazi deportations of Jews to extermination camps emptied many of its houses.

Armen's great-uncle Rouben had worked in a factory before it was bombed by the Allies. His wife Gasia was a cleaner of public buildings. They now lived on their savings and her meager wage. They had very little, but they willingly shared what they had with Armen.

The war had left France with few young, healthy, unwounded men, so Armen found work easily. Already fluent in Armenian, Russian and Turkish, he learned French quickly. He arranged to attend some *lycée* classes to prepare to study chemistry at the university. Great advances had been made in the science of chemistry during the war. Knowing chemistry, he thought, it would be easy to find a good job in the post-war economy.

In the autumn of 1968 Armen Bagratian was 44 years old and a lecturer in chemistry at the Sorbonne.

He was unhappy. His childless marriage had ended in a bitter divorce.

He didn't have good relations with his students. After what he had been through—growing up in a poor country, the horrors of war —he just couldn't understand this self-absorbed, self-entitled generation of young people.

His colleagues at the university found him increasingly difficult to work with, and he heard rumors that the administration was taking steps to transfer him to a new university in one of the former French colonies in Africa.

He needed a new direction in life.

A younger Armenian-French colleague invited him to attend a discussion group about the Great Tragedy, the mass murders of Armenians in the twilight years of the Ottoman Empire. He listened discontentedly as a few fledgling firebrands argued about arcane political matters—Soviet Armenia, Lebanon, Palestine—and hinted at grandiose, unrealistic plans for revenge. Armen had been a Soviet soldier in a crack unit. He knew what real fighting was.

He left the meeting in disgust, but the seed of revenge for the Great Tragedy was planted.

His friend and mentor, History Professor Aram Manouchian, noticed the changes in Armen, and worried about him.

One sunny summer day, they sat at a café on the Boulevard Saint-Germain. Around them, neighborhood regulars sipped coffee, wine and beer. Old men read newspapers and racing forms, a second glass of red wine ready to hand. Young couples looked dreamily into one another's eyes. Only Armen and Professor Manouchian wore serious expressions on their faces. Armen had raised the subject of the Great Tragedy.

"Other subject peoples of the Ottoman Empire achieved independence, but we Armenians did not," the professor said. "The sultan's government looked upon us as a 'fifth column,' ready to aid the Russians again in World War I. And we were! If only they would help us gain independence. I was a boy in Constantinople when the Armenian revolutionaries occupied the Ottoman Bank. They claimed that this attack would get the notice of the Western powers, and they would intervene with the Ottoman government and pressure it for Armenian independence. But what happened?"

He stared at Armen, who was silent.

"The revolutionaries attacked the bank with guns and bombs," the professor went on. "Dozens of people died. What did they accomplish? Their attack gave the reactionaries an excuse to hunt down Armenians! I saw it myself! It made the wave of murders of innocent Armenians worse!"

Armen slapped the café table with the flat of his hand.

"What would you have us do, be slaves forever?"

"Armen, we placed our hopes in Russia, but Russia failed us. It sent its armies into Armenia and Thrace in 1877, promising us independence, but their real purpose was not to help us. Their real goal was to control Constantinople and the Dardanelles."

"But… they didn't," Armen said.

"No. The Russian armies got as far as Ayastefanos, a few kilometers west of Constantinople, but then the European powers intervened. Britain and France threatened war if the Russians took the city, so they stopped."

The professor sighed, lifted his glass of wine, swirled the liquid around in the clear glass bowl and admired its color. He sipped, set the glass carefully on the marble table, and continued.

"The Russians built a huge war memorial at Ayastefanos, supposedly to commemorate their fallen soldiers, but in reality it was a warning to the Turks: 'We can take Constantinople anytime we like!'"

He chuckled to himself.

"The Turks dynamited the monument in 1914 because the Ottoman and Russian empires were on opposite sides in the war. November 14th—I remember the day."

He looked at Armen.

"So much for Western intervention. My young friend, the Great Powers want great things: oil, sea routes, great cities, fertile land. We Armenians had none of those things, just poor soil in a harsh climate. They do not help oppressed people out of the goodness of their hearts. They cared nothing for us."

"All of this changes nothing," Armen said. "We need revenge."

Armen took a packet of *Gitanes* from his pocket and offered a cigarette to the professor, who declined. Armen lit one for himself. As he lifted the match to his face, Professor Manouchian saw the flame in Armen's eyes.

He looked away. Such anger was alarming. He was afraid for his younger colleague.

"If you can find alive any of those responsible for the massacres, bring them to justice!" the professor said, "but do not let the poison of hatred rot your soul. Look what hatred and 'revenge' have done to Europe: Germany conquered France in 1871, and attacked again in 1914. France won, but Germany rose again and attacked France in 1940. In every one of these wars, millions died! This is insanity! The cycle of revenge must be broken! "

"The only way for the cycle to be broken is through an independent Armenia that can defend itself!" Armen growled. "When we are strong enough to deter invaders, we will have peace."

The professor sighed and looked directly at his younger friend.

"Armen, I was there! I lived through it! I know what I'm talking about!"

He paused for emphasis, then continued.

"We cannot control the past, but we can shape the future. The United Nations may give us hope: all the nations of the world, large and small, discussing global problems and arriving at solutions in concert. This is a better way."

Armen hadn't drunk much of his wine. He stubbed out his cigarette, drained his glass in one long pull and put coins on the café table in payment.

"Goodbye, professor."

United Nations? World government? *Merde!* Armen had learned in the Soviet army that power—raw force—was all that mattered. Those who had power won, and got respect. Those who did not, had nothing.

17

Kamanbay

"My name's Bruce Harmone. I'm here to see Mr Kamanbay."

"Yes, sir. Welcome. I will let Mr Kamanbay know that you are here."

The office reception area was sleek and modern, with a panoramic view of the Bosphorus. A door opened and a heavy-set Turk in his 50s emerged: dense black hair swept back, greying at the temples, bushy black eyebrows above active dark eyes, prominent rectangle of dense black hair on the upper lip. He extended his hand.

"Welcome! I am Ahmet Kamanbay. *Buyrun!*" He waved his arm toward the doorway and the vast private office beyond. "Please!"

"*Buyrun!*" Kamanbay indicated a chair across the desk from him. The guest chair featured a view of the boss backed by an even more spectacular view of the Bosphorus. It seemed a pity to Bruce that the boss didn't have that view. Maybe he had it everywhere else, all the time.

The rest of the walls in the office, and the shelves, and the cabinets, and any extra floor space, were filled with Turkish art objects: colored tiles, inscriptions, framed fabrics, large vases, marquetry tables and chairs, mosque lamps, even jewelry in frames and glass boxes. It was truly a museum of Islamic arts, and not a small one. Bruce didn't know much about Turkish and Ottoman art, but he guessed that this private collection was worthy of a small museum anywhere in the world.

"You teach English," Ahmet smiled. "*Evet…*" He held out his hands as though waiting for Bruce to give him something.

Bruce wasn't prepared for this. He had expected a short get-acquainted meeting. Soon he guessed that the English Ahmet had just spoken was over half of what he knew, and must have been grabbed from a phrasebook or dictionary. Bruce's Turkish was barely that of a three-year-old, so communication was primitive.

Thinking quickly, Bruce began with vocabulary. The objects in the office—desk, chair, lamp, telephone, window, door, glass of water. Walking, running. Body parts: head, chest, arm, hand. The half hour went quickly.

"T'ank yoo!" Ahmet said, walked him to the office door, shook his hand. "Goot-bye!"

The receptionist smiled at Bruce and handed him an envelope.

"Your next appointment is in two days, at the same time."

Out of the office, Bruce opened the envelope. Wow. Look at that cash. This was going to work! He'd be better prepared in two days.

Another lesson for Ahmet Kamanbay today, Bruce thought. Things are going along well enough. Ahmet Bey had absolutely no facility for languages, and it looked to Bruce like he would never learn English, but the executive seemed delighted with his progress, and the envelopes full of cash were going to be Bruce's mainstay.

"I friend has," Ahmet said at the end of their lesson. "Friend English learn wants. *Ama* friend no—childs."

Ahmet Bey wrote down a name and phone number and handed it to Bruce.

"Teşekkür ederim, Ahmet Bey!" Bruce said.

"T'ank yoo meens!" Ahmet Bey translated, and smiled broadly.

On his way home Bruce stopped at the grocery shop and called the number Ahmet Kamanbay had given him.

"Efendim," the voice answered.

"Hello, Mr Halepli? This is Bruce Harmone. Mr Ahmet Kamanbay gave me your number. Do you speak English?"

"Yes," said Devin Halepli. "Thank you for calling. Yes, Ahmet Bey said you might call."

"Would you like private English lessons for your children?"

"That's right. My children are six and eight years old. I would like you to come to our house in Ortaköy to give the lessons. I guess it's best if you come and see us, meet the children, and we can discuss the schedule. I will give you our address. Do you have a pen?"

Bruce wrote down the address. The next day he took the bus north up the Bosphorus shore.

He got off the bus in Ortaköy, went into a shop and showed the address to the shopkeeper, who pointed up the hill opposite to a large house, raised his hands and spread them apart.

"Büyük!" he said. Big house.

Bruce climbed the hill and saw a large, modern villa surrounded by trees except on the Bosphorus side. The view would be breathtaking. He got to the heavy metal driveway gate and touched the button on the intercom.

"Buyrun," a voice said.

"Bruce Harmone for Mr Halepli," he said.

With a click, a motor whir and a grumble of metal wheels, the heavy gate slid slowly to the left. He walked through the fence, along the cobbled driveway, and up the steps to the front door.

The door opened. The man who opened it smiled at him and said "Welcome! Please come in."

It was the same handsome man in shaded glasses he had seen at the Casablanca with Astrid.

Bruce arranged to take the bus to the Halepli villa twice a week in the afternoon to give the children their lessons. The kids were cute: six-year-old Bülent and his eight-year-old sister Pelit. Bruce bought some illustrated Turkish picture books and wrote English translations beneath the Turkish captions. It was a good way to start. The kids learned quickly. Later, he covered up the Turkish and ask them to read the English. It was like a game to them. They loved it.

Usually, Halepli was not there—at work, or traveling. The housekeeper or another member of the staff—there were a lot of them—would let him in. The kids always greeted him excitedly. They loved the fact that this was "school" but they didn't have to wear school uniforms or sit at desks or behave themselves as stiffly as they had to in a real school.

Things were going well.

* * *

On the same day that Bruce was teaching the Halepli kids in Istanbul, 240 kilometers to the west in Edirne, a black hearse returned to its garage on a dead-end street. After the hearse driver had departed, a man closed the heavy garage doors, then two others began to remove the rear bumper and tailgate of the long vehicle. Removing the bolts holding a thick steel plate, they exposed a large empty space beneath the coffin platform. The man who had closed the garage doors then wheeled an industrial cart loaded with cardboard boxes up to the back of the hearse. The other two men unloaded the boxes from the cart and pushed them carefully into the hearse's hidden cargo space. When all 24 boxes had been loaded, they bolted the steel plate back in place, re-attached the rear bumper and tailgate, and polished the entire rear of the vehicle to remove fingerprints.

The two men then placed a simple pine coffin—empty—on the high coffin platform and quietly closed the tailgate and window. The shipment was ready to depart tomorrow morning to Bulgaria, the first leg of a long journey to waiting markets in Europe and America.

18

Rakı Masası

Dave Coughlin sent a note to Bruce: "Want to join us for the Rakı Table that Director Yılmaz promised you? Give me a call."

Bruce called the consulate from the grocery shop. They agreed on tomorrow evening, 8 pm, Çiçek Pasajı in Galatasaray.

At 8 pm, Bruce was at the front door of the Çiçek Pasajı, the one-time flower market in Galatasaray Square, now a gathering of beer shops and *meyhanes*—Turkish tavernas. As Dave Coughlin and Ralph Graves walked up to Bruce, Hikmet Yılmaz got out of a police car across the street.

They all shook hands and Yılmaz led them into the 19th-century building to the Kimene Restaurant. The *maître d'* was expecting them. He led them through the ground-level dining room to a stairway and down to a subterranean chamber. Large barrels crowded one wall, leaving enough room for only six tables, three of which were already occupied by diners. The other diners' table tops were so crowded with small white plates of appetizers that some plates perched atop others two and three high. Glasses of milky-white rakı were at each place.

Bruce and the others sat. The waiter came and Yılmaz engaged him in a lengthy and earnest conversation, Yılmaz asking questions, getting answers, making decisions. Finally the waiter left, and within five minutes several waiters returned with nearly two dozen small plates of Turkish hors d'oeuvres—*meze*—and the rakı equipment: tall glasses, bottles of spring water, an ice bucket, and a bottle of *Yeni Rakı.*

Yılmaz nodded to the original waiter, then at Bruce. The waiter then opened the bottle of rakı, and began to pour. When the glass was about a third full, Bruce nodded. The waiter poured water, and Bruce nodded when the glass was two-thirds full. Then the ice cubes, enough to fill the glass.

The waiter repeated the ceremony for each of the other men.

Yılmaz, Coughlin and Graves lifted their glasses, and Bruce did the same. Looking into one another's eyes, they smiled, said *Şerefe!*— In your honor!—clinked glasses, and took a sip.

Ah! The *rakı* signalled its arrival with the satisfying contrast of chill and warmth.

Yılmaz intoned the Turkish name of each meze dish as he pointed at it: cheese fritters, white sheep-milk cheese, eggplant purée, white beans vinaigrette, tomato and cucumber salad, yellow cheese, pickled bonito fish. Bruce would never remember all the names, but he would remember the look and the flavors.

They ate, drank and chatted. Coughlin asked Bruce about graduate school.

"So, what is it that fascinates you about religion? Do you see that as your profession?"

"No, actually not. I'm not the clergyman type, I guess. Well, my father is a Baptist pastor. I grew up in a totally religious household. That, for me, was normal. Then I went to UC Berkeley. It was like entering an alternate reality! But later I came to think of my childhood home as the alternate reality, and Berkeley as the real world."

"Some people might dispute Berkeley being the 'real world,'" Coughlin joked. "Do hippies live in the 'real world'?"

"Don't ask me!" Bruce smiled. "I just study the supernatural!"

But the joke was on Bruce. He had a flash of insight: is religion part of the 'real world'? If it isn't, why am I studying it?

They were silent for a minute, sipping their rakı. Yılmaz broke the uncomfortable silence by suggesting that Bruce tour Cappadocia, where he had grown up, because of its 'moonscape' topography and medieval painted churches.

After a half hour of chit-chat, Graves got down to business.

"Bruce, in May the US government finally signed the UN's Drug Traffic Flow Treaty. It was ratified by the UN six years ago, but we didn't get around to signing it until now. It's been a big help to us in getting Congress to spend more money on interdicting the flow of drugs to the US. Some of that money goes to the Turkish government and thus to Director Yılmaz's security service, which is a help. We Americans can't take any direct action here in Turkey, of course. We're foreigners with no legal authority outside the US, but what we can do is coordinate intelligence with Director Yılmaz and give his officers information that can help them in their work."

"So. Information," Graves said. "If you come across any information that may help us in our work, please let us know. Don't get me wrong. We're not employing you! You're not 'spying' for us, and you're certainly not supposed to put yourself in any danger. We're just asking you to keep your eyes and ears open."

"If you notice anything interesting," Graves went on, "the best way is to tell us face to face, at times like this. At the consulate, in a café or restaurant. We'll buy you a rakı! It's better not to write things down or telephone them unless you have to. Don't be afraid to call us at the consulate and tell us you'd like to meet. Any time."

Coughlin and Graves picked up their glasses and sipped. Yılmaz did the same. Bruce did too. That, he guessed, was the end of the business meeting for which they had organized the Rakı Table.

Yılmaz, glass in hand, lifted it, looked at Bruce and said *"En kötü günümüz böyle olsun!"*

"May the worst day of our lives be as good as this!" Coughlin translated and, smiling, clinked his glass to Bruce's.

19

Büyükada

Bruce was tired of being cooped up in his apartment. After breakfast he used the phone at the grocery shop to call the PCVs' school and leave a message: want to do something this weekend? Call the grocery shop, leave a date, time and place message. I'll do whatever you like.

That afternoon the grocer handed him a slip of paper: *Pazar 10.00 Köprü Adalar Feribot Mayolu.*

Bruce translated "Sunday 10:00 am, Galata Bridge, Princes Islands ferryboat," but what was *mayolu?* He looked it up in his dictionary. A *mayo* is a *maillot* (French), a bathing suit. *Mayolu* means "with bathing suit." Got it.

On Sunday morning he walked onto the lower walkway of the Galata Bridge and saw Sarah in front of the ticket counter for the ferries to *Adalar,* the Princes Islands in the Sea of Marmara.

"James and Jim are off to Bursa and Çekirge today to go to the Turkish baths, so I thought you and I could go to the islands. Have you ever been?"

"No! This is perfect! I've been wanting to go, but I haven't taken the time to figure out how to get there or what to do."

"Pretty simple," Sarah said. "You take this ferry to Büyükada— the Big Island—then you bargain with a *calèche* driver for a tour, and you ride in his horse-drawn carriage around the island. You take a picnic and maybe have a swim. I have the picnic. You brought your bathing suit, right?"

"Right. Underneath. Thanks for the heads-up."

The ferry was waiting.

They stepped along the rickety gangway, climbed the stairs to the upper deck, turned and walked to the open stern deck.

"Sun or shade?" Sarah asked. "If we want sun we have to sit where there's shade now, because the ferry will turn."

"Sun," Bruce said. They sat.

Bells rang, a siren sounded, mates cast off the hawsers, the big diesel engines revved, shaking the decks, turning the props, churning the water. The ferry pulled away from the bridge, the domes and turrets of Topkapı Palace on the starboard side, Galata and the Galata Tower to port.

"How are Jim and James?"

Sarah smiled. "They're fine, as always. The perfect happy couple. Like two old ladies."

"Old ladies?"

"I don't mean to be catty. I love them, I really love them, they're my best friends, but there's no space between them."

"Space?"

"Bruce, THEY'RE IN LOVE! WITH ONE ANOTHER! They're fruitcakes. Did you look in their bedroom?"

"No."

"There's *only one bed, one big bed!*"

Bruce didn't know any homosexuals, or anything about them. He knew they existed. Suddenly he wondered if some of his high school and college friends had been "homos." One pair of guys always together in school....

"But I love them, too. They're the nicest guys I've ever met." She glanced at Bruce. "You're nice too, Bruce, don't get me wrong. But I don't know you very well. Maybe after today...." She smiled.

Sailing across the Sea of Marmara on a bright sunny day.... Bruce was in heaven! As they rounded Seraglio Point, the domes and towers of Topkapı Palace gave way to the enormous dome and four minarets of Hagia Sophia, then to the domes, semi-domes and six minarets of the Sultan Ahmet, the "Blue" Mosque. Up the Bosphorus to port, Leander's Tower stood out in the channel and the vast expanse of Dolmabahçe Palace spread along the European shore.

They talked: what was it like growing up on a farm in Illinois corn-country, what's San Francisco like, do you like graduate school, what do you think of Istanbul. A pause, then, what are your dreams, where do you want to go from here. He's interesting, Sarah though. She's interesting, Bruce decided.

From the ferry dock in Büyükada they walked uphill through the town to the *calèche* stand. Sarah's fluent Turkish and no-nonsense manner were easily up to the task of browbeating the carriage driver to forget his dream of an exorbitant fee from the foreigners. He finally quoted her the going rate and they mounted the rickety one-horse carriage.

Sailing on a ferryboat is one thing, Bruce thought. Riding in a carriage with a girl close beside you, behind a horse and a driver with his back to you... I wonder if this is the Turkish equivalent of the "parking" we had done in high school: borrow the car, pick up the girl, go to a scenic overlook or just to a deserted stretch of road if overlooks were in short supply, and make out.

They didn't talk much during the ride. The steady clip-clop, the jangling harness, the creaks and groans of the antique carriage didn't encourage it. When they stopped, it was by a beach.

"We can walk back to the ferry from here," Sarah said. She paid the driver and he jangled off.

They found a quiet place beneath the pines and plopped down the picnic bag.

"Don't look!" Sarah said as she walked away, wrapped a big beach towel around her, expertly shed her clothes and emerged in a modest one-piece bathing suit.

Bruce took off his shirt and trousers to his swim trunks underneath.

They walked to the shore and Sarah slipped a bottle of wine into the water.

"Keep it cool," she said.

The water was chill but refreshing, the sun and clear air exhilarating. They laughed and swam and splashed and joked.

"I'm hungry!" Sarah said. They retrieved the bottle of wine and its label which had come loose in the salt water, walked up into the pines, dried off, spread the beach towel and laid out the picnic: flaky cheese-filled *börek,* black and green olives, fresh sourdough bread, tomatoes and a cucumber for salad, olive oil and a lemon for dressing, fruit, a bottle of white *Çankaya* wine and two glasses.

"Is this stuff any good?" Bruce asked, eyeing the bottle critically.

"The best in Turkey, which is to say, not bad. Do you know Turkish wines?"

"I've heard of a white called *Güzel Marmara.*"

Sarah exploded with laughter. *"Guzzle Marmara!* Peace Corps swill! Turkish rotgut! Actually, sometimes it's fine and sometimes it's undrinkable, you never know. It's certainly cheap at *iki-buçuk.* It's made by Tekel, the government company, so there's no quality control. *Çankaya* is made by Kavaklıdere, a serious wine company."

İki-buçuk?"

"Two and a half. Liras, that is. About a quarter US, and a half-lira of that is deposit on the bottle."

Bruce opened the bottle and poured two glasses of *Çankaya.*

From the first sip, he knew the wine was good. After the second glass, as he lay there next to this girl on a bed of pine needles made fragrant by the sun slanting in over the sea, he knew the day could not be better.

20

Sultan's Revenge

Dave Coughlin had sent a letter to Bruce's apartment by messenger asking Bruce to come to the consulate for a chat sometime. Bruce phoned him and they set up an appointment for Wednesday afternoon.

On the way to the consulate, he stopped in the Galatasaray fish market for a bite of lunch. Looking around for what to eat, he was approached by a man carrying a tray of what looked like mussels. The meat of the mussel had been removed from the shell, mixed with rice and spices, and replaced on the half-shell. They looked good.

The man offered him a free sample. They *were* good! He bought and ate several more.

When he got to Dave's office, Ralph Graves was there.

"Coffee or tea?" Dave asked.

"Coffee, please."

"So, how's the teaching going?" Dave asked.

"Pretty well," Bruce said. "I'm making a living, and my clients are gracious. I'm impressed by Turkish hospitality."

"It's exceptional! We've all noticed it. So—you have Ahmet Kamanbay and Devin Halepli's two kids, right?"

Bruce didn't remember telling Dave who his students were. He must have guessed from the names he had given Bruce just after he arrived.

"Mr Kamanbay is nice to me, and he pays generously. I don't know whether he's going to learn English, but slow progress doesn't seem to bother him. The Halepli kids are a delight, and fast learners."

"Good, that's great," Dave said.

They talked about other things: current events, his Peace Corps friends, Turkish food, where to go on weekends—a friendly ten minutes.

Then Dave said "We're kind of interested in Ahmet Kamanbay for a variety of reasons. He's an interesting man. Speaks Bulgarian. His family—ethnically Turkish—left Bulgaria after the war and immigrated to Turkey. Smart move. Turks aren't treated so well in that communist paradise where everyone's supposedly equal. He's done very, very well for himself here."

Dave took a sip of coffee.

"Halepli, too," he went on. "Robert College graduate, speaks perfect US English. They work together. They're important, and we like to keep up to date on prominent citizens. For reasons of protocol they aren't on the consulate's invitation list for social events —no business relationships with the States—so we don't get to see them here. As we told you, we'd appreciate anything of interest you might mention to us."

Bruce got the picture. That's why Ralph was there. Holy smoke! That's who I'm dealing with?

Leaving the consulate, Bruce didn't feel right. His stomach felt queasy. Too much coffee? He stopped at the grocery shop to buy some drinking water.

"How are you?" Marina asked as she walked into the shop.

"Terrible," Bruce answered. "Something's wrong with my stomach."

"What have you eaten in the last 24 hours?"

Bruce mentioned a few things, including the raw mussels at the fish market.

"Bacteria bombs! That's probably it. Could be food poisoning. It's common here. You could get quite sick," Marina said, now in nurse mode. "Go straight to your apartment and get in bed. I'll come in about half an hour and tell you what to do."

She came with Tetracycline antibiotics, dry toast, chicken broth, yogurt, bottles of water and a few other things.

She pressed her forehead to his to feel his temperature.

"Your temperature is high and your skin is dry. How's your stomach?"

"Awful! I threw up after I climbed those stairs. I've got diarrhea."

"Food poisoning: staph, vibrio or salmonella. The sultan's revenge! You'll have a bad 24 hours, then a weak 24 hours, then a few days to recover."

She got a Tetracycline tablet and a glass of water.

"Take one of these every six hours. Don't miss a dose! Drink a lot of water with it. Don't stop until you've taken all the pills, even if you feel better. There's enough for a week."

"But I've got to teach! I have a student tomorrow."

"Give me his phone number. I'll call him as your medical person and cancel. Stay in bed. Keep drinking water. Put a little salt in it as electrolyte. I'll come tomorrow and check on you."

Late in the afternoon the next day, Marina knocked on his door.

"How's the patient?" Marina asked as she walked in. He looked better, but tired.

"I'm exhausted, and sweating like a pig."

She leaned toward him and pressed her forehead to his.

"Your fever's broken, that's why you're sweating. This is good! The bad buggies are dead, but now your body has to recover. Are you drinking lots of water? I see you're taking the Tetracycline. Let's see if you can keep down a little broth."

"Marina, I can't tell you how I appreciate this. You saved my life."

"Not likely!" she laughed, "but it's good not to be alone when you're sick. That's why nurses were invented."

"Can you stay a little while?"

"Bruce, I'd love to, but medically it wouldn't be the best thing for you. You still need lots of rest, and if I'm here, you'll concentrate on the other person in the room rather than just forgetting everything and resting. No, it's best I go. You'll probably sleep a lot, which is good. I'll check in tomorrow."

This time when she came to his apartment in the afternoon, the door was unlocked and he was dressed and groomed, sitting in a chair, reading. A glass of water was on the table next to him.

"So. Crisis passed!" she said.

"But I'm so HUNGRY!" he said.

"No surprise," she answered. "You're completely empty! I'll make more broth and rusks, and you can have some yogurt now. Maybe a little plain tea, no milk or sugar. In a few days I'll take you to a restaurant and fill you up again."

He ate. She sat and watched him, smiling. He finished, and he looked at her. She came over and pressed her forehead to his.

"Healthy young man," she said, and pressed her lips to his.

PART TWO

OCTOBER

21

GRU

Lieutenant Colonel Boryana Nikolaievna Ermolayevna, heavy-set, roundish face, short light brown hair, slightly slanted eyes, lifted a long-tubed Belomorkanal cigarette from the ashtray on her desk and took a deep drag. As she looked at Vladimir Mikhailovich Petrovsky on the other side of her desk, the smoke shot from her nostrils.

Ermolayevna was the Istanbul agent of the Soviet Army's Main Intelligence Agency, the GRU. Behind her desk were framed photos of Lenin and Brezhnev. Facing it on the wall in front of her was a large hand-colored photograph of the Russian war monument erected at Ayastefanos just outside Constantinople in 1898. Ayastefanos was now called Yeşilköy, Constantinople was now called Istanbul, and the Russian monument was long gone.

"You will help us in an important mission," she said. "It is a mission of the highest importance. It has been approved by Yuri Vladimirovich personally. It will change the world."

"I serve the Soviet Union," Vladimir repeated by rote.

"Russia and the Soviet Union have always considered Turkey to be one of the most important countries on our borders, as you know. If we have influence here, it strengthens the USSR greatly and gives us unfettered access to the Mediterranean and beyond—all the oceans of the world. If we do not, it weakens us."

"Unfortunately, Turkey is now a NATO country," she went on, setting the scene, "which means NATO has influence, not us. The Soviet Union must claim more control over Turkey. The mission I will describe to you can and will give us that control."

Vladimir nodded.

"You see the Ayastefanos War Memorial there," she said, pointing to the photograph on the far wall. "It was a magnificent tribute to the glorious Russian troops who fell for the fatherland in 1877 and 1878. Our armies could have taken Constantinople then! We had the power! Had they marched on, today the people of this city would be speaking Russian instead of Turkish! But the countries of the West, always ready to gather against us, persuaded the tsar's weak government to stop at Ayastefanos. The traitors who allowed this defeat should have been punished. Instead, at least they constructed the magnificent monument at Ayastefanos as a reminder that we could seize Istanbul anytime we wanted and, sometime in the future, we would!"

"But the monument is no longer there," Vladimir noted, trying to follow her logic. "And the Republic Monument in Taksim Square includes the figures of Frunze and Voroshilov…"

"No, our monument is no longer there! It was destroyed by the Turks in 1914 at the start of the Great War—wanton destruction of a work of beauty, and desecration of the hallowed graves of our fallen soldiers! It is an unforgivable act of barbarism! It will be avenged! The monument will be rebuilt even higher, even more magnificent, in commemoration of an even greater victory!"

"As for Frunze and Voroshilov," Ermolayevna continued, "they are in the Republic Monument because of Soviet aid to Mustafa Kemal. Because of *our* assistance to *them!* At that time we were working together against the Western powers. We were building the future together!"

"The Turks cannot make up for the destruction of our monument just by putting two faces on their own monument," she went on, "not when they participate in the criminal NATO alliance. They stab us in the back!"

"The time for rebuilding our monument is not yet here," she said with a frown, "but we can prepare the way for it with this mission. The goal is to turn the government and people of Turkey against NATO so that the USSR can fill the void with its influence. You are familiar with the program whereby we bring in small arms from Bulgaria and distribute them to dissident groups?"

"Yes."

"This program, though useful, has not succeeded as we wished.

The influence of the Western powers, particularly the degenerate capitalists of the USA, has been surprisingly effective. It is this influence in particular that is targeted by the mission I will describe to you. With its success we will convince the Turks that America is not an ally to be relied upon. We will build on the distrust that America has already engendered by its vicious capitalist war in Vietnam. We will also avenge the destruction of our Ayastefanos monument," she said, looking up to the photograph, then back at Vladimir.

"If this can be accomplished, it will be of the highest importance, as you say, but how is this to be done?" Vladimir asked.

"To compensate for their destruction of our great monument, we will destroy the greatest of Turkish monuments! It is important not just to Turks but to the whole world. It is one of their treasures. It is also a prime symbol of their religious superstitions. By destroying it, we will also strike a blow against the folly of religion in both Turkey and America!"

Vladimir shifted in his chair, unsettled. This sounded like madness!

"We destroy a monument in Turkey and the Turks fall under our influence? You will forgive me, Comrade Colonel, but that does not make sense!"

"Control yourself!" Ermolayevna barked. "It will be 'the Americans' who cause the destruction! We will manipulate the intelligence reports to point to NATO and the USA. We will provide 'evidence' of NATO's responsibility. There will be no evidence that the Main Intelligence Agency of the Soviet Army was involved at all. This highly important mission will make it impossible for any Turkish government, or the Turkish military, to continue their close ties to NATO. We will force the Turks to see that their future lies with us, not with the West."

"You must explain the plan to me," Vladimir demanded. "It appears…difficult."

Ermolayevna opened her box of Belomorkanals, took out another, lit it with a Soviet Army lighter, inhaled deeply, and went on.

"Listen carefully! The explosive employed in the mission will be American-made. After the destruction the investigation will reveal this to the world. NATO, and specifically the Americans, as Christians and Jews, will be suspect. Intelligence reports —'evidence'—linking the Americans to the destruction will be pre-positioned so as to be discovered by various agencies during the investigations following the event. Of course we will also create our own 'intelligence' linking NATO and Christian religious organizations to the deed which will agree with the pre-positioned disinformation and confirm it. This work is already under way."

"No operatives from our organization will be involved in the active phase of the mission," she went on. "Not even *Spetsnaz*. It will be carried out by others already under our control who are ignorant of the actual mission."

"But that's dangerous! Not having our own agents perform the mission may risk failure!"

Ermolayevna banged her fist on the desk.

"Having our own people perform the mission risks its exposure! If we are seen as having *any* role in this, the result will be disaster. Exposure would *strengthen* the bond between Turkey and NATO! No, we must use others, those who are already working for us in the small arms transport program. They have been vetted and found acceptable. This gives us deniability." She looked intently at Vladimir. "We will use agents who are expendable. They will not survive the mission. That link to us will disappear in the explosion."

She explained the details of the plan: access to the necessary materials, transport, positioning, result, disinformation and aftermath.

She paused, giving herself time enough to think of her great-grandfather, who had been a young soldier in the tsar's army and who had died by an enemy's bullet in the last days of the march toward Constantinople. Had it not been for his death, her family might have been much more numerous and influential, with many more offspring and branches in the family tree. The actions of the western powers had cost her not only this, but also the victory for which her ancestor had fought and died. The monument to his sacrifice was a monument to her family's loss as well.

"Your task is to coordinate and oversee the active phase of the plan, to control the agents, make sure the explosive device is properly transported, positioned and detonated, and that no one suspects us of any involvement."

"You have not mentioned the target. What is it?"

"It is the most perfect one, within easy access of our resources in Bulgaria."

Ermolayevna smiled at him. "They destroyed our beautiful monument, we will destroy theirs."

"You don't mean...?"

"Yes! Edirne. The Selimiye mosque. It's perfect."

Marina stood at the high, heavy metal gates of the Consulate-General of the USSR on İstiklal Caddesi. The guard unlocked the gates and let her in. She went to the second set of gates and another guard unlocked them. She walked across the courtyard and entered the consulate, glanced at the guard standing behind the reception desk, and said in English to the grey-uniformed receptionist, "I am here for my regular appointment with Mr Petrovsky for English lessons."

It was a ceremony they went through each time for the hidden cameras and microphones.

Marina signed the logbook, walked down the hallway to a doorway marked "Consular Affairs," and knocked three times.

"Come!" she heard, in Russian.

Vladimir was sitting behind his desk. He looked up when she came in, smiled, and gestured to the chair opposite the desk.

"How are you today, Miss Schiller?" he said in English, smiling broadly. "I hope you are well."

"I am very well, thank you, Mr Petrovsky. And how are you?" She smiled in return.

It was their little game.

She took some papers out of her briefcase and put them on the desk in front of him.

"Today we will study adverbs," she said. "I only have one copy of the lesson so, if you don't mind, I will look over your shoulder."

She got up and went around behind him and the desk, giving her a clear view of all the papers on it.

During the lesson, Vladimir's intercom buzzed several times. Twice he apologized to his teacher and left the office for a few minutes. Marina leaned over the desk as though studying the papers she had given him. She fingered a button on her blouse several times as though trying to close it and a hidden microfilm camera made several exposures.

After they had studied English for a half hour, Marina left Vladimir's office and walked out through the multiple barriers. As she stepped onto İstiklal Caddesi, a man sitting behind a lace-curtained window in the second-floor restaurant across the street looked up. Seeing her, he pressed the shutter button on a small camera sitting on the table that was aimed at the consulate gates. He made a note in his notebook.

22

Flora & Julien

Julien couldn't take his eyes off her as she sauntered along the Boulevard Saint-Germain, her light cotton flower-print dress swathing her slender torso, leaving her long golden-tanned legs and arms bare. When she came to the café terrace where he was sitting in the sun, his fingers on his espresso cup, his heart leapt as she sat at the table next to his.

"Herbal tea," she said to the waiter.

"Pardon?" The waiter looked at her blankly.

"Herbal tea, please."

"Une tisane," Julien said.

The waiter nodded at Julien, and went to put in the order.

"Thanks," she said, smiling at him. Her long straight hair, caught in the sun, was an extraordinary color between red and blonde.

"You are American?" Julien asked.

"Yes."

"Are you a hippy?"

Her sunny smile clouded over.

"No. I used to be a hippy. Now I don't think I am…. I'm from California—San Francisco. I'm an art student. Do I look like a hippy?"

"No, I think not, but I do not know. I only see photographs of hippies."

"You're French, but you speak English. Do you live here in Paris?"

"Yes. I am studying to be a sculptor."

"Oh wow! Far out! We're both artists!" she said as she took a

101

chair at his table. "I want to see all the great art museums here. Which ones should I see?"

The waiter brought her *tisane*.

"I'm Flora," she said, offering her hand.

"Julien."

She lifted her cup and looked at him over the rim: slender, handsome in a boyish way, black hair and lively eyes constantly darting here and there, taking everything in.

"So, I guess the first place to go is the Loover."

"You can see the Louvre anytime. Do you like Monet? If so, you must go to the Orangerie."

"Wow! Yeah! I *love* Monet!"

They talked about Paris and after they had finished their drinks, Julien guided her along the Rue de Seine to the Quai Voltaire, across the Pont Royal and through the Jardin des Tuileries to the Orangerie.

They spent more than an hour there. Flora wanted more.

"Musée Marmottan Monet," Julien said, and took her by Métro to La Muette, then on foot to the museum on the outskirts of the Bois de Boulogne.

While Flora filled her eyes and heart with Monet, Julien filled his with Flora.

Finally, she was satisfied, and told him she was ready to go.

"Where to next?" she asked, her eyes shining.

"A surprise!" he said, leading her from the museum along the forested paths of the Bois to the boat dock on the Lac Inférieur. They rode the launch across the smooth lake to the Île Supérieur and took a table in the bougainvillea-clad garden of the Chalet des Îles restaurant. He ordered *champagne en apéritif* and as they sipped it they talked about their dreams.

"I can't get over how Monet used color!" she said. "Those water lilies are more real to me than the real thing."

The waiters smiled to themselves at the young couple, infatuated with one another, oblivious to everything but themselves. They kept the service slow, with few interruptions.

"How is California?" Julien asked in the silence of their thoughts.

"You mean, what kinda place is it?"

Flora told him her story—her passion for art, the early exhilarations of freedom at San Francisco State College, the ecstatic Human Be-In in January in Golden Gate Park, then the July cover story in *Time* magazine that signalled the end of innocence for the Bay Area hippy community, followed by the tidal wave of would-be pseudo-hippies flooding in and ruining everything.

"It all went bad. I had to get outta there. I hope it's better here."

Julien, as a Frenchman, was totally unprepared for the complete personal openness of Americans. French people did not blurt out their entire personal histories to total strangers, not even after decades of acquaintance, but Flora had told him all about herself. Intoxicated by the excitement of such immediate intimacy, Julien told her things he had never told anyone else: his dreams of changing the world through sculpture, of making avant-garde works that would embody emotions never before captured in stone or metal.

"Next I must show you some sculpture. Paris is filled with it! But I don't want to make statues of generals and poets. I want to create shapes like no one has seen before."

His head was spinning over this girl. He felt that his life had changed completely in a single day.

The light was fading. A waiter approached and whispered that the restaurant was closing. The last launch of the evening was about to depart for the lakeshore dock.

Stepping off the launch, they wandered in the forests of the Bois, hiding from the *gardiens*.

His parents were sick with worry when their ever-obedient, *très propre* son came home to the spacious apartment in a prestige *immeuble* on the Rue de Rennes early in the morning, disheveled, with this 20-year-old hippy from California, intent on breakfast and a nap. Who was this…*unconventional* person? Where had he been? Why hadn't he just come home as he always did?

There was a scene.

Julien's mother stood stone-faced and grim.

Julien's father raised his voice, gave orders and handed down punishments.

"I am 21 years old, almost 22!" he shouted at them. "I am not a child!"

It pushed Julien over the line. He would no longer take orders. In Flora he glimpsed a completely different world, one of utter freedom.

He took Flora to his room, slammed the door, grabbed his passport from a drawer, snatched a duffel bag from the closet, stuffed it with clothes, toiletries and his sleeping bag, and while his parents argued in the kitchen, Julien and Flora fled.

They sat in a café over croissants and coffee.

"Are you sure?" she asked.

"I want to do what you are doing. I want to go and see the world. But…where should we go first?"

"Kathmandu. It's where everybody's going!"

"Where is it?" Julien asked.

"In India, I think. Somewhere in India. You start by going through Europe to Turkey. That's what the kids at the hostel are saying."

"We will need money," he said.

"I have travelers' checks."

"Yes, and I can take money from my bank account. I was saving it for… but that doesn't matter. I can get my money."

"Let's just do it!" Flora said. "We'll make it happen. I can make drawings and sell them. You can make statues and be a translator!"

They left the café and walked along the Boulevard Saint-Germain. He went to his bank and withdrew his savings. They resumed their stroll.

"Here is a travel agency," he said. "Wait here."

He went inside, and returned in three minutes.

"The train to Istanbul departs from the Gare de Lyon at 23:50 tonight."

"Twenty-what?"

"Twenty-three fifty. Uh, ten minutes before midnight."

"Oh, okay…. What do we do until then?"

"I will show you."

They walked down Rue Bonaparte to the Jardin du Luxembourg, sauntered beneath the trees, watched the children playing, other lovers strolling, old people sitting in the sun. They found two of the small steel-and-wood chairs and sat, holding hands. Soon an old woman approached them and demanded 20 centimes each. She held out a pack of tickets.

"What's this all about?" Flora asked.

"We must pay for the use of the chairs."

"What?!"

"It is not really for the use of the chairs. It is a way to support old people who have no money."

Julien handed her a few coins, she gave him two tickets, and shuffled away.

The sun was growing hot. They walked north along the Rue Garancière to the cool, dusky interior of the Église Saint-Sulpice and sat in silence, thinking and dreaming. The confusion and doubt in their minds was buried deep under a blanket of romantic infatuation. Whenever a worry surfaced, it was immediately overcome by a surge of emotion and excitement.

"Have you seen Notre-Dame?"

"No!"

They walked north on Rue Mabillon to Rue de Buci. Among its market stands they found a bistrot and sat in the cool interior for lunch. The afternoon was slowly passing, but they barely noticed the time.

Rue Saint-André-des-Arts, Boulevard Saint-Michel, the Pont Saint-Michel, and the vast glory of Notre-Dame, grimy from the ages outside, glorious with gold and lights inside. The priests were celebrating mass. They listened to the call and response, the chants and hymns.

Julien looked at his watch,

"One more place to go!"

He took her by the hand. They took the Métro to the Trocadéro station, walked through the courtyard of the Palais de Chaillot and stood gazing at the Eiffel Tower.

"Wow! I've always wanted to see it!" Flora said. "Can we go to the top?"

"Of course!"

The wind was brisk at the top. He wrapped his arms around her. Their eyes drank in the banquet of sights below as they swayed back and forth, holding tight.

"I think we must now start our journey," Julien said.

They rode the Métro to Monge. He waited in the park while Flora went to her hostel and changed from her dress into jeans and a bright yellow T-shirt with a picture of the Louvre sketched on it in blue paint. Beneath the drawing was a slogan: "War is poor. Art is smart!"

Jamming the rest of her things into her backpack, they took the Métro to the Gare de Lyon.

Julien wrote a note to his parents and mailed it at the station post office.

They bought their second-class tickets and supplies of bread, pâté, cheese, fruit, wine and water, then went to the waiting room and sat on a hard wooden bench.

* * *

"Orient Express to Lausanne, Milano, Venezia, Trieste, Beograd, Sofia and Istanbul, ready for departure on Platform 3."

Startled by the loudspeaker announcement, Julien jerked awake. He looked at his watch, gasped, shook Flora by the shoulder, and they ran to the train platform awkwardly bobbling their luggage. Racing along the line of carriages, they clambered into the second-class carriage for Istanbul.

In their compartment, Julien leaned out the window and scanned the platform. No one he knew. Only the station master in his red cap, raising his whistle and signal stick.

The shrill sound of the whistle, the slamming of carriage doors, the rattle and clunk of the heavy train couplings, the jerk of the carriages, and the Orient Express pulled slowly out of the Gare de Lyon.

Julien pulled his head back into the compartment and took his seat across from Flora.

"We are free!"

"Istanbul! Here we come!"

They leaned toward one another, embraced and kissed, a fervent, lingering kiss.

Their first big adventure! They stared at one another with huge dopey grins. Their hearts were pounding with emotion. They opened a bottle of wine, poured two cups, toasted one another and their future together.

They had barely slept in 36 hours. Before the wine was finished, before the train cleared the suburbs of Paris, they were out cold.

Three days after leaving Paris, Flora woke up in the Yücel Hostel in Istanbul. A clerk from the hostel had approached them yesterday afternoon at Sirkeci Station as they got off the train. He asked politely if they would like a clean, safe, cheap hostel right across the street from Hagia Sophia. They said yes. He led them along a narrow street, up a hill, and into the modest hostel building with the huge church looming opposite.

"Miss, you will be in the girls' dormitory, and Mister, you will be in the boys' dormitory," the agent said.

"What? You mean we can't stay together?" Flora asked.

"No, if you are not married, it is against the law. To stay in the same room you must show us a marriage certificate."

Exhausted after the 2-1/2-day train trip in a second-class compartment with four other people coming and going, smoking and talking all night, they dropped their packs at the heads of beds in the separate dorms, fell into bed and slept for 14 hours.

Flora got up, washed and dressed, and went to the breakfast room where Julien was already sipping tea. They ate a simple breakfast—bread, butter, jam, white and yellow cheeses, sliced tomatoes and cucumbers, an egg, and tea—then walked out the hostel door.

It was warm and sunny, promising to be hot later.

Directly in front of them rose the massive stone bulk of Hagia Sophia. Four tall minarets marked its corners, and its huge dome crowned the top of what had reigned as the greatest church in Christendom for a thousand years.

As though in a trance the two artists stood in awe.

"I'm gonna draw it!" Flora whispered.

They turned right and walked to the Byzantine Hippodrome, now a long park. They strolled through it and stopped at an Egyptian obelisk.

"We have one like this in Paris," Julien said. "The Obelisk of Luxor in Place de la Concorde. These sculptures are marvelous! They had no proper tools. The stone is so hard! But look at the perfection of the work!"

Around the park were old cars and vans, and their hippy owners. They chatted with some of the hippies, from the USA, Canada, Europe, Australia.

"Mellow!" Flora said, excited. "It's just like the good old days in the Haight! Mellow! The police don't bother you?"

"Not really, unless there's a lotta noise or a fight or heavy drugs or something. They let us be," one man said.

"They don't like us," a young woman added. "The cops and the suits. Actually, most Turks don't like us, except a few of the Turkish kids, but the old guys don't interfere if we don't make trouble."

"I'm not sure all Turks don't like us," another young woman said. "They just don't get us. Can't figure us out. Think we're from Outer Space. We're kind of a curiosity. Live and let live, huh?"

Flora and Julien walked to the far end of the Hippodrome, turned and walked back.

"If we had a van like these people, we wouldn't have to pay for two separate beds in the hostel," Julien said, "and we could sleep together."

Flora gave him a smile.

A few steps ahead they saw a white-and-blue VW microbus covered in dust. Scraps of old newspapers and litter gathered around the tires. They stopped and looked at it. They looked at one another.

A young man was standing near them, frowning at the van.

"It's been here for over a month."

"Whose is it?" Flora asked.

"Who knows?" the young man said. "I come and go to Istanbul, and I've seen it here for over a month. It must be abandoned."

"Why would someone abandon a car?" Julien asked.

"Who knows? They took the train to Europe. They went with other people to Iran. They decided to stay in Turkey. They got sick and are in hospital. They got arrested for selling drugs and are in jail."

"It's a pity," the young man said, frowning. "It's a good vehicle when it is kept properly."

He walked off.

Flora looked at Julien.

Julien wiped the dust from a window in a side door and peered in: a VW camper with a fold-out bed, fold-out table, a little sink and, beneath it, an icebox. He tried the door handle. It turned. He opened the door. They looked in.

They stepped in and sat.

"So we move here!" Flora said. "This could be our room!"

"What if the owners come back?"

"So we move out!"

They walked back to the hostel and asked to borrow a broom, a bucket and some rags. They got water from the public toilets by the tourist office. At the end of the morning the microbus was tidy.

They checked out of the hostel and moved in.

"Home!" Flora cheered.

Julien smiled at her. Their first home, on the Byzantine Hippodrome in Istanbul.

23

Ikbal

Bruce was sitting on the terrace at Mustafa's café sipping a cool —only slightly cool—Tekel beer when an old, bearded, white-haired man approached. He had a colored cloth wrapped around his head, a colored vest over a homespun shirt and old-style Turkish baggy trousers. He was a picture-perfect stereotypical Ottoman Turk, but despite the folksy costume he didn't look Turkish.

"Salaam-un aleikum" he said to Mustafa who came out to shake his hand and welcome him with a bow. "Peace be upon you!"

Mustafa took the old man's hand, kissed it and touched it to his forehead.

"Aleikum salaam, Ikbal Beyefendi!" Mustafa answered. "And upon you, peace, Lord Ikbal. Please! What can I offer Your Exalted Personage?"

Ikbal sat at a table on the terrace.

"Tea, please, and your venerable notebook," he said in Turkish, smiling.

"At once, O Exalted One!"

Mustafa brought out a glass of tea, a gift of baklava, and the notebook. Ikbal sipped his tea, took a bite of baklava, and began leafing through the notebook.

Bruce couldn't resist.

"Pretty interesting notebook," he said.

"Surpassingly interesting!" Ikbal said in Oxford-perfect British English. "Have you examined it?"

"I've paged through it," Bruce answered. "A lot of it is just day-to-day stuff, but entertaining. Some of it I don't understand—perhaps because it's in so many languages."

"Indeed! And the impenetrability is more than linguistic. It is much more than a hippy daybook."

"How so?"

Ikbal smiled. "Keep after it. You may find surprising things. Are you American?" he asked, forking another bite of baklava.

"Yes."

"Military? Peace Corps? Consulate? Tourist?" Another bite.

"A tourist, I guess, but also a teacher. Of English. I give private lessons."

"Ah, yes, Turks are mad to learn English now. Amusing. The language of Chaucer and Shakespeare, so much a language of the past, seems to be the language of the future!"

"Well, at least of the present," Bruce smiled. "That's what pays my bills."

Bruce took a chance.

"You're not Turkish," he said.

"Not originally."

Last bite. Ikbal wiped his lips with his handkerchief and took a sip of tea.

"I was born and raised in London, but very soon after I came here, oh many years ago now, I felt myself truly to be Turkish. I married a Turkish girl, raised a family. I just knew this is where I belonged."

Mustafa appeared, bowed respectfully, set down a glass of fresh tea and removed the empty plate and tea glass, bowing as he did so.

"Mustafa certainly thinks highly of you," Bruce said.

"Mustafa is a gem among men. He welcomes all comers, no matter who, no matter from where, no matter if they can pay or not. The hippies make a lot of noise about universal brotherhood. Mustafa practices it without a fuss. The world could take a lesson from him. Yes, he treats me with deference. I think of him in the same way."

"Some of our Turkish mystics see him as a sort of saint," Ikbal went on. "Do you know Zen Buddhism? How the revered Zen master may bow down to a simple working man or woman, mystifying his students? He sees the inner goodness in a simple soul, what most of the world ignores as naïveté, simplicity, ignorance or a humble station. The workman is as mystified as the students because he is not *trying* to be good, he simply *is* good. His heart is pure."

"I know some Buddhism. I was studying religion in graduate school." Bruce said. "So...do these mystics come here and write these things in the notebook?"

"They do. They write or draw a sort of blessing, a prayer, a talisman, to abide here in this place made holy by one man's goodness, and not even Mustafa can understand them. He would not be interested if he could. He would not accept that he is special. That is what makes him special!" Ikbal smiled broadly.

"Can you read these Arabic writings? Do you understand them?"

"I do. You are a sensitive young man. Some day I may tell you more," Ikbal said.

He put some coins on the table and covered them with his tea-glass saucer.

"Mustafa won't let me pay, so I have to hide it!" Ikbal chuckled, winking at Bruce.

He stood up, nodded to Bruce and walked away.

24

Yergat

The *Orient Express* rolled southeastward through Switzerland, Italy, Yugoslavia. In his second-class seat, Armen Bagratian considered his plan.

He had decided to adopt the *nom-de-guerre* "Yergat"—Armenian for 'iron'—to describe his will for revenge. After he had accomplished his mission in Turkey, he would escape to Armenia and work for its liberation from the Soviet yoke.

At the Bulgarian border, the train stopped for yet another passport check. Two Bulgarian Immigration officers entered his compartment and demanded passports, speaking in Bulgarian and French.

Yergat handed his French passport to the officer, who studied it and compared the passport photo to Yergat's face. Noticing Yergat's Armenian name, he showed the passport to the second officer.

"Where were you born?" the second officer asked in French.

"Yerevan, Armenian SSR."

"Why do you live in France?"

"I am a scientist. I was permitted to move there to explore French scientific education and bring the results back to Armenia."

The officers looked at one another. The second officer said "We will return your passport to you in a little while."

They left the compartment.

Fifteen minutes later, the second officer returned, and handed

Yergat his passport without a word. After a few minutes, the train jerked forward, toward Sofia.

Yergat gazed through the window.

By the time the train reached Plovdiv, he had his plans in order. His first task would be to orient himself in Istanbul, to plan his movements, and to augment his financial resources. He would do it all in the quickest way.

Bruce and Sarah sat at a café in a park uphill from the Hippodrome, sipping Turkish coffee.

"What's that little building over there?" Bruce asked, pointing to a small structure at a corner of the park.

"The *muhtarlık*," Sarah said, reading the sign on the front of it. "The city office for this neighborhood. The *muhtar* is the neighborhood headman. That's where he works. Neighborhood stuff."

A truck pulled up on the street beside the park. Bruce read "Gündem Transport" on its side. He watched as two men got out and went into a hotel carrying cardboard boxes.

Sarah signaled to the waiter. Two more coffees, light sugar.

"Somebody told me there was a cistern underneath this park," Sarah said.

"A cistern?"

"Yeah, left from the Byzantines. They had these big cisterns underneath the city to store water."

The waiter brought the coffees.

"Is there a cistern underneath this park?" Sarah asked the waiter in Turkish.

"Yes, *Binbirdirek Sarnıcı*," the waiter answered in Turkish, "but it's closed. You can't go in."

"He says it's called 'the cistern of a Thousand-and-One-Columns,' but it's not open."

"Isn't there a cistern right down by Hagia Sophia?" Bruce asked.

"Yeah. *Yerebatan Saray*. The Sunken Palace. I think you can get into that one."

"We should go see."

* * *

Yergat sat at another table in the same café watching the men unload the boxes from the truck. After they had made several trips into the hotel, he paid for his tea.

He calculated their rhythm. There was a 30-second interval when both men were away from the truck and in the hotel. He strolled along the park to the far side of the truck, and when the second man walked toward the hotel, Yergat came around the side of the truck to the back, snatched two smallish cardboard boxes marked *Musluk Malzemeleri*, disappeared around the side of the truck again, and walked nonchalantly across the street, the boxes clutched tightly to his chest, out of sight of the truck.

Faucet parts. Oh well, he had to start somewhere. By selling these he'd get into the network of fences, the guys who bought stolen goods. Maybe he'd do a jewelry store next. Turks are trusting. There doesn't seem to be a lot of retail robbery. If he stole enough stuff and sold it, he'd soon have the money he needed for his plan.

Back at his hotel, he opened one of the boxes. Inside was a plastic bag tightly wrapped around a mass of white powder. A typewritten paper label was stuck to the bag with a date, lot number, other record-keeping info.

Yergat knew immediately what he had stolen. His heart pounded. He couldn't believe his luck. It was just what he needed! Instead of faucet parts which might bring a hundred liras, this would bring a fortune! Instead of the weeks of theft he had planned on to build up his money supply, he had gotten all he needed in less than a minute!

After it was sold, he could move quickly.

Bruce and Sarah paid for their coffee, walked down the hill along Divan Yolu and found the entrance to the Yerebatan Saray cistern. The door was locked, but soon an old man appeared. He sold them tickets, unlocked the door and turned on an electric light. A rickety wooden staircase descended into damp, murky gloom. They walked down to a small wooden platform at the bottom.

The floor of the cistern was covered in two feet of water. Extending into the darkness were ranks and rows of stone columns.

"Isn't this the one that was in that James Bond movie, *From Russia With Love?*" Bruce asked.

"I think so."

"Bond got in a boat and rowed to a place underneath the Russian consulate, then looked into a periscope that came up in a fireplace."

"Yeah, but the Russian—the Soviet—consulate is over in Beyoğlu, nowhere near here. No way you could see it from here."

"Cinematic license," Bruce said.

They climbed back up the stairs to the entrance. Sarah chatted with the guard.

"I asked him about that Binbirdirek cistern. He says it's big, and the floor is dry, but it's not open. He says there are lots of cisterns in Istanbul. The Byzantines built them underneath most of the important buildings to ensure a supply of water if there was war or drought."

"Pretty good planning," Bruce said.

"Life or death," Sarah pondered. "Makes you think of what you really need."

At Gündem Transport, Danny was nervous. Talk was going around the office that "some goods" were missing from a delivery. Several kilos. The clerks looked nervously at one another as they paged through the records, trying to trace the lost boxes from the shipment. If they didn't find them, the boss would be furious—and vicious.

25

Cisterns

Bruce asked Mustafa when Ikbal was likely to come to the café.

"Cuma. Friday. Sometime he do *hütbe* and *namaz* in Sultan Ahmet Camii. After come here drink çay. "

Bruce made a point of spending time at Mustafa's on Friday afternoons. Sure enough, Ikbal came the next Friday afternoon after the sermon and prayers at the Blue Mosque.

Bruce asked him about cisterns.

"Cisterns? Lots of them," Ikbal said. "Under every important Byzantine building. Most of them are still there, but inaccessible, or mostly inaccessible. I look forward to the time when they will be restored and open to the public."

"Wait a minute," Ikbal went on. "I think I have an archeological plan of the Byzantine city somewhere, in a book. It might show a lot of the cisterns. If I can find it, I'll bring it to Mustafa's tomorrow so you can see it. Let's meet at 10 am."

"Thanks," Bruce said. "I'd really like to see it. I'll be here."

The next morning Bruce arrived early. A few minutes later Ikbal walked up to the café with a large-format book under his arm.

"Here's the plan I found," he said. "There were at least 100 cisterns and reservoirs in old Constantinople. They were fed by a vast system of aqueducts nearly 400 kilometers in length. Some of the aqueducts extended almost to today's Bulgarian border. It's an astonishing accomplishment of hydraulic engineering! Huge quantities of water came to the city and were stored in a hundred places."

Bruce looked at Ikbal's map of Byzantine Constantinople at the height of its glory. He was right. Cisterns were hidden beneath dozens and dozens of buildings.

"This plan is not up to date, I'm afraid. There's been a lot of new building in Istanbul, and archeological features present a problem for construction companies," Ikbal said. "If they start an excavation and find an archeological feature such as a cistern, they are required by law to stop and call in the archeologists. This costs them a lot of money—all those work crews and expensive machinery just sitting around while professors and graduate students excavate artifacts with tiny trowels and toothbrushes—so sometimes when builders come upon something old, mum's the word and they just build over it. Hence, lots of unknown cisterns."

"Is it possible that the people in the newly-built buildings would know about the cisterns?"

"Certainly! Imagine that a mysterious draft is making your house or shop cold or damp, or if you see water condense on your tile floor. You look for the source of the draft. You find a small opening in the floor with air coming through. You widen the opening, shine a light in, and see a vast space and a forest of stone columns. This is not unusual in the Old City."

"So…you discover you're living over a cistern. You cut a hole in your floor, put down a ladder, and you've got a huge storage area," Bruce said.

"Why not? If the cistern is dry, that is. They were made to hold water, remember? Have you been to the Yerebatan Saray there, across the street?"

"The James Bond movie cistern? Yes, I've seen it. It's got water in it. I've heard there's another one just up the hill, the Bin… something."

"Binbirdirek, the Philoxenos. It's not open to the public these days. There's another one, the Theodosius, just west of the Philoxenos. I've actually seen the inside of that one."

"How did you get in?"

"Oh, years and years ago there was a teahouse there. I stopped for a glass of tea and noticed a strange stone structure in the middle of the room, like a huge pot or jar about 70 centimeters high and a

meter across. It reminded me of a well opening. It had boards on top
of it and empty tea glasses. I asked what it was. The *çaycı*—the tea-
man—said it was a *sarnıç*, a cistern. We removed the boards and
looked in. There was a rickety ladder. I asked if I could go down into
it. He hesitated, but then brought me a candle. I went down. It was
dry and, oh, perhaps 40 meters long, a big space. I looked around a
bit but I couldn't see much with just a candle."

Ikbal lifted his tea glass and took a sip. It was cool. He looked for
Mustafa, Mustafa nodded and in seconds brought fresh glasses of tea
for both Ikbal and Bruce.

"What about the Sphendoneh?"

Ikbal smiled.

"Ah, that!" It looks like it's solid, just a support for the
southwestern end of the Hippodrome, but behind the wall I've read
that it's all arches and chambers and ramps—at least it was in
Byzantine times. Below the Hippodrome's surface, within the
Sphendoneh, is where the charioteers prepared for the races. I don't
know what's down there today. Perhaps nothing, although the way
people seek out usable space in this teeming city, I'd be surprised if
there was some old space that was not occupied by a carpentry shop
or brass foundry or junk dealer!"

He smiled and took a sip of tea.

"I'd love to see the Sphendoneh restored. I'd love to see it used
for chariot races!"

They both laughed at the thought, then looked out toward the
Hippodrome, surrounded by hippies and their jalopies. They laughed
again, even longer.

"A warren of huge rooms and tunnels, a subterranean
Constantinople beneath ground-level Istanbul...."

Bruce strolled along Divan Yolu from the Grand Bazaar toward
the Hippodrome thinking about Byzantium. He decided to stop for a
glass of tea at the teahouse on the little park above the Binbirdirek
cistern, but then changed his mind. Ikbal had said that there was
another cistern, the Theodosius, just a few streets to the west.

He turned right and walked down a side street.

Halfway down the hill on the left side, some men were loading boxes into a truck. Gündem Transport. The truck was parked in front of a building with steel double doors, both open. Inside were piles of boxes. At the center of the storeroom was a low big-jar-like structure with boards on it. As Bruce looked at it, two men stopped moving the boxes and stared at him—glared would be a better word. Gündem Transport, Bruce thought. Better move on.

At the next corner he saw a café. He took a seat on the sidewalk and ordered tea.

Several tables away, two Turks were chatting in Turkish with lots of English words interspersed. At a pause, he went to their table.

"Excuse me, do you speak English?"

"Sure, mate!" Australian accent. "You American?"

"Yes."

"Come on, join us," the man said. "My name's Galip—they call me Gallup down under—an' this larrikin here's Göker—Gooker. Siddown, mate, have a çay."

Bruce grabbed his tea glass and moved to the Turkish-Australians' table.

"I'm Bruce."

He sat down.

"You sound Australian, but you're Turkish?"

"Right you are, mate. Born and raised right here in this neighborhood. We took ship years ago, end up in Sydney, jump ship, go walkabout, get jobs, start our own business, do pretty well. My mum's doing poorly at the moment so we came back to check on her, see the old neighborhood, eat some real *kebap*."

"I've heard there's a cistern around here somewhere—*sarnıç.*" Bruce knew the word by now.

"*Sarnıç. Şerefiye Sarnıcı.* Theodosius Cistern."

"Yeah, that's the one."

"Basically, you're right above it, mate, or at least above a corner of it. It's below this whole area," the man said, turning and waving his arm up the hill toward Divan Yolu. "Not open to the public, though. Hasn't been since we grew up here decades ago. *Yerebatan*

Saray, the one at the end of the Hippodrome, that one's open. You can go into that one. Just look for the caretaker, he'll let you in. "

"Yes, thanks, I've seen that one."

Galip signaled to the waiter for fresh tea.

"The cistern here. Have you seen it?"

Galip smiled and looked at Göker who looked back with a conspiratorial grin.

"Well, here's the dinkum. It was closed up tight, right? But boys will be boys. One of our mates back then was the son of the *çaycı*— the tea shop owner. One day when the old guy wasn't looking the kid takes us to the loo in the back, lifts off the wood panel that hides the plumbing and leads us into a kind of cave-like place. We squeeze through a crack in the stone wall into a big room fulla rubble. Couldn't see much. Came out filthy, caught hell from me mum. Went in a few more times just for the hell of it, but it wasn't much fun. Dirt. Mud. Rats. Dunno what we expected, but we think to ourselves we'd rather be out in the sun playin' footy."

They chatted some more. Bruce finished his tea, offered to pay, was refused, and walked up the slope to Divan Yolu.

The next morning, Bruce pocketed his Swiss Army Knife, bought a flashlight and batteries at the grocery shop, took the T1 bus from Taksim Square to Sultan Ahmet Square and walked up Divan Yolu and through the side streets to the teahouse above the Theodosius Cistern. The place was crowded with morning tea-drinkers. Newspapers were unfurled everywhere and the chatter of dice and clack of pieces slapped down on backgammon boards filled the air.

Bruce slurped a quick tea, dropped a coin in the saucer and went to use the toilet. He looked for where the pipes went into the wall, put the blade of his knife under the thin plywood panel and turned it. The panel popped out. The space was tight but he squeezed through and pulled the panel back against the wall as best he could.

It was dark. He found the crack in the foundation wall and aimed the flashlight's beam through it. No filth, dirt, mud, rats. He saw a wood floor and walls, electric lights, stacks and stacks of cardboard boxes, and a pulley-and-winch contraption for lifting the boxes through the well hole in the ceiling.

He moved the beam around the room. Small scales, some other machines. Bundles of plastic bags. Jesus!

He heard steps. The toilet door opened. Piss. Flush. Faucet. The door again. He waited for silence, then quickly pushed the panel out, crawled out and locked the toilet door from the inside. He carefully replaced the panel, looked in the mirror, brushed some dust from his shirt, flushed the toilet, unlocked the door and left.

26

Agnete

After another lesson at Halepli's villa in Ortaköy, Bruce took a bus to Sultan Ahmet Square. He walked over to Mustafa's.

The tables were full. A young woman sat alone at a table in the shade. Bruce hesitated.

"Bruce! *Buyrun!*" Mustafa said, and pointed at the empty chair at the shaded table. "Agnet, he is Bruce," he said. "Amerikan."

"Hello," she said. "Agnete. Please sit down. You are American?"

"Yes," Bruce said. "And you?"

"Danish."

"Do you live here?" Bruce asked.

"No. I don't live anywhere. I live in the world," Agnete answered.

She had lively, dark eyes, pale white skin, finely sculpted features, shoulder-length dark brown hair. Her hands were rough. Her jacket was crude brown suède worked with brightly-colored wool appliqués of flowers, stars, moons, occult symbols.

"The world's a good place to live," Bruce joked. "But what does that mean?"

"It means I don't stay in one place. I live in the world. I travel here and there and back again."

"How long have you been 'living in the world'?"

"About four years now."

Mustafa brought two glasses of tea. They each plopped in a cube of sugar, stirred, lifted the hot glasses by the rim and sipped.

"Hot tea on a hot day," Bruce said.

"The Turks think it cools you. You perspire, it evaporates, this cools you."

"So...where have you traveled?"

"Oh, I have been around Turkey and to Israel and Egypt, to Iran and India. I've been to Nepal. I go to Europe sometimes, but it is more expensive there. I have not been to Africa yet. I want to go there. I can show you where I have traveled," she said.

She stood up, brought the notebook to the table and opened it in front of him. She paged through until she found what she was looking for. She pointed to a long list of countries and dates.

"That is Agnete's trip in the world," she said.

Impressive. A real hippy wanderer, Child of the World.

"Don't you get lonely or homesick?"

"No, I am not lonely, mostly. I meet people, lots of people. I have many, many friends."

Bruce paged through the book looking for something.

"You're Danish. Can you read this?" Astrid had told him this note in the notebook was 'Just some comments about Istanbul.'

Agnete leaned over and looked at the paragraph. Her smile faded.

"Someone had some trouble and this is a warning about it," she said. "Something about the mafia, Turkish mafia here in Istanbul. They sell drugs and you shouldn't buy because the mafia want to trap you. They take your money and then if you stop buying they tell the police you have drugs and the police arrest you and find the drugs and you go to jail. The police pay the mafia a reward for finding a drug smuggler. Even if you aren't a drug smuggler, they don't care. I guess the police think this will stop the drugs, but it's just a game they play."

"Do you use drugs?"

"I did sometime, but I do not use them now."

"Are there a lot of drugs in Istanbul?"

"Yes, of course, if you want. This is an opium country. They grow it here. One town is even named 'opium.' Afyon."

"Yes, I've heard of that. The Black Castle of Opium."

Bruce sipped his tea and turned the pages of the notebook. The variety was astonishing: an entire informal history of Istanbul's 1960s hippy invasion. But it was chaotic. He'd see a note in French, in green ink, and then a few pages later see the same ink and hand again, but mostly it was one-time outpourings. Everyone was moving, no one stayed around long enough to write more than once.

Two-thirds of the notebook's pages had been filled. Visitors were still opening it to the next blank page and continuing the hippy saga. As Bruce approached the latest entries, one thing kept appearing: a quick, crude drawing of some sort of archway, beneath it four numbers, two pairs separated by a period. The drawing was small, and always in the lower right corner of the page. Bruce turned pages. The drawing showed up every few pages, right up to today.

It was odd. No flowers or effusions about love and joy or jokey portraits of hippy groups bound for Kathmandu. Just the same crude arch and the numbers.

The latest page was nearly blank, but there in the lower right corner was the drawing of the arch and the numbers.

"Do you know what this means?" Bruce asked Agnete.

"I do not know. Just drawing. It's normal."

But it wasn't normal. It didn't fit.

"More tea?" Mustafa asked.

"Yes, please," Bruce answered. "Mustafa, do you know who drew this arch?"

Mustafa leaned over and looked at the arch.

"Denni," Mustafa answered. "Duh pees korps. He just here. I see him write."

"What about the numbers?" Bruce asked.

"23.45? Is too late," Mustafa said. "I close hour twenty-two. Not open 23.45."

The café overlooking the Hippodrome was open until midnight. Late at night, hippies sat and drank beer. Sometimes there was a guitar. So long as they played and sang quietly, the staff didn't mind.

Bruce sat by himself and waited. At 11:30—or 23.30 in European time—, three men and two women got up and left. He saw others walking through the Hippodrome in the same direction. Bruce paid for his tea and followed them at a distance. They walked the length of the Hippodrome, turned left and walked down the hill.

The group turned right on a narrow side street and entered a small hotel, the Sifendoni. Bruce waited a few minutes, then walked by the hotel and glanced in: no one in the lobby but the desk clerk, a young black-haired Turk with a bushy moustache.

Bruce went in the front door.

"Good evening," the clerk said.

"Hello. What do you charge for a room?"

"Pardon. We are fully book. There is no room."

"It's not for tonight," Bruce said. "I want to come back to Istanbul later. What would it cost next week?"

"If we have room, rate is 50 Turkish liras for two people. But we fully book this week, next week."

It was impossible. No Istanbul hotel was fully booked for two straight weeks at this time of year, except maybe the Hilton, by a convention. And 50 liras? That was an insane price for such a plain, simple hotel.

"My friends who just came in here told me I could get a room for 15 liras," Bruce said.

The clerk was silent. He didn't move. His eyes stayed on Bruce's face. Finally, he said, "They wrong. We fully book. Goodbye."

He lowered his eyes to the desk and shuffled some papers.

27

Danny's Den

Bruce was at Mustafa's when Danny walked in.

"Hi Danny! Say, I have a question for you," Bruce said.

He got up, found the notebook, and sat at a table next to Danny. He opened the notebook and pointed to the little arch in the lower right corner of a page, the arch that he believed had something to do with the Hotel Sifendoni.

Danny laughed.

"Yeah, that's me. It's the symbol for our meeting, with the time. If you see that on a recently-blank page, it means we'll have the meeting that night at the time indicated."

"Where's the meeting?"

"So you want to join us! Good! Be at the Sifendoni Hotel ten minutes after midnight tomorrow and I'll take you to the meeting. Here's the address. You'll like it."

Bruce knew where the hotel was.

He arrived right at midnight. As he entered, the same desk clerk looked steadily at him.

"I'm waiting for Danny," he said.

The clerk nodded and returned to his work.

Danny walked into the lobby.

"Come!"

Bruce followed him. They went down a corridor and descended a flight of stairs to a cellar storage room. Danny unlocked a door, switched on a flashlight, and they walked into a cave, a man-made arched cave of bricks and stone. They turned a corner, walked along a narrow passageway, and into another, larger barrel-vaulted subterranean room lit by kerosene lanterns.

This was not a cistern. It had to be part of the Sphendoneh that Ikbal had told him about—the structure that held up the end of the Hippodrome. Ikbal was right: it wasn't empty. The Byzantine charioteers had been replaced by hippy drug users.

It smelled of damp earth, stale air and mildew. The dirt floor was spread with soiled carpeting. Piles of cushions and small wooden three-legged stools provided seating. Nargile water pipes, small gas burners and other objects stood on shelves in a corner.

"Have a seat," Danny said.

Soon others arrived, mostly hippies. Danny greeted some of them. Bruce recognized two of the hippies he had seen leaving the Hippodrome café to come to the Sifendoni the other night.

A young woman got out nargiles and lit burners. Some of the hippies lit cigarettes that smelled of hashish. The woman handed around small opium pipes and nargiles.

"What's your pleasure" Danny asked Bruce.

"I'll have a nargile, a light one," Bruce said, but he had made up his mind. When the nargile came, he would make it look like he was smoking, gently sucking, then blowing, to make the water bubble, but he was not going to inhale the smoke.

After a half hour, most of the group were deeply drugged, lying back on the cushions, eyes staring or closed. Bruce went up to Danny.

"A few days ago I got food poisoning. I'm still on antibiotics. Now the smell in this cave is getting to me. I don't want to make a mess. I'd better go."

Danny frowned, and hesitated.

"Okay. All right. I won't charge you this time. When you're better, you can come back. Just look for the sign in Mustafa's notebook. Good luck."

The next afternoon, Danny was just leaving Mustafa's when Bruce arrived.

"Hi Danny."

"Hi Bruce. What's up? Will we see you at the meeting again?"

"I'd like to talk to you about that," Bruce answered.

"Okay. Let's take a walk."

They walked along the Hippodrome.

"Aren't you afraid of the cops?" Bruce asked.

Danny gave him a patronizing smirk.

"Bruce my boy, the cops here are witless. And they don't care. We've got the perfect set-up: the hotel, the cave in the Sphendoneh. If Turks were there doing drugs, maybe they'd be concerned. But a bunch of foreign hippies? The cops don't give a damn. Besides, they get a cut."

At the southwestern end of the Hippodrome they turned right and walked downhill through the back streets. Bruce spotted a white truck marked Gündem Transport.

"Hey, isn't that one of your trucks? The company you work for?"

Danny chuckled.

"Yeah. Gündem Transport, servicing the million-dollar minaret."

"What?"

"Never mind," Danny smiled.

"No. What did you mean by 'million dollar minaret'? That minaret near the truck—it looks like it's in ruins. Top's knocked off. How could it be worth a million of anything?"

"It's not the minaret, it's what's *beneath* the minaret." Danny gave him a sly look. "I can't say any more."

Bruce didn't push it, but he thought Danny was a little too smart for his own good.

28

The Love Bus

Flora and Julien were sitting in their VW microbus home with the side doors and all the windows open. It was hot. Flora was wearing her yellow T-shirt. This time it bore a multi-colored sketch of her face and the motto "Artists think in color!!!"

Flora had made pen-and-ink drawings of the Blue Mosque, Hagia Sophia, a Turkish water seller, and a watercolor of a carpet. They hung the drawings on the doors of the van beneath a hand-lettered sign, bordered in drawings of flowers, that read "For Sale!!!"

A young woman walking by stopped and looked in. Beside her was a guy with a guitar on his back.

"Can we sit with you?"

"Want to buy some drawings?" Flora asked. "They're all originals."

"Not right now, honey," the woman said. "Maybe later. We've got some great weed but we don't want to smoke it in public. We'll share."

They climbed in, lit up and passed it around.

"Denise," she said. "This is Odie."

"Odilon," the man said. "Odie for short."

Denise was short, olive-skinned, and crowned by a nimbus of wiry black hair which, though not technically an Afro, came as close as possible on an Italian-American girl from South Philadelphia. Odie looked New World Hispanic: short but powerful build, darkish skin, longish black hair, and a serious look.

Each took a deep toke as the joint went around.

"Nice to have a van," Odie said.

"We don't know who it belongs to," Julien said. "It was sitting here, for a long time we think. It was not locked. So we cleaned it and we are here now."

"Shit, that is GREAT!" said Denise. "Down with private property! Does it run?"

Flora and Julien looked at her blankly.

"We do not know. We do not have the key."

Denise handed Odie the joint, got out of the side door and went around to the driver's door. On the way she passed a neatly-dressed young man who was staring at the van with a frown.

Denise lifted the driver's side floor mat, and there was a key. She picked it up, sat in the driver's seat, put the key into the ignition slot, stepped on the clutch pedal, turned the key, pumped the gas, and the van sputtered.

"Oh wow! Far out!" Flora said. "It works! Outta sight!"

"Don't get your hopes up, honey. It sounds like it's gonna die," Denise said.

"Maybe that is why it is here. Maybe that is why it does not belong to anyone," Julien said.

"Maybe it can be fixed," Odie said.

The well-dressed young man came to the side door.

"Did I hear it start?" he asked. His English seemed perfectly American, but there was the faintest of accents. German?

"Well, kind of," Denise said. "It turned over, but it sounded like death."

The young man went around to the back of the van and opened the engine compartment.

"Try it again," he said.

Denise turned the key and pumped the gas pedal. The engine sputtered, made encouraging sounds, then died.

"The valves are too tight. It needs a tune-up for sure," the young man said. "The fuel is old, maybe it is thick and blocking the fuel line. It must be cleaned."

"Where can we get this tune-up?" Julien asked.

"I can do it."

"In that outfit?" Denise said, looking at his neat clothing.

"I am a mechanic. I have mechanic's clothes also."

"We don't have much money," Flora said.

"If you pay for the parts, I will do it. It bothers me to see it in this condition. It's a good vehicle. You cleaned it well. A tune-up is not a lot of work. It deserves this. But there may be other things wrong. I can't tell until it is tuned and it has clean fuel."

"What will the parts cost?"

"Not much, maybe twenty liras. Let me know. I'm around. My name's Wolfgang," he said, and walked away.

Denise crawled to the back of the van and sat. They passed the joint.

Two young men neatly dressed in sport shirts and trousers walked by the open doors of the van. They stopped to look at Flora's drawings.

"These are pretty good," the taller one said. Americans. He looked closely at the ones of the Blue Mosque: a general view from a distance and a dozen close-ups of architectural details. The compositions were excellent, the precision and shading gave them depth and brought the drawings to life.

"How much?" he asked.

"A dollar each," Flora said.

"That's a lot," he said.

"I worked hard on them. You can tell."

She was right. They were very good.

"Yes, I can," he said. He thought for a moment, then said, "I'll take all of your Blue Mosque ones."

Flora took down the eight drawings and held them out to him, thought a moment, then ran to a neighboring van. She came back with the drawings wrapped neatly in a piece of newspaper.

"Thanks," the young man said. He handed her the money.

"Thank YOU!" Flora said, excited.

"By the way, I like your T-shirt. 'Artists think in color'... I like it."

"That's the thought for today," Flora said. "It changes."

"You have lots of T-shirts?"

"No, only a few. But when I wash them, the paint comes out and I paint a new picture and a new thought. It's my philosophy."

The young men wandered off. Flora jumped up in the air holding the money and yelled "Yippee!"

The two young men looked back at her, chuckled, and walked on.

A warm morning, promising an even hotter day.

Flora was decorating the outside of her new VW microbus home with paint: paisley-like psychedelic patterns, rainbow arcs and big multi-colored flowers. On the front she painted LOVE BUS in big, elaborate graffiti-style puffy letters.

Today her T-shirt had a picture of the Love Bus on it, and underneath "The future lies ahead—and then some!"

"This your van?"

"Kinda," Flora said. The young man had spotted the winsome hippy blonde standing by the VW microbus and had taken an interest. Then Julien emerged from inside. Oh well.

"Hi. My name's Ricky."

"Flora."

"Julien."

"So… is it your van or not?"

"We don't know," Flora said. "It was here, kinda left on its own, in bad shape. We cleaned it up and moved in. Cheaper than the hostel. We wanna get it tuned up, but we don't have much money. For the parts."

"If you got it tuned, what would you do?"

"Go to Kathmandu!" Flora threw her arms up in triumph.

"I don't know about Kathmandu, but maybe I'd go with you at least for awhile, if you agree. I didn't come here to see cities. I want to see the countryside, the farms. The agriculture. What if I paid for the parts and then we shared the gas?"

Flora and Julien looked at one another.

"Well, we're not gonna get out of here otherwise. I'm trying to sell my drawings, but the hippies aren't buying. Two American guys bought some, but so far they're the only ones."

"I've got an American Express card. We'll get some other people. It can hold five, six, even more if somebody's got a tent. We'll all share the gas. You contribute the van. "

"Far out! Let's go!" Flora exulted.

"Flora, my love, first we must have this tune-up thing or we will go nowhere."

29

Wolfgang

Hagia Sophia. *Ayasofya* to the Turks. The great church of Justinian. This was the second time Bruce had explored it, strolling among the porphyry and breccia columns, watching the sun cast god-rays through the high windows to the marble-slab floor. The echoes alone were worth the experience, but the glittering mosaics and the sense of history were worth an empire. He drank it all in.

He stood in the middle of the *omphalos,* the circle-in-a-square composed of colored marble shapes that marked the site of the coronation throne for the emperors of Byzantium—the Eastern Rome—in the 8th and 9th centuries. The great church itself dated from the year 548. The oldest religious buildings he knew in California, the Spanish missions, dated only from the late 1700s. Bruce imagined himself in the church a thousand years before: the hundreds of oil lamps, the clouds of incense, the echoing chants of the priests, the throngs of worshippers, the emperor and his court resplendent in bejeweled robes and crowns.

Was it the building's great age that seemed to sanctify it? Or its architectural genius, with its soaring dome, semi-domes and glittering mosaics? Or was there still something left of its sacred character, the holiness with which it had been imbued by its creators and the millions who had come here to feel the presence of God?

Out in the bright sun again, Bruce wandered over to Mustafa's, sat and sipped a beer, then strolled over to the Hippodrome and along the row of hippy vans.

"Yank! Hand me that spanner!"

"What?"

"The spanner! The wrench! Hand it to me."

Bruce looked down. A hand reached out from under a VW microbus toward a pile of tools too far away. He stooped, picked up a big open-end wrench and put it in the hand.

"No, not the big one, the little one, the ten-millimeter."

Bruce found the small wrench and put it in the hand.

"Thanks."

After a minute the mechanic wriggled out from under the van, stood up and stretched out his hand.

"Wolfgang. Call me Wolf."

"Bruce. Hey, how'd you know I was American?"

"Your shoes, Yank. You've got Yank shoes. Turks don't wear shoes like that."

Bruce looked at his shoes. Normal shoes.

"What's wrong with your VW?"

"It's not mine. Fixing it for friends. Just a tune-up at this point. Replace the points and condenser, adjust the valve clearance, gap the plugs, set the dwell. It's not my van. My van is over there."

He pointed to another VW microbus down the line.

"You're giving this one a tune-up right here?"

"Where else?" Every 3000 kilometers. If you don't, things go wrong. Bad for the engine."

"Where are you from?"

Wolfgang laughed.

"Wolfgang! VW! Where do you think? Germany! West Germany to you."

"But you speak perfect American English…except for 'spanner.' That's British."

"I went to an American high school in Germany. My father works on the base at Ramstein. One of the perks is that his son could go to the American high school. Come, I'll get you a beer."

"I just drank one," Bruce said.

"So?"

Wolfgang opened the VW's side door, looked in the icebox, grabbed two bottles, pried off the tops and handed one to Bruce.

They settled on the curb in the shade.

"Where are you going?" Wolfgang asked.

"Nowhere. I'm staying in Istanbul."

"Staying? Aren't you on the road?"

"I came here from Paris because Istanbul seemed interesting. Figured I'd stay awhile. Don't know much about it except it's cheap and friendly, the food's great and I like it so far."

"So. Are you working here?"

"I'm teaching English. Private lessons. I did some teaching back in the states. What about you?"

"I go back and forth to Germany. Sometimes to Iran. Depends."

"How do you pay for it?"

"I started out fixing Volkswagens. I'm a mechanic. When I'd run out of money, I'd stop and work in a garage for awhile. Volkswagens are everywhere. I don't have to speak the language, just do good work. Good work's the language. Everybody needs mechanics. These jokers here, for example. This Type 2," he waved at the Love Bus, "has the typical 1200cc stand-up engine. On its second rebuild at least. I can tell. If you overhaul the engine every three hundred thousand or so, it'll last a long time. But this one's been badly mistreated."

"Type 2?"

"The van. The VW microbus. Transporter. Kombi. Technically, in VW-speak, it's a Type 2. The Beetle is Type 1. The little 1200cc is mounted in both Types. It can push this big metal box okay, but not so fast. My Type 2 is…a little different." Wolfgang smiled.

"Different how?"

"Well, it has a much bigger engine—Porsche—and other modifications. You wouldn't know to look at it, but it goes like a rocket. It outruns the little Renaults the Turkish police use and the silly Moskvitches of the Bulgarian and Yugoslav police. I can be in Munich tomorrow if the bribe-hungry Bulgarian border guys don't slow me down and if the Yugoslavs don't sell me bad gas."

"Let me show you a *real* Type 2," Wolfgang said, putting his tools down.

They walked from the Love Bus along the row of vehicles parked on the Hippodrome to a flawless silver VW microbus.

"I've never seen a silver one," Bruce said.

"Special finish. But look back here." Wolfgang took Bruce to the back of the van, lifted the engine compartment door, looked at Bruce and smiled broadly.

Bruce saw a motor.

"Porsche 2-liter, single overhead cam, fuel-injected 6 cylinder, 12-valve. 170 horsepower at 6800 rpm. Five-speed manual transmission. I took it out of a wrecked Porsche 911S."

"Good...I guess."

"Good? It makes the clumsy Type 2 a rocket! Sure, it can't beat a 911S, the Type 2 doesn't even have the aerodynamics of the Beetle, let alone of a Porsche, but it can beat most everything else on the highway between here and Germany."   Wolfgang winked. "And nobody knows this."

Bruce glanced inside.

"It's full of carpets."

"That's what I do now. It pays a lot better than working on cars. I buy them here and in Iran and sell them in Switzerland and Germany. They're mad there for 'oriental carpets.'"

Several days later Bruce wandered through the Hippodrome and saw Wolfgang standing by the Love Bus with a small group of hippies.

"Bruce!" Wolfgang said. *"Wie geht's?* What's up?" He introduced Bruce to the group.

"This is Ricky, and Julien, and Flora, and Denise, and Odie. They're in the Type 2 that I was working on when we met."

"Yeah, Wolfie's a handy man to have around. Fixed it up just great," Ricky said. "You just passing through?"

"I'm living here for the time being," Bruce answered, "teaching English. Better than shooting people I don't know in Vietnam."

"Very good! Down with the *militaires!*" Julien said.

"Make love not war!" Flora cheered, raising her arms.

Silence.

"So...you're all traveling?" Bruce asked.

"Kathmandu or bust! Wolfie's tuned us up, Danny's turned us

on, now we're gonna drop out to Kathmandu!" Flora laughed.

"Well, good luck!" Bruce waved to them and walked on.

"I dunno," Ricky said. "I'm all for an adventure, but the five of us in this jalopy... I doubt we'll make it."

"Good point about the five of us," Denise said, "is that we're not six. Won't be so crowded."

"The problem won't be the van," Wolfgang scolded. "The Type 2 is a solid machine. Yeah, this one's got some years and kms on it, but it's just had its tune-up and it is good for another 3000 kilometers. Check the oil every day, change the oil and give it another tune-up after 3000 kilometers and it will be good for yet another 3000—if that old fuel pump doesn't fail. You might want to take a new fuel pump with you. You should also get some new spark plug cables somewhere. I have heard there are many VW mechanics like me in Nepal," Wolfie smiled. "The problem is not the van, it is you jokers!"

They all laughed.

"Make love and border crossings!" Flora laughed.

"Ricky, come here and I'll show you how to check the oil," Wolfgang said.

"J'ai besoin d'un p'tit verre," Julien mumbled, opening the icebox and taking out a bottle of Güzel Marmara white wine.

"Julien, it's only noon. Have some food first."

"Does anybody want some?" he asked.

"Later," Denise said.

"I'll have some Guzzle Marmara!" Flora said.

Odie joined them in a glass.

"So Wolfie. How do we go to Kathmandu?"

"What do you mean, 'How do you go'? You get in the van and drive."

"How do we know what road to take?"

"Scheiss und himmel! You get a map and follow it! You follow the signs! You ask people the way to the next city on your route."

"What if we run into trouble? Robbers? Bad cops?" Odie asked.

"You deal with it, with whatever happens. It's not the destination, it's the journey," Wolfie said with mock profundity.

"I want peace and love," Flora said. "Peace and love! Make love not war! Why should they give us trouble? We're mellow."

"Not everybody is like you, Florie," Ricky said.

"Why not?"

"What's the next country anyway, Wolfie?"

"That would be Iran, but before you get there you've gotta go through about 1500 kilometers of Turkey. Then 2000 kilometers of Iran, then another 1500 kilometers through Afghanistan to Peshawar, Pakistan, then down to Lahore, then Delhi, then to Lucknow in India —more thousands of kilometers, and finally way up into the mountains in Nepal."

"WHAT the FUCK?" Denise shouted. "Shit! That'll take weeks!"

"Of course," Wolfie grinned.

"And we gotta get this piece-of-shit microbus fixed as we go? We can't just drive there?"

"If you want to get there, you will have to maintain your vehicle. And then you will probably want to drive back."

"But that's bullshit!" Denise yelled. "I just wanna have fun! I don't want breakdowns and flat tires and robbers and mean cops and running out of money in all those different countries! What *is* this?"

"It's the new summer of love, Denise, the new summer of love," Ricky smiled. "Get with the program. Guzzle some Marmara."

The next morning Wolfgang was up early, driving out of the Hippodrome well before dawn on a normal carpet run: Edirne, Plovdiv, Sofia, Niš, Belgrade, Zagreb, Salzburg, Munich, Stuttgart, Karlsruhe, and home to Kaiserslautern. He'd contact his friends at the airbase, invite them over for beer, pretzels and a carpet viewing. Americans were crazy for oriental carpets, and he could offer them far better prices than any other source in West Germany. They could actually afford these luxury items on an airman's pay. Besides, he'd happily accept payment in dollars, the international currency, rather than Deutsche marks, so the airmen saved the expense of currency exchange.

A lot of the guys who showed up the next evening were old friends from Ramstein High School.

"Go Royals!" Wolfgang toasted as he raised his glass.

They all laughed and cheered "Go Royals!"

"Whaddaya got for us, Wolfie?"

Wolfgang put on a traditional Turkish carpet display, unfurling the rolled carpets with a snap as he flung them onto the growing pile in the center of his parents' living room floor. If a particular item caught the eye of an airman or his wife, they'd speak up and he'd put it aside for later consideration.

The evening was successful. Wolfgang sold at least half of all the carpets he had brought, taking in several thousand dollars. He'd find outlets for the others, or store them in his parents' attic for later sales.

After the purchase-and-sale details were finished, the group sat and chatted. Wolfgang noticed that his oldest friend from high school, Andy Dietrich, wasn't saying much.

"What's up, Andy?"

"Nothing, Wolfie. Just stuff at work."

"Not going well?"

"I'm fine, but there's a problem. Let's just say something's missing and the MPs and plainclothes suits are all over the place looking for it. They get in everybody's way. Lockdowns everywhere. It's a pain in the ass. That's all I can say."

The next morning at breakfast, before Wolfgang headed back to Istanbul and his father went off to work on the base, Wolfgang asked him about it.

"Not good," his father said. "Serious. Very serious. I don't know for sure, but I get the idea that what's missing is a weapon."

"Not a nuke!"

Wolfgang's father said only, "It's not supposed to happen. Ever."

30

The Deal

Yergat wandered through the Hippodrome, thinking. He saw the hippies standing, sitting in and around their vans, smoking. He smelled tobacco, hashish. The hippies looked crazy to him: crazy hair, crazy beards, crazy clothes, crazy cars. He had seen some in France. What would his parents in Armenia have thought of such youth? They had no idea of the hard life lived by most people on the earth. A year or two of life in the Soviet Union would change their attitude.

He came to a polished silver VW minibus. Perfect condition. German plates. A properly-dressed young man with a well-trimmed beard was sitting in the driver's seat examining a map.

"Bonjour!" Yergat said.

Wolfgang answered the same. His French was not fluent, but he could get along. He had repaired many French vans in the past few years.

They chatted. When Wolfgang told Yergat he was in the business of importing carpets to Germany, Yergat drew closer and said "What if you imported something that was much more profitable?"

"What would that be?" Wolfgang asked.

Yergat smiled and said *"Poudre blanc."*

Wolfgang frowned, then stared at Yergat.

"Who are you?" Wolfgang demanded. "You can't frame me! I don't get involved in that stuff. Try some of the hippies. *Va-t-en!"*

Yergat didn't leave.

"I am not police," he said. "I am not a drug dealer. Look: I will take a chance. I will tell you everything, the truth. I stole the packages. I don't use drugs, I don't need them, I need money, lots of money, and I need it quickly. My wife is having a baby and she is very ill. If I do not get money quickly, both she and the baby will die. I stole the packages to get money. If you have money right now, I will sell them to you for a fraction of their full value. You can make a fortune from them. I need money now, right now!"

"I cannot sell them here," Yergat went on. "I don't know who is who. But you could sell them easily in Germany. You can take them there. The police won't suspect such a clean van. You leave them in a locker at a train station in Germany and take the key. You hide the key, make the sale, tell the buyer where to leave the money, then where to find the key. You need never see the buyer."

"How do I know what you're selling?" Wolfgang asked. "I will also be honest and tell you the truth. I don't know anything about drugs. You could sell me flour or sugar and I wouldn't know. I could end up with cornstarch and you could end up with all my money."

"Find someone who knows drugs and give them a sample," Yergat said. "Anyone you want. There must be some hippies here who know. They can tell you."

"Look," Yergat continued, "I will take a big chance. I will trust you. I will put my fate completely in your hands. I must save my family! I will bring the packages here tomorrow in the morning at 10 o'clock. You can have someone check them, any test you want. I will accept their decision. If you want them, you will pay me one thousand dollars. These kilos of drugs are worth at least ten times that on the street, much more if you cut them with other powders."

"I really am putting my fate in your hands," Yergat went on. "Tomorrow, you can call the police and they will arrest me. You can tell me you will not buy and I will go away. Or you can buy them and be rich for the rest of your life. The choice is yours."

"Go away!" Wolfgang shouted.

"*À bientôt,*" Yergat said. "I will come tomorrow at 10. If you are not here, I will know your answer. But I hope you will say yes. Help me!" he pleaded.

He walked away.

He's conflicted, Yergat thought. He may come around. If he does, I can put my plan into operation within days.

* * *

The conversation with Yergat upset Wolfgang. Were the cops out to get him? He didn't believe so. He was the only normally-dressed person in the Hippodrome. Turks respected proper dress and behavior. His late-model van was a fancy car here. He was obviously not a hippy. Everyone had seen him buying carpets and driving them to Germany. Several times. No one had ever seen him with any drugs, not even the ubiquitous hashish. He was legit.

But then…if he did buy the drugs and sell them in Germany, he could be rich. He wouldn't have to drive to and from Turkey ferrying carpets. The profit in Germany would be a hundred times what the stranger wanted for the drugs. Just one sale, one big score and he could do whatever he wanted. Not after working 20 or 30 or 40 years, but *right now*, while he was still young. He could buy a real Porsche, he could open his own garage, he could do both! He could live in Germany as a rich man!

Then he thought of the heater boxes. The Type 2 has big metal tubes underneath to carry heat from the fan-cooled 1200cc engine to the front of the vehicle to warm the feet of the driver and passengers. It was a simple system, and it kept the passenger compartment kind of warm down to about 10°C. Lower than that—and it was often lower than that in a German or Balkan winter—the weak heat wasn't much help. Wolfgang's 911S engine was air-cooled as well, but much more powerful. He had designed and installed his own system of insulated heating ducts and booster fans to heat the interior. The old ducts and heater boxes were still there, but he just used them as an auxiliary cooling system for when the 911S engine was heating up at particularly high revs, like when he climbed a steep mountain or drove 150 kilometers per hour along the autobahn on a hot day.

He could put the cargo in the heater boxes. No one would suspect. All VWs had the heater boxes, and they were for hot air. When the Customs guards rolled their mirror under the car, they'd only see what they saw on every other Type 2 they ever checked.

Using the heater boxes for a shipment was not like what the ridiculous amateur drug mules did, hiding their shipment behind the trim panels of the doors. Fools! That's the first place the cops would look.

The stranger's plan for disposal of the cargo was simplistic—and dangerous. But there were other possibilities. For one thing, he wouldn't have to dispose of the cargo right away. He could hide it in Germany until he had studied the situation there and figured out a safe way to sell the cargo. He had plenty of capital from selling carpets. He could easily buy the drugs and have enough money to pay his expenses until the big payoff.

But who was this stranger? If he wasn't a cop, who was he? He spoke French, but with an accent. Was this a setup or the biggest opportunity of his life?

Wolfgang didn't know.

31

The Sale

It was 9:45 in the morning. Wolfgang had decided not to chance it. He would drive out of the Hippodrome. The stranger would find him gone, and that would be the end of it. Still, it was difficult to drive away from what could be lifelong financial independence. He got in his van.

"Hi, Wolfie!"

Danny was walking through the Hippodrome on his way to the Sifendoni Hotel.

"Danny, *wie geht's?*"

"Good, good," Danny said. He stood beside the van and put his elbows on the driver's side window ledge.

"Still ferrying dusty carpets to Germany?"

Wolfgang frowned. Then he had a thought.

"Say, Danny, tell me something. I've heard of your little 'club,' and…"

"Want to come join us?" Danny smiled. Another customer.

"Not just yet. But I wonder if I could ask a favor."

"Sure. What?"

"You know something about…various substances, right?"

Danny smiled, a sly grin.

"I guess I know some things, yeah."

"A guy says he has some stuff. If you see it, can you tell how good it is?"

145

"Well, there are certain tests. A few of them are simple, pretty easy. Yeah, probably. Say, are you going into the trade, Wolfie? Giving up the old dusty carpets?" Danny sensed an even bigger customer or a colleague—or a competitor.

"Not really. I'm just doing a favor for this guy," Wolfgang said.

Wolfgang looked in the sideview mirror of the van and saw the stranger walking toward the van wearing a big backpack.

"Hop in the van," he said to Danny, rolling up the driver's side window and locking the door. He crawled over to the side doors and opened one. Danny got in and sat on the carpets. Half a minute later the stranger arrived, hoisted the backpack in, climbed in and sat.

No names were exchanged. The three men looked at each other. Without a word, Yergat opened the backpack and took out one of the cardboard boxes. Danny's eyes grew big, but at once he controlled himself and put on a poker face. So this is what happened to the shipment.

Yergat looked at Wolfgang. Wolfgang looked at Danny.

"I don't have to test it," Danny said.

"What do you mean?" Wolfgang said, surprised, exasperated. It was a cardboard box labeled Faucet Fixtures.

"I know where it came from, and I know the quality. It's top-grade, pure stuff. It's worth a bundle."

He looked at Yergat, then at Wolfgang, and said, "Ask him if the boxes were sealed when he got them."

Wolfgang asked.

"*Oui.*"

"If that's true, then this is top-grade stuff."

"Test it," Wolfgang said.

Danny turned back the flaps of the box that Yergat had opened before, and saw the shipping labels. The missing shipment, for sure. He took out a pocket knife, made a little hole in the bag, squeezed out a tiny amount of powder, licked his finger, touched it to the powder, sniffed it gently, and touched it to the tip of his tongue.

"Best there is," he said. "100 percent."

Yergat took the second box out of his backpack. Danny said, "That one too."

They all looked at one another.

"Thanks," Wolfgang said to Danny." See you at the club."

Wolfgang opened a side door enough for Danny to get out, and he did. Wolfgang closed it again, crawled to the back of the van, unscrewed the bolt on a small tool compartment and took out a wad of 20-, 50- and 100-dollar bills. He counted out $1000. Yergat took the wad of bills, jammed it in his pocket and held out his hand to Wolfgang, but Wolfgang only opened the side door and barked, *"Va-t-en!"* Get out!

Wolfgang immediately started his van and drove out of the Hippodrome, down to the Galata Bridge, across the Golden Horn, up through the Beyoğlu district to Taksim Square, around the square and into the little grid of streets called Talimhane, a residential and commercial neighborhood. At least half of the shops here sold spare parts for automobiles and trucks.

He parked on Lamartin Caddesi near two auto parts shops, went into one and bought a few items. Then he put a drop cloth under his van, shoved the boxes under, took some tools and crawled underneath. When the "repairs" were done he tore up the cardboard boxes, shoved them into a rubbish bin, and drove away.

Danny was proud of himself. Now he knew something that no one else in his organization knew: what had happened to the missing shipment. What he did not know was how the guy in Wolfgang's van had come into possession of it. Did the delivery guys sell it to him? If so, they were as good as dead. The boss would track them down. It would be efficient. They would disappear. Others in the organization would have nightmares about what had been done to them before merciful death came.

Was it stolen? That was possible: stuff "falls off the back of a truck" all the time. If you're pretending that a shipment of goods is faucet fixtures, you can't have guards that would draw attention. But Gündem Transport's delivery men were good. They never should have allowed a theft.

So all Danny knew is that the shipment had gone astray either through disloyalty or carelessness. Either one was bad.

Knowledge is power. He considered how to use it.

He could stay mum and see how things developed. But the boss was furious and everyone in the organization was afraid. When the boss was furious, nobody could be sure what would happen.

Everyone was under suspicion, from the manager of operations through the clerks and accountants and pistol-packing hitmen down to the lowest delivery man.

On the other hand, he could tell the boss what he knew. Some people would be disciplined. Delivery men, probably, lowest of the low. But he, Danny, would be a hero, the man with inside knowledge, the man protecting the organization, rooting out disloyalty and incompetence. This good work would be worthy of a promotion—and a raise, a big raise.

Danny smiled and held that thought.

As Ahmet Kamanbay's secretary was handing Bruce his pay envelope, Devin Halepli walked into the office. The secretary greeted him in Turkish.

"Hello, Bruce! Nice to see you." They shook hands. "You're here to give Ahmet Bey his lesson?"

"Yes, sir. He's a willing student, and generous."

"Good! I'm sure he will learn fast, like my children."

After Bruce left, Halepli went into Ahmet Kamanbay's office, sat down, and told his boss about the missing shipment.

"Danny tells us he found out what happened to the shipment," Halepli said in Turkish. "He says it was stolen."

"Stolen?!" Ahmet frowned and grimaced. "Impossible! We have rules and procedures for moving product. Our men are not careless. With so many depots, it's essential to have a completely secure operation."

"It is unlikely, I admit," said Halepli. "The other possibility is that Danny stole the shipment to sell on his own. He has that little opium den in the Sphendoneh which we ignore. He thinks we don't know about it."

"I don't mind his little hobby so long as it doesn't impact our operations," Ahmet mused. "On second thought, why should we permit it? It only increases our exposure. Close it down."

"Ahmet Bey, whoever stole the shipment, Danny or someone else, this American is not trustworthy. The opium den is an indicator of that. He is supposed to work for us, only for us. He is to do what we tell him to do. We pay him generously. We did not tell him he could have a 'hobby' on the side. And now that he has told us his story of what happened to the shipment, many others in the organization hate him. They think he stole the shipment to sell in the Sphendoneh, but that they, especially the delivery men, will have to pay the price."

The two men looked at one another.

"Danny is no longer an asset to our organization," Kamanbay said. "It is time for Danny to leave our employ."

Bruce got off the bus in Ortaköy and walked up to the Halepli villa. The housekeeper greeted him as usual, but this time Devin Bey was at home. He greeted Bruce and said he'd like to see how the children were doing with their English.

He sat in on the lesson, which was fine with Bruce. He was suave and gracious and cultured. That he was Astrid's lover—probably—Bruce put out of his mind. Or tried to.

The phone rang. The housekeeper came into the salon, meaning that the call was for Devin. He got up from his chair and went into the next room to take it.

It was Pelit's turn to read from the book. As she did, she pointed to each picture, said its name in English, then pointed to the English caption and spelled it—in English.

Bruce could hear Halepli on the phone in the next room, speaking Turkish.

"Danny," Bruce heard Halepli say, and then "*…gitmesi lazım.*"

By now Bruce knew enough Turkish to understand what that meant. Or at least he thought he did.

32

Heaven's Garden

Bruce ran into Marina in the grocery shop.

"We've got to stop meeting like this!" he joked.

"So let's meet some other way," she winked. "What about dinner? I promised you I'd fatten you up after your stomach bug."

Hmmm… What to do. Sarah and I are…interested in one another, he thought, but I owe Marina, and I like her as a friend and neighbor.

"Sure," he said. "Definitely beats eating my own cooking."

"*Cennet Bahçesi*. Heaven's Garden. D'you know it? You walk west on Saray Arkası, the street turns left down the hill, and the restaurant is right there at the bottom where the street turns right. Seven-thirty tonight?"

"See you there."

The restaurant had a garden terrace with a spectacular view of the Bosphorus and the minarets and domes of Old Istanbul. They decided to dine outside to enjoy the view.

"Why didn't I know about this place?" Bruce exclaimed. "It's just down the street!"

"Stick with me," Marina smiled.

They ordered a dozen plates of *meze* appetizers and a bottle of *Çankaya* white wine. The waiter filled their glasses, they toasted *Şerefe!* They sipped and poked at the appetizers.

"So what's new with you, Bruce?"

"I've been meeting people, seeing things. I've been to Rumeli Hisarı and Kadıköy, and to the islands. Even Kasımpaşa!"

"Good god, Kasımpaşa! That's a pretty tough neighborhood. Why would you go there?"

"Oh, a friend invited me to a café there. It was all right." Bruce was not going to mention Danny's opium den in the Sphendoneh.

The waiter refilled their glasses and asked whether they'd like to order a main course. Marina ordered bluefish. Bruce did the same.

They sipped, admired the view and talked about the historic buildings: Topkapı Palace, Hagia Sophia, the cisterns....

"How are things at the hospital?" Bruce asked after a silence that was getting uncomfortably long. He was enjoying himself. Marina was good company. He didn't want her to feel uncomfortable. He noticed that the wine bottle was empty. He signaled to the waiter for another.

Marina sighed and said "They're good. It's fine there. I enjoy the work." She left it at that.

The waiter came, opened the second bottle of *Çankaya* and filled their glasses. They each took a sip. The food and wine were delicious, the soft autumn evening equally so, the view across the Bosphorus and the Golden Horn to Old Istanbul simply magical. So why that sigh?

"Well...maybe I'm wrong, but it seems to me you have something on your mind. I'm a good listener if you want to vent," Bruce said.

Marina had been drinking a little faster than Bruce. She did want to talk....

"Well, the problem... I don't remember if I told you, I also give English lessons to a guy at the Russian consulate."

"So what's the problem? That would seem the perfect moonlight job for you! Your English is native, and your Russian probably almost as good."

"They don't know I speak Russian," Marina said. "I figured they'd work harder if they thought they couldn't ask me questions in Russian. Total-immersion in English, right?"

"Yeah, that's best. Do everything in the target language. Otherwise everybody gets lazy and talks about the target language in some other language. Not good practice. But what's the problem?"

"Oh, just that Soviet mentality, you know? Constant suspicion and inferiority complex covered up by braggadocio. 'We're the best, we're the future!' Khrushchev's 'We will bury you!' and all the time they don't believe it, they're feeling inferior. Two realities: the fantasy reality they can talk about, and the real one they can't. It just gets tiring to keep track of which is which."

"Where do you give him the lessons?"

"In his office at the consulate. The big Soviet consulate on İstiklal. You know it, right? Huge! It was built as the Russian Empire's embassy to the sultan."

"That place is like a fortress! Double fences, klieg lights, guards. They let you in?"

Bruce took a sip of wine.

"What's it like in there?"

"Well, kind of like any diplomatic, bureaucratic place: guards, and lackeys in black suits, and forms and protocol. They're nice to me because they're curious, I think. Some of them have met Americans but most haven't. I like the guy I teach, but the atmosphere is *heavy* there."

The evening was soft and lovely, with a gentle breeze. They sipped the wine and gazed at the view. Marina looked at Bruce as well as the view. He was conscious of her gaze. It made him feel good and uncomfortable at the same time. Marina was…well, she was at least several years older than he, not exactly pretty, but quite attractive in a mysterious, alluring way. This evening perhaps she had a bit too much wine, but in general she was calm and self-possessed. There was a sophistication, a worldliness about her that impressed him. It might almost go to his head that a woman like Marina would take an interest in him.

They had finished their dinner. The sun had set, it was dark and the breeze was becoming a little too cool. They asked for the bill, paid it, and Marina said, "Let's walk to the edge of the garden and take a last look at the lights."

They strolled to the railing. The lights of the Old City twinkled across the Golden Horn. Marina put her arm around his waist. Automatically, it seemed, he put his around hers. They stood for awhile, savoring and fearing that delicious romantic tension in which you don't know what will happen next. Would the next moment bring excitement, exhilaration, disappointment, or disgust? There was no way of knowing. The tension made them both breathe harder.

She drew him close, looked at him and offered herself. He kissed her, a short kiss. Then a long kiss. Then a long, long, thrilling kiss.

The next morning Vladimir Petrovsky checked into the German Hospital for his periodic examination. An aide led him to an examination room and said, "The nurse will be with you in a few minutes."

Five minutes later Marina entered the room. They smiled at one another, embraced, and indulged in a long, ardent kiss. Marina rubbed sensually against him and felt immediately his arousal and excitement. Without a word they commenced the examination and intimacy which, every two weeks, Petrovsky eagerly anticipated. It was their only opportunity.

Twenty minutes later, after Petrovsky had left, she filled in the report with his vital statistics, her observations, and the progress of treatment, as required.

Bruce was in a quandary. The dinner with Marina at Heaven's Garden had been wonderful, just like all of the other time he had spent with Marina. Well, always good, and sometimes wonderful.

But he had to be honest. He had to level with her about Sarah.

He made up his mind. He'd go to her apartment and have a talk. She said she gets up late on Saturdays, so she'd probably be there.

He walked to her building and up the steps to her apartment. He was about to press the bell when he heard voices. There was someone with her. The voice was male. Their conversation was a steady back and forth: he would speak, she would speak, he, then she, like question-and-answer.

He pressed the bell.

The conversation stopped. He waited for Marina to open the door.

Nothing happened. No sound of steps, no 'Just a minute!'

He waited, then rang the bell again.

After a few minutes he was ready to ring a third time, but thought again, quietly walked down the steps and out of the building.

33

Passport

Astrid finally realized that she was a prisoner. Devin was not going to give her back her passport. Bulut and Ali were with her whenever she left her apartment or the club. Devin would come to her apartment, take her to bed, then leave on another business trip— or wherever he went.

She was his mistress. She might as well be in his harem. Actually, she was—a one-woman harem. Or did he have others?

It had been exciting at first. She thought she was going to be a successful business woman. She dreamed of returning to Kongsberg in triumph, the girl who had made it in the Big World.

She even thought she might be in love with this rich, movie-star-handsome man with fine manners who made her laugh and who made love to her like no other.

But now she knew: this was it, living in a luxury prison, doing the boring work of a bar girl, servicing her boss when he wanted her. And what happened if or when he tired of her? Mistresses don't last forever. Men get tired of them and get rid of them and get new, younger ones. What then?

She remembered that note in Danish in the notebook at Mustafa's: a foreigner writing about a close call with a drug gang, warning "Don't go to nightclubs! They're run by the mafia!"

And what was the Casablanca? Devin came to it only

occasionally. He was always away on business—she had met him flying back and forth to Copenhagen. A man didn't travel like that to run a nightclub. He had some other business and Astrid thought she knew what it was. She had overheard things at his table in the club. Where else would a businessman get so much money without people knowing what he did? You didn't get this rich from a nightclub, but a nightclub was a good way to keep in touch with people who could help you in your "business."

Her temper rose within her. She would *not* be a slave! She was in good physical condition and could run faster than any of them. But where would she run? And…she could not outrun a bullet. Devin sometimes put a pistol on the dresser when he came to her. She knew Bulut carried a pistol too. She had seen it stuffed in his waistband and in the car. People in the club had pistols. She had just assumed it was for protection from robbers, but now it all added up.

This was dangerous! Astrid realized that getting away was not the big challenge. The big challenge was getting away alive.

34

Bursa

"Wolfie, we're on our way!" Ricky said as Julien, Odie, Flora and Denise piled into the Love Bus.

"Wish us luck!"

Wolfgang smiled and waved. Under his breath he murmured "You'll need more than luck."

Ricky started the Love Bus and pulled out of the Hippodrome.

"Where now?" he asked.

Odie was looking at a city map he got at the tourist office.

"I guess we look for a bridge across the Bosphorus, but I don't see any bridge."

"There isn't any bridge, you Mexican. You have to take a ferry," Denise chimed in pleasantly.

"So…where is the ferry? Will it carry cars?" Julien asked.

"If it doesn't take cars, how would cars get to the other side? You think they only have horses—or elephants—on the other side? They've got cars there. I'm sure they've got cars." Flora was proud of her deductive powers. Today her T-shirt had sketches of the Eiffel Tower and the Blue Mosque. The slogan was "You can't be in both places at once, so try later!"

"Look!" Odie said. He pointed to two signs. One pointed left and read *AVRUPA*. The other pointed right and read *ASYA*.

"Does *ASYA* mean Asia? Isn't that where we want to go? Isn't Kathmandu in Asia?"

"I thought it was in India," Flora said. "Is India in Asia? Is there another big thing like that out there?"

Ricky figured if he went downhill he'd get to the water, and if he got to the water they'd find the ferry. He did, and they did.

A line of cars was waiting to board. Ricky got in line, shut off the motor and got out to pay the fare.

"Where do we go when we get to the other side?" Flora asked.

"Damn it, Flora, there will be signs!" Denise frowned.

"What will the signs say?" Julien asked. "Kathmandu?"

"There probably won't be any signs to Kathmandu," Denise calculated. "We're not close enough. There'll be signs to other places."

"Which places?" Julien asked.

"Who knows? We'll read them when we get there."

They arrived at the Harem dock on the Asian side and drove ashore.

"Is this the Harem?" Flora asked. "I thought the Harem was in that palace back there on the other side. What's a ferry dock doing in the Harem? If I lived in a harem I wouldn't want a ferry dock there."

"Flora, shut the hell up!" Denise raged. "There are lots of harems! The sultan had lots of harems! He was a misogynous pig! He kept thousands of women prisoners! This was just one of his harems."

"Bursa!" Julien said, pointing to a sign. "Isn't that in Iran? Maybe we should go that way. We don't want to go to Ankara. That's the capital."

Ricky turned the van toward Bursa. Odie took out his guitar and began to play The Mamas and Papas' *Look Through my Window*, and they all sang: ...*see the people hurryin' by, someone to meet, somewhere to go....*

The Love Bus trundled eastward some distance inland from the Sea of Marmara shore. At a place called Gebze, signs to Bursa pointed to the right. At Eskihisar, the road came to an end at a ferry dock. Ricky got out of the van, bought a ticket, and drove the Love Bus onto the ferry.

"What is this, a big river, like the Rhône?" Julien asked. "I see the other side over there."

They drove off the ferry. Signs pointed to Bursa. Ricky drove on.

Two hours after they had left Istanbul, they were at another ferry dock in a place called Yalova.

"This is another ferry dock. What are we doing at another ferry dock? We already took two ferries," Flora said.

"Flora, the first was to cross from Europe to Asia, the second was to cross some Rhône-like thingy. Now we're gonna cross the Sea of Marmara," Denise said.

"Oh."

They drove onto the ferry and got out of the van to enjoy the sea breeze and the view.

"Wow. The Sea of Marmara is BIG!" Flora said.

After half an hour they saw land on the horizon.

"Is that Bursa?" Julien asked. As they sailed closer, they saw domes and minarets poking skyward. "Bursa looks like Istanbul."

"It's a Turkish city!" Denise said. "They all look like that, with minarets and domes and stuff. That's how they make them."

The ferry rounded Seraglio Point and docked at Eminönü.

"This IS Istanbul!" Ricky murmured glumly. "We're back where we started!"

"SHIT!" Denise spit.

"Cool!" Flora said. "We went in a circle!"

"We can't go back to the Hippodrome. They'd all laugh at us," Ricky said. "Wait! I have an idea."

He got out of the van and talked to a crewman.

"All set!" Ricky said, smiling.

The crewman signaled him to pull the van over against the wall of the ferry. All the other vehicles drove off.

"We're gonna sail right back!"

Ricky drove the van off the ferry and asked the way to Bursa. They drove over the mountains and across a broad, fertile plain, and saw ahead a city perched halfway up the slope of a long, massive mountain. Soon they were in the city, which was good because the sun was setting. They drove until they saw a sign that read *Çekirge Oteller.*

"*Oteller!* That's kinda like *Otel* that I saw on all the hotels in Istanbul. Maybe it means there are hotels and hostels and stuff that way," Flora said. Flora the pathfinder.

They saw lots of hotels in Çekirge. They picked one that looked cheap. Actually, it looked old and rundown, which probably meant cheap. Julien went in to see if it had rooms available.

"He says he has rooms. We cannot stay together. Men must sleep with men, women must sleep with women. A three-bed room for the men. A two-bed room for the women. He also says do we want mineral bath."

"What's a mineral bath?" Odie asked.

"I do not know," Julien answered. "We will see."

They shouldered their backpacks and went into the hotel.

"*Pasaport!*" the desk clerk commanded. They all took their passports out and handed them to the clerk. He tried to read the unfamiliar names as he copied them into the register.

"REEJ-HARD LANT-BROOK-EHR. ZHOO-LEE-EHN ZHOSS-AH-LEE-NEH. OH-DEE-LON TEN-OH-REE-AHS. DEH-NEE-SEH JAR-SO-LEE. GER-TROO-DEH BEH-AH-TREESS-SEH SEE-LEE-TOH-EH.

"What the fuck?" Denise said. "Who the hell is Gertrude Beatrice Sillitoe? Flora, is that you?"

Flora's face blazed bright red. She stared daggers at Denise.

"Gertrude Beatrice Sillitoe!" Denise shouted. "Gertrude Beatrice Sillitoe! You can't make this up!"

"Denise, those are my grandmothers' names, and my father's last name. I'm named after them, but I hate those names! I'm Flora Solaria now."

"Denise, calm down. Don't be so nasty," Ricky said. "Flora is Flora."

Odie put his arm around Denise, pulled her close and shushed her. Julien took Flora's hand, squeezed it, and kissed her on the forehead.

As they took their backpacks to the rooms, they saw hotel guests walking around in thick, bulky terrycloth bathrobes. They found bathrobes in their rooms. They undressed, put on the robes, and followed the other guests. They came to a big indoor swimming pool. Flora dipped her toe in.

"Whoo-wee! That water's *hot!* Last one in is a rotten egg!"

She threw off her bathrobe and jumped in naked. The others did too.

Pandemonium among the other bathers, all of whom wore modest bathing suits. The pool emptied in a single minute except for the hippies.

"Far out!" Flora shouted. "We have it all to ourselves!"

"They didn't have to call the police. What'd we do wrong? We were just being natural," Flora grumped. "Thank god for Denise!"

"Yeah, otherwise we'd be in the slammer," Ricky said. "Thanks, Denise."

"Fuckin' assholes!" Denise fumed. "We were just taking a swim! The others didn't have to haul ass. They could've taken off their stupid bathing suits, just like us."

"Weren't you afraid of the cops, Denise?"

"Odie honey, they think just because they're wearing stupid uniforms they've got some power. Underneath they're just normal jerks."

"Yeah, they should've taken 'em off and jumped in the pool with us!" Flora laughed. "Turkish cops and hippies in a hot tub! Outta sight!"

"But…I mean, when you went after them you were a force of nature! They looked stoned! They had no idea what to do."

"Serves 'em right! But what do we do now?" Denise asked. "That hotel and all the others around it are no-goes. Where are we gonna sleep?"

"We can always sleep in the van."

"Sleep? SLEEP? On top of one another? With you pigs snoring, there's no sleep! We need rooms."

They had left Çekirge and were driving through Bursa. They saw a hotel. There was a cop standing in front of it.

"Flora, light the burner and make some tea. Make it strong. We're just gonna drive," Ricky said.

"I can drive too if you like," Julien said.

"Julien! Let a fuckin' Parisian drive?" Denise fumed. "Over my dead body! Or it would be dead if we let you. I've been to Paris.

Tried to cross the street. The assholes almost flattened me."

"I can drive," Odie said.

"A goddam Mexican? No way!"

"I'm not Mexican, Denise, I'm Chicano. You know that."

"Odie, you're a sweetie and you play far-out guitar and I love you, but there's no difference between a Mexican and a Chicano. A Chicano's just a misplaced Mexican."

"Denise, I'm from L.A., not Mexico. I know how to drive."

"L.A.??? THAT'S WORSE! No Mexicans driving, especially if you're from L.A. And Flora? Hah! And I'm not gonna take it on," Denise said.

"Ricky's gonna drive," Denise said. "Ricky's from Minnesota."

Within 20 minutes, except for Ricky, they were all dead asleep, making more noise than the hard-laboring 1200cc engine.

Ricky sipped his dark, strong tea and drove.

35

Cappadocia

Millions of years ago, volcanic Mount Aergius shot huge quantities of hot boulders and stone dust into the air. Settling on central Anatolia, the dust formed a layer of soft rock half a mile thick.

Over millennia, wind and water carved the soft rock into unearthly formations: sinuous valleys, flat-topped buttes, and jutting rock pinnacles.

Humans have lived here for at least 6000 years. Using simple tools, they carved cave homes from the soft, tawny-colored stone. Medieval monks found it the perfect place for quiet, secure monasteries and for cultivating vineyards in the well-drained, mineral-rich soil under the generous sun. They chipped away at the soft rock and made great caves to be used as churches, dormitories and refectories, decorating them with colorful frescoes of scenes from the Bible.

Since the 6th century BCE, it has been known as Cappadocia.

In 1968, Cappadocia was just being discovered by modern travelers. Services were simple, but the people were friendly and the surreal volcanic "moonscape" unforgettable.

Ricky drove through the night. He followed the main road. In a few hours he could see light appearing in the sky on the horizon.

"Where are we?" Flora rubbed her eyes and ran her fingers through her long hair.

"I don't know. Somewhere east of Istanbul, or Bursa, or wherever," Ricky answered.

"East?"

"Yeah, east. The sun comes up in the east, right? So when I saw the light, I was going in that direction. I figured I'd just keep going that way. Iran is to the east."

"I see signs for Ankara," Julien said sleepily. "We don't want to go there. Ankara's the capital."

"What's wrong with the capital?" Flora asked.

"It's boring. Capitals are where governments are."

"Oh."

"Okay," Ricky said. "The sun's farther to the right anyway. We'll go that way."

They came to an intersection. Ricky turned right. Flora went back to sleep.

A few hours later she woke up.

"Where are we?"

"Anywhere but Ankara," Ricky answered with a chuckle.

"Wait! Look at that funny thing over there!" Flora pointed through the van window. "The funny rock thing, like a tower!"

"More like a penis," Denise said, rubbing her eyes, stretching her arms and smirking.

"There's another one!" Flora said. "And another, and, oh wow! Lots of them! What are they? They're so cool! Ricky, stop! I wanna look at them!"

Ricky slowed down and spotted an unpaved road going in the direction of the rock towers. He turned, drove along it, and stopped at the base of a tower. They got out.

"FAR! OUT!" Flora shouted. "Look at that! There's a DOOR in it! We can go inside!"

The rock tower was 30 feet high, with an open doorway at ground level and steps cut from the rock ascending into its core. She went in. In less than a minute she emerged 12 feet above them, peering out through a window-like opening.

The others followed. They climbed to a medium-sized room cut right into the rock: rock walls, rock ceiling, rock floor. Flora's long rectangular "window"—just an open space—looked out across a tower-filled moonscape.

* * *

"Oh wow! I mean…OH WOW!" Flora was in ecstasy. "This is, like, psychedelic!"

Ricky went back down the steps to the van and got his sleeping bag and pillow. He rolled it out on the floor of the cave room and crawled in.

"I kill the first person who disturbs me," he said.

Denise set out in the Love Bus to find a town and buy supplies. An hour or so later she drove slowly back up the dirt road to the tower. She got out with two string bags.

"The people in the town are nice," Denise said. "They thought I was weird, but they were okay. I got bread, milk, some kinda cheese, cukes and tomatoes, eggs, fruit, some meat to grill, bottled water and six bottles of Güzel Marmara. The icebox is fulla ice."

"Denise, *eres la mejor!*" Odie said. "We'll have to find some way to roast the meat. We'll leave it on ice. For now, it's eggs," and he went to get the burner and a pan to make some omelets for supper. Flora rolled a joint and passed it around.

"Save some for Ricky," Denise said, "if he ever wakes up."

The next day the sun woke them, shining in their eyes and reflecting off the walls of golden stone. Ricky was up early, having slept twelve hours. He put the kettle on the burner for tea.

Odie gathered up the plates, cups and pans from their late supper, washed them in the van's little sink, and set out the same food for breakfast just as Denise emerged from the rock tower.

"So…what are we gonna do today?" Denise asked, pouring herself some tea. "Anybody got a plan?"

"I really like this place. Too bad there's no swimming pool here," Flora said, leaning out the rock window, her long hair dangling Rapunzel-like over the edge. Her T-shirt read "To be is to be how it is!!!" over a sketch of a yogi meditating.

"If there was a swimming pool or a hot tub, it'd be perfect. Maybe we should go get that one in Bursa and bring it here! Ha ha!"

They all smiled at the memory of what they had come to call the Up-Tight No-Night Hotel.

"I wanna look around and do some drawing," Flora said, emerging from the tower with her sketchbook. "This place is so psychedelic! I'll draw when I'm stoned and when I'm dry, and see how they're different. Maybe I can sell some of the drawings. I wonder which ones'll sell better, stoned or dry...."

"I see vines, Julien said, looking through their hole-in-the-stone window. "I wonder what grapes they grow. They must make wine! Why else would someone grow grapes?"

"People eat grapes, y'know," Ricky said. "They make vinegar. They're not just for wine. Maybe we'll stay another night or two so Flora can draw. I don't want a long drive like that again right away."

Breakfast done, Denise watched Odie gather up the cups, plates and utensils and wash them again.

It was a treat to watch him. What a guy! No Italian Stallion in South Philly would have been caught dead washing dishes or cleaning up. That's women's work, they'd say.

When he was finished, Odie sat down next to Denise.

"Thanks, love. Yer a keeper. I never seen a guy clean up in my life."

"I'm one of eight kids, Denise. I'm the third oldest. My mom and dad worked all day out of the house. We had to help. We all did stuff. We older kids took care of the little ones, got 'em washed and dressed and off to school, kept the house nice for when my folks came home from work. They were both beat from working all day to support us. A lot of the time we kids'd fix dinner, then clean up. It's normal."

"Jeez, my dad woulda gone ballistic if my mom had worked outta the house! In South Philly, the papa's s'posed to bring home the money, the mamma's s'posed to take care of the house and kids."

"Fine if there's enough money, Denise, but for us there wasn't unless both my mom and dad worked. Eight kids! But it was good. We didn't need a lot. We got along. We're a real family. Now it's easier because all the kids are old enough to help and some of us aren't crowding the house anymore."

Ricky fussed around the van: cleaned the windows, checked the oil.

Flora and Julien went out for a walk.

* * *

"Our vineyards are different," Julien said as he and Flora wandered along a dusty dirt track among the tawny rock towers and between rows of vines laden with purple grapes. "These vines are so close to the ground. We make them grow up, along wires to give them more sun and air. But here the ground is a bright color. This yellow volcanic sand must give the grapes good reflected light."

They came to some mountain-peak-like stone formations with door openings and little windows. Flora peeked inside.

"Oh wow! Julien, look! There's painting on the ceiling! Guys and angel-girls and stuff!"

They stood inside the stone peak and looked up at the colored paintings on the ceiling and walls.

"It's a church," Julien said. "Look, they've sculpted the rock to look like it was built with separate stones. Incredible!"

Flora sat on the floor, opened her sketchbook and began to draw.

When Flora and Julien returned to the rock tower, they had handfuls of grapes.

"Try them!" Julien said, offering them to the others. "They're... *acide* but also some sweet. They have much tannin."

"We found this great cave-place," Flora said. "The ceiling was all painted with, like, angels and saints and guys. I made a lot of drawings."

"Let's see 'em," Denise said.

Flora showed Denise her sketchbook.

"Flora! These are *so good!*" Denise exclaimed. "You got the gift, honey."

She showed the drawings around. Everyone agreed. Julien smiled like the proud boyfriend. Flora blushed.

Silence. The late afternoon sun, reflected off the tawny rock and yellow sand, was warm. They rolled out their sleeping bags beneath the rock tower and took a nap.

36

Campfire

"How're you gonna cook this meat, Odie?" Flora asked. "We don't have a stove."

"Denise got some spits," he said, reaching for some long flat metal skewers. "All we need now is a fire."

"I saw a quantity of old vines in the vineyard," Julien said. "They cut off some of the vines and burn them in Provence, so I think they will be good for a fire." He left to get some of the vines before the sun set and the light faded.

After sunset they sat around the fire, holding their meat-laden skewers over the low flames.

"This reminds me of when I was a kid," Flora said. "My mom and dad were back-to-the-earthers. They quit their jobs in SF and we moved to a cabin they built outside of Weed, this little town up in the mountains near Shasta. The town had a big sawmill, that's about all. Everybody had campfires all the time coz there was so much wood."

"So your parents were hippies too?" Julien asked.

Flora laughed.

"I don't think they called 'em hippies then but yeah, they were kinda hippies-before-there-were-hippies. They grew some weed. Ha ha! Grew weed in Weed! But that was only for us and some friends. They really made their money making magic wands."

Silence.

They looked around at one another, eyes meeting uncertainly.

Julien was going to ask, "What is a magic wand?" but didn't.

Ricky was going to ask "Have you been smoking some of that weed?" but didn't.

"MAGIC FUCKING WANDS??" Denise shouted. "What the hell are you talking about?"

"Magic wands," Flora said calmly. "They were kinda gold tubes with jewels on 'em. You could open 'em up at the end and put your drugs in."

"What drugs?" Odie asked.

"Coke mostly, I think. We'd take 'em down to SF and sell 'em to rich cokeheads. My dad said some of them were rock stars."

"What'd these magic wands cost?"

"Oh god, some of them went for, like, a thousand dollars I think, or even more. But my mom—she was the jeweler—needed all this expensive stuff to make them: tools, the gold, the jewels. They were real jewels. So we had to pay for all that stuff. My dad would go down to the Bay Area, take orders, then buy the stuff she needed to make them. I went with him sometimes when I was older, and I knew that's where I wanted to be, so after high school I went to SF State coz it's an art school."

"Unbelievable," Denise murmured.

"You didn't have magic wands where you grew up, Denise?" Flora asked, a slight edge in her voice.

"In South Philly? In South Philly, the only magic wands were in the guys' pants. There were drugs around in Philly, but why risk the cops when you could light up on booze? Ripple. Thunderbird. Four Roses. We were Italian Catholics. We drove around and drank booze and screwed."

"Boy, that sure sounds like fun," Ricky joked. "Why'd you leave?"

"Because all we ever did was drive around and drink booze and screw. And the future was for the girls to live on the same street they grew up on and get pregnant and have lotsa kids and cook and take care of 'em and get fat while the guys drove around and drank booze…and probably screwed, but not us. Screw that! I wanted out."

"Your meat's done," Odie said to Flora and Julien. "I think maybe they're all done."

He ran the lumps of meat off the skewers onto plates, added some cut-up tomatoes and cucumbers and handed the plates around.

Julien got up and grabbed another bottle of Güzel Marmara from the icebox. They ate.

"God, this is good!" Denise said. "Odie sweetie, you're a chef!"

"It's good lamb," Odie said. "I never had lamb this good at home, but then we usually ate beef, pork, chicken. Anyway, with meat this good all you have to do is not ruin it."

They ate.

"So how'd you end up in Turkey?" Ricky asked Denise, putting down his plate and picking up his cup.

"I figured I'd go see what the real Italy looked like. Our church ran a charter flight outta Philly to Rome for $205. I had money from my babysitting and waitressing. In Rome I met Mr L.A. Mexican there. We got it on. Here we are."

Odie smiled, collected the plates and walked toward the van to wash them in the sink.

"Bring another bottle of Guzzle," Denise yelled after him.

37

Flee!

I'll have to tell Dave what I heard Halepli say on the phone, Bruce thought. Maybe Dave knows Danny is into drugs, but that doesn't matter. If an American citizen is in danger, the diplomats are supposed to help.

Bruce had a fleeting thought about Astrid. He had seen her with Halepli at the Club Casablanca. Was she involved in the drug business? He doubted it. But perhaps he should get in touch with her and see if she needed a warning.

He called the consulate from the grocery shop phone.

"Can you come right now?" Dave asked.

When Bruce got to Dave's office in the consulate, Ralph Graves was there. He told them what he knew.

"I think Danny is in danger, and I don't know how to warn him," Bruce said. "I thought of going to where he works, but..."

"Don't do that," Ralph said. "You were right to come to us."

"Look, we know about Danny," Ralph went on. "We've had our suspicions about Halepli. We're in Turkey, subject to Turkish law. We couldn't touch them if we wanted to. But if they're doing what we think they're doing, we're very interested because somebody's moving a lot of product and a lot of it ends up in the US. Danny is small beans. They'd dispose of him in a minute, which would be a shame for the young guy and a headache for us. From the legal standpoint we can give Danny what's coming to him if he ever returns to the US."

"Right now we need him to get out of here," Dave said. "The consulate can help American citizens, but we can't be seen as an accessory to crime—particularly not drug-smuggling!—so we're limited in what we can do. If we can get an anonymous message to him, we'll let him know he's in danger and warn him to get out of Turkey. Maybe it'll scare him enough so that he quits the business. For his sake—and ours—I hope so."

Danny read the mysterious note again and again. After reading it the first time he thought it was a bad joke. After the second time, a quandary. It couldn't be from Gündem Transport. They loved him there, at least the bosses did. He had found the lost shipment. Could it be from a rival organization, trying to get him to leave, and weaken Gündem?

He puzzled over it.

If the anonymous note had been from a rival organization, Danny thought, maybe it was a veiled offer of a job with them. He had been in the business for awhile, he had learned the ropes. Maybe another organization would lure him away to work for them for even more money! That's how businesses worked, wasn't it? You hire the best talent away from your competitors. That not only strengthens your own organization but weakens the competition.

Danny decided to go to the Hippodrome and see if he could find out. If he made himself available, the meaning of the message might become clear. Someone would approach him and he'd find out what it meant.

Bruce was sitting on the terrace at Mustafa's, paging through the notebook and talking with Agnete, when he saw Danny walking toward the Hippodrome. He leapt from his chair, grabbed Danny and pulled him inside the tiny restaurant.

"Danny, what are you still doing here? You've got to get out RIGHT NOW!"

"Hold on, Bruce old boy," Danny said, shaking free of Bruce's grip. "What's all the excitement? Let's have some tea." He started for the door, but Bruce grabbed him and pulled him back inside.

"Danny, you don't get it. You're dealing drugs and the people you work for are going to kill you!"

Bruce told him about Halepli's phone conversation.

"*'Gitmesi lazım,'* he said." Doesn't that mean 'Danny has to go?'"

Danny's mind raced. He searched his memory for the various meanings of the Turkish words. 'He must go,' was clear. But what did 'go' mean? Were they going to send him to another company office? His blood ran cold, his heart pounded. No, they would have said that differently. He thought of the note telling him he was in danger.

"Did you write me a note? An anonymous note?"

"No," Bruce answered. He said nothing about the consulate.

Danny broke into a sweat. His eyes nervously swept the vicinity for suspicious activity.

"You mean…somebody might be trying to kill me right now?"

"Yes! Danny, they're after you. You've got to leave this minute!"

"But…where do I go? They know everything about me!"

He thought for a minute.

"You're right. I can't take a chance. I'll get my passport, go to the airport and take a plane out."

"You don't have your passport with you?"

"No. It's in my apartment."

"You can't go back there! That's the first place they'd look for you. They're probably waiting outside. If they think you know they're after you, the airport is the second place."

Danny felt in his pocket. He had a thick wad of dollar bills. He could afford to run. But how?

"Midnight Express," Danny said to himself.

"What?"

"The Midnight Express," Danny said. "It's a night train that goes from Istanbul to Edirne. Part of the way, it goes through Greece."

"Through Greece?"

"It's what they call a 'corridor train.' The old Ottoman train line between Istanbul and Edirne—when the empire fell and they made the republic, they drew a new border with Greece. Part of the train line ended up across the border in Greece, but since the train is starting and stopping in Turkey, and not stopping in Greece, it's legally a Turkish domestic train. You don't need a passport to take it. You're not really 'entering' Greece."

"If it doesn't stop in Greece, what good is it? Don't you want to get out of Turkey?"

"You jump off the train in Greece! The train isn't really an express, people just call it that. It's a *Posta,* the slowest kind of Turkish train. It leaves around ten o'clock at night and takes ten hours to go 300 kilometers from Istanbul to Edirne. When the train goes slowest, you jump off. I know the best spot to jump. I researched it for my work."

"It's how people convicted of drug offenses get out of Turkey," Danny went on with an ironic smirk. "The US wants drug dealers convicted. The Turks catch them and convict them, but they don't want the headache and expense of keeping them in prison for years. They let the convicted guys out on bail—without their passports—while their cases are appealed. The guys come to Istanbul, get on the Midnight Express, jump off in Greece, and go their merry way."

"Everybody's happy!" Danny continued. "The Turks have lots of convictions to show the US Congress, but don't have to pay the drug guys' living expenses for 30 years. The drug dealers go back into the business in some other country. The drugs keep flowing, so druggies are happy. It's a beautiful system!" Danny smiled.

"What about a passport?" Bruce asked.

"You go to the US consulate in Thessaloniki, tell them you lost yours, or it was stolen, they give you another one. It's a hassle with lots of forms, but they always do it if you can prove you're American. They have to."

"So you go down to Sirkeci," Bruce said, "into the station, buy a ticket and get on the train. After it's started, one or two guys come into your compartment with guns in their pockets, or knives, or garrotes—whatever. You end up off the train in Greece, but not alive. That's not a plan," Bruce said.

"Yeah, good point. Thanks for that. But I can take a suburban train to Halkalı and get on the Edirne train there. They won't be looking for me at Halkalı. I'll make sure I'm not followed."

"That might work! If I were you, I'd do whatever I could to disguise myself, go to Halkalı right now, and hide out until the train comes."

"Come with me," Danny said. They went into Mustafa's tiny toilet and struggled out of their clothes. Bruce came out in Danny's silk shirt, gabardine trousers and expensive sweater, Danny came out in Bruce's three-year-old Oxford shirt and chinos. Danny took off his flashy Rolex, handed it to Bruce and said "Gimme your Timex."

Danny went up to a hippy with a broad-brimmed hat, slapped $20 on the table and said "I'm buying your hat."

His head down, the hat pulled low, Danny walked out the back of Mustafa's café and down a side street.

Danny was scared. Now he felt certain the threat to his life was real. The jolt took him out of his fantasies and he thought clearly. After sneaking out the back door of Mustafa's, he sprinted down a narrow passage a car could not enter, turned and went into a doorway. No one came sprinting out of the passage after him. He waved down a taxi, got in, and said "Florya."

He walked to the train station in Florya and got on a suburban train to Halkalı. There he went into a small back street hotel, rented a room, then checked the layout for exits, especially rear exits. He went to the top of the stairs and found a terrace from which he had a 360-degree view of the surrounding streets and most of the town.

He walked from the hotel to the train station. It took six minutes with a fast stride. He bought a ticket for the *Posta* to Edirne, and confirmed the departure time: 10:57 pm.

"Is this train usually on time?" he asked the ticket seller in Turkish.

"'Usually," the man answered.

He walked back to his hotel. Six minutes. He bought a few food items in a grocery shop, went to his room, and waited.

Agnete watched unhappily as two Turks in suits and ties came into the café and talked to Mustafa. She couldn't understand what they were saying, but Mustafa looked tense and worried. He clasped his hands in front of him and kept bowing to the men. They had grim faces and poked their fingers at him. When, finally, they left, he was sweating profusely, and his face showed fear.

Devin Halepli was angry. It was unusual for him because he was nearly always in control. He ran a tight organization, it made him rich and powerful, and he enjoyed that. He was not used to things going wrong, like this business with Danny.

When Danny was out of the way he would be happy again. But the phone didn't ring, giving him the news that the job was done, and done correctly, and that things were back to normal.

"After you finish the lesson, I'd like to talk to you for a moment."

Devin Halepli had greeted Bruce with this when he arrived to give the children their first lesson of the week. Halepli wasn't smiling.

"Sure," Bruce answered. "Of course."

A chill went down his spine. He hid his thoughts.

What did Halepli want? Was it about the children and their lessons? No, it was going to be about Danny.

Bruce was distracted during the lesson, thinking of what to say, and what not to.

"I wonder if you know an American named Danny," Halepli said when the children had gone off to play.

"You mean the former Peace Corps Volunteer?"

"That's the one."

"I've met him. Don't know much about him."

"Have you seen him recently?"

"No, I don't think so."

"Do you remember the last time you saw him? I've got some money to give him, and I'm having trouble finding him. Imagine! Worrying about getting rid of money!"

Halepli smiled at his own joke. Bruce forced a grin.

"Sorry, I can't really remember. We were not friends or anything. I just knew him to see him."

Bruce thought of Sarah, James and Jim and didn't want Halepli contacting them.

"I know he didn't keep in contact with the Peace Corps Volunteers who are in Kadıköy. I know them pretty well. I keep in touch with them. I think they didn't appreciate his leaving. They had to pick up his class load. They're not happy with him."

Halepli thought for a minute. He smiled and said, "Oh well, I guess I'll just have to keep his money! If you run into him, let me know, okay? I really do want to pay him."

"Sure."

38

Hurufism

Bruce and Sarah were sitting on Mustafa's terrace in the warm October sun, paging through the notebook, when Ikbal walked up, smiled, and greeted them warmly. He started to move toward another table, but Bruce got up, grabbed another chair, brought it to their table and signaled for Ikbal to come. Ikbal smiled in satisfaction and sat.

Mustafa appeared, he and Ikbal slowly bowed low to one another, and Mustafa placed three glasses of tea on the table, a first one for Ikbal, a second each for Bruce and Sarah.

Bruce paged through the notebook, looking for something. He turned the book toward Ikbal.

"Do you know what all this Arabic is?"

"This isn't Arabic," Ikbal said glancing at the page. "It's in Arabic script, certainly, but the language is Ottoman Turkish. Turkish was written with the Arabic alphabet until 1929, when it was changed to Latin characters."

"What about these pictures of birds and mosques and so forth made out of Arabic letters? And this face?"

Bruce pointed to a drawing that filled an entire page. Arabic letters were beautifully drawn to form a stylized human face.

"It reminds me of Mustafa," Sarah said.

"Ah, Hurufism!" Ikbal exclaimed.

"Bless you!" Bruce joked. "Sorry. What was that? Roof-what-ism?"

"Hurufism. It's an Islamic Sufi mystic philosophy. *Harf* is Arabic for letter—of the alphabet. *Huruf* is the plural. Hurufism is the study of the special significance, the mystic significance and numerical values, of Arabic letters. Numerology. It was first conceived by the mystic spiritual thinker Fazlullah in 14th-century Iran."

"That is indeed a Hurufi letter-portrait of Mustafa," Ikbal went on. "You know, of course, that 'graven images'—statues, portraits, representations of any living being, human or animal—are prohibited in Islam as idolatry. This makes the holy writ all the more important! Calligraphy is among the most significant arts in Islam because it is essential to communicate the holy words of the Qur'an in as beautiful a way as possible. As with the Hebrew and Christian Scriptures, the Word is the most important thing, because it is the communication we have from God."

"But isn't this letter-drawing of Mustafa a representation?" Sarah asked.

"Ah, yes. Well, the Arabic letters are themselves holy because they are the means of forming the holy words and sentences of the Holy Qur'an. So no fault can be found with the letters themselves. And the long history of Arabic calligraphy, of studying the proportions and flow of the letters, of creating illuminated capitals, and so forth, lends itself to seeing the letters as graphic symbols that are sanctioned by doctrine and tradition. Hurufis would say that the letter-shapes seen in the faces of men are put there by God when he creates men, and so they cannot be idolatrous."

"Is this Fazlullah a saint, then?"

Ikbal gave a rueful chuckle, sipped his tea, and plunked the glass down on its saucer with a clink.

"Hardly! He was put to death as a heretic in 1394, but his theories and teachings spread from Iran to the Bektashi dervish lodges in the Ottoman Empire. Some lodges, like the one in Edirne, became famous for their Hurufi knowledge and wisdom. Nur Baba, the current sheikh of the Edirne lodge, is perhaps the greatest Hurufi numerologist in centuries."

They sat in silence for a moment, surveying the Hippodrome. The sun was warm. A slight breeze was starting to bring down the autumn leaves on the few trees nearby.

"Speaking of centuries," Ikbal went on, "sacred numerology is one of the reasons that medieval Muslim mathematicians practically invented, and certainly named, *algebra*. Our term *algorithm* is derived from *Al-Kwarizmi*, the name of a great Muslim mathematician working in 12th-century Baghdad. He worked out the first systematic solution of linear and quadratic equations. One of these solutions he termed *Al-jabr*, from which we get *algebra*. In fact, it was Al-Kwarizmi who popularized the use of so-called 'Arabic' decimal numbers. Without Al-Kwarizmi, we might still be counting on our fingers, or with Roman numerals and no zero!" Ikbal laughed.

"So what's this relationship between letters and numbers?" Sarah asked.

"Each Arabic letter has a numerical value, and combinations of letters such as words, phrases and sentences can have complex numerical formulas and meanings, usually related to words, phrases and meanings of the Qur'an. D'you know anything about Kabbalah, the Jewish esoteric discipline?"

"I studied it a little in grad school before I left," Bruce said. "I get the idea."

"Kabbalah is probably the closest in concept to Hurufism. According to Hurufis, the numbers, rightly understood, can explain the hidden meanings in the Qur'an, a gift of God that explains all of His creation. The Qur'an is the key to the meaning of everything in the universe."

"But…why faces made of Arabic letters?" Sarah asked.

"A Hurufi studied in the practice of facial assessment can look at your face, 'read' the shapes in it as letters and by their meanings and numerical values assess your personality, your prospects, even your destiny! The letter-faces you see in the notebook are a Hurufi's interpretations of people he's met."

"You said somebody was a sheikh in Edirne," Bruce said.

"Nur Baba. He is the current sheikh of the Edirne Bektashi lodge. An extremely wise and spiritual man! He is Turkey's most knowledgeable and practiced Hurufi—a Sufi *pir* really—an elder or teacher. I'm confident that one day he will be regarded as a saint. Have you been to Edirne yet?"

"Not yet."

"You must go! Edirne's Selimiye Mosque is the most beautiful and spiritual sacred building in the world! Some mosques are larger but none is finer or more harmonious. The Selimiye has a particular spiritual power which you must experience to appreciate."

"Can we meet this Nur Baba?"

"Of course! He has a bookshop in the Selimiye *arasta*, the row of shops below the mosque. So go down there and ask for the shop of Nur Baba. Everyone knows him. When you visit, please give him my greetings."

39

Selimiye

Edirne's Selimiye Mosque, opened in 1574, is the masterwork of the greatest Ottoman architect, Mimar Sinan. It is one of those buildings like the Parthenon, the Coliseum, Hagia Sophia, and the Palace of Versailles, that defines architecture and human achievement.

It is large, but not the largest. It is a standout, but not showy. Although it is effortlessly impressive to the eye, its genius is not apparent until you enter the holy space and abide in its center. Harmony of the soul, after all, is that rare conjunction of the physical, the spiritual and the human that gives respite, at least momentarily, from the chaos and clashing forces of the ordinary world.

Some people believe that harmony is power: achieve harmony, and you strike a chord deep in humanity that exalts you above others, that holds you up as the one who can bring "the peace that passes all understanding," that engenders bliss. Art, music, athletic triumph, religious ecstasy, psychotropic drugs—all these seek to achieve, if momentarily and incompletely, that sense of triumph and completion that gives full rest to the heart and mind, engenders bliss, and gives earth-bound humankind a glimpse of heaven.

But only architecture, inspired by and in harmony with nature, can represent in grand, solid form the union of human and divine powers. Only it, by its size and solidity, can approach the power of love to bring harmony to the soul. Only architecture, among the works of humankind, offers the possibility of creating a livable space in which bliss is accessible in the world of humans.

Just a handful of places in the world allow the acquisition of inspiration, of the breathing-in of the divine. Most are in nature. Some are human-made. Most of these are religious. The Selimiye Mosque is one of them. It was not built by a ruler as a testament to his glory, or even to the glory of a religion, although it serves those functions. It was built by a human, gifted and inspired, to exalt the human spirit so that it could glimpse, for a longer moment than most, the purity and harmony of heaven.

"I want to go to Edirne," Bruce said to Sarah as they sipped tea in Kadıköy. "Have you been there?"

"No. I guess because we're on the Asian side of the Bosphorus, we always think of traveling east, not west."

"I want to see the Selimiye and meet this Nur Baba guy."

"Me too! Tomorrow's Saturday. Let's go."

The next morning they took a bus. It traveled over rolling farmland swathed in sunflowers, then into a small city that the Romans called Adrianopolis, and which in the 1300s, as Edirne, served as the second capital of the Ottoman Empire.

Because of its history, Edirne has an astonishing variety of historic mosques, but the Selimiye is the epitome. Set on its hill in the city center, it is visible from everywhere, the city's visual and spiritual symbol.

They got off the bus with their daypacks and strolled through the small city. At lunch in a simple restaurant, Bruce said, "Let's save the Selimiye for tomorrow morning. Save the best for last. There are lots of other places to see."

They wandered through the *Kapalı Çarşı* (Covered Bazaar), the *Eski Cami* (Old Mosque), the ruined Great Synagogue, neighborhoods of wooden houses constructed in the fancifully-decorated *Edirnekâri* Ottoman-Victorian style.

They walked down to the Maritsa River and across the bridge to the ruins of the first Ottoman palace.

By late afternoon they were tired. It was time to find a place to stay.

They had passed several small hotels. They chose one with signs in English and German, thinking that the staff would be accustomed to Europeans driving through the Balkans and stopping here for the night on their way to Istanbul.

"Two single rooms, please, for one night," Sarah said.

The next morning, after a late breakfast, they went out to the base of the hill and gazed in wonder at the Selimiye's astonishingly tall, slender minarets. They strolled up the hill to the mosque. Removing their shoes at the door, they padded into the main hall.

It was not prayer time. The mosque was empty.

They sat on the soft carpets between the *müezzin mahfili,* the cantor's platform, and the *kıbla,* the niche showing the direction of Mecca.

They sat in the stillness and listened, not to the distant, nearly inaudible hum of the city, but to the sacred space.

A sense of peace fell upon them. They both felt it. They knew that any movement, or speech, would be sacrilege. They felt that nothing was necessary, nothing was urgent, nothing mattered except being there, feeling the peace.

They sat.

The sun poured through the windows, the rays imperceptibly inching across the carpet, through the sacred space.

Time stood still.

Finally, the time came to move. Bruce shifted his weight. Sarah turned to look at him. Their eyes glistened as they smiled serenely at one another.

They understood that the moment had ended, that like everything on earth—and especially the beautiful—it was over, at least for now. But they had felt it, they had lived it, and they would remember it for the rest of their lives.

Slowly they rose and walked out in silence.

40

Nur Baba

"Where is Nur Baba's shop?" Sarah asked a shopkeeper in Turkish. He pointed into the shops below the mosque and explained how to find the shop.

Soon they were there.

Through the doorway they could see a man sitting behind a desk surrounded by gilt-bound books. He was of middling stature and weight, perhaps in his late 60s, with grey hair and beard, and glasses. On his head he wore an embroidered white skullcap, as many Muslims do at prayer time, and the particularly devout wear all the time.

Bruce knocked. The man looked up from his reading.

"Buyrun!" he said and motioned for them to enter. Here and there on the walls were picture frames holding large, elaborate calligraphic figures: Arabic letters shaping a bird, a ship, a face, and a particularly large, beautiful one of a mosque. The Selimiye?

"Wilkommen!" he said loudly, waving his hand in the direction of the shop's only guest chair. Bruce looked at it uncertainly, then at Sarah. Nur Baba looked from Bruce to Sarah and back, then picked up the telephone, said a few words, and in less than a minute a neighboring shopkeeper brought in another chair.

Bruce and Sarah sat down.

Nur Baba looked first at Bruce, at his face, intently, concentrating on it for at least a minute. Bruce and Sarah were starting to feel uncomfortable with the staring. Was he partially blind?

Then he looked at Sarah the same way, with great intensity, his animated pupils moving quickly all over her face as though in search of something. Was he trying to decide if he had seen them before?

Then he smiled, a broad, welcoming smile, even a look of glee.

"*Wilkommen!*" he said again.

"*Hoş bulduk!*" Sarah answered.

"Ah! So you speak Turkish!" Nur Baba said in Turkish. "How surprising! I assume you are German? Would you like *çay?*"

"*Amerikan,*" Sarah said, and in Turkish, "yes, thank you, we would love some çay."

"Well then, we can speak English if you prefer," Nur Baba said. "I picked some up during my lecture tours in various English-speaking countries."

"Picked some up?" Bruce exclaimed. "You speak it fluently!"

Nur Baba smiled and nodded in thanks at the compliment.

"Ikbal in Istanbul suggested that we meet you when we came to see the Selimiye."

"You are welcome! How is Ikbal? May Allah keep him in health and happiness!"

"He is well, thank you, and he sends you his greetings."

"I receive them with the greatest pleasure and appreciation. He is a man like no other."

"*Nur Baba Efendi,* he says the same of you," Sarah said.

"I pray to Allah that I may be worthy of such sentiments."

"Is this shop your library?" Bruce asked.

Nur Baba smiled. "Yes, in a way. But all of these books are for sale. However, selling is just a way of making them available. The money from sales goes to our lodge."

"What sorts of books?"

"Works of mystical exegesis, interpretations of calligraphy, religious treatises, Qur'anic commentaries. I have written some of the books. It is my purpose in life."

"Interpretations of calligraphy?"

Nur Baba smiled broadly.

"Ah, yes! You see, Qur'anic calligraphy is the Key to all the secrets of the universe. Allah keeps nothing from us! Everything we need to know is available to us. He has given us the key to the treasure-house. It is the *Qur'an-i Kerim,* specifically the 28 letters of the Arabic alphabet and the 32 letters of the Persian alphabet. If we wish to know, we must learn how to use the Key. When we know how it fits in the Lock, all is clear!"

He smiled.

"You have come to Edirne to see the Selimiye?"

"Yes. We have seen it, and we are in awe of it. Just now we sat in the mosque and we felt something we have never felt before."

Nur Baba grinned, a blissful, open-mouthed grin, raising his eyes.

"Yes! The Selimiye is unique. I am glad you have experienced its magic. Much of the Selimiye's power is unseen, however, unlocked only if you use the Key. The *müezzin mahfili,* the platform in the center? It represents the sacred *Kaaba* in Mecca. The architect, the great Mimar Sinan, determined its dimensions by the sacred letters: 45 *arşın—arşın* is an Ottoman measure, less than a meter. 45 is the cipher for Adam, the first man. The measure for the minarets is 66, the cipher for The One." Nur Baba raised his eyes to heaven. "All is determined using the Key."

He turned to the wall and gestured toward the calligraphic representation of a mosque. "It is all explained in this calligraphy."

Bruce and Sarah looked at the calligraphic mosque. It was beautiful, the letters gracefully, intricately intertwined to resemble the Selimiye. The calligraphic proportions were perfect.

"What does it mean?" Sarah asked. "Do the letters make words?"

"Of course!" Nur Baba answered. "The words are important, but they constitute only part—a small part—of the letters' significance. Each letter has certain qualities, certain characteristics. Combinations of letters have even more and greater significance. If you interpret these qualities correctly, they reveal the deeper meaning."

A boy came in the door carrying a tray with tea. He picked up a glass to serve Nur Baba, but the sheikh signaled for him to serve Sarah first, then Bruce. Lumps of sugar were dropped into the ruby liquid, little spoons stirred. They sipped.

"How does...the Selimiye...how does it have that effect on people?" Bruce asked.

"The secret of the Selimiye is a deep one, my young friends. It is a divine harmony: from Allah, through humans, to us. I don't blame you for seeking an explanation. An explanation can lead to understanding which, one might believe, may lead to the possibility of re-experiencing. Anyone who has had such an experience wants to have it again. And it is possible! But the possibility springs not from explanation or intellectual understanding—not even from *Hurufiya*, which is merely an aid to comprehension, a trail of stepping-stones, if you will. Ultimately, the possibility comes from spiritual purity, from the purity of the heart. Rather than seeking a superficial explanation, I would counsel you to look deeply into your own hearts. When you find peace there, you will understand the peace of the Selimiye."

They sat quietly sipping their tea.

After simple thank-yous, they left the shop. Nur Baba asked them to convey his warmest greetings to Ikbal in Istanbul, and to visit again, then returned to his reading.

Bruce and Sarah walked down the hill and back into the busy city.

"I...I don't know what to say," Bruce said.

Sarah took his hand and held it.

Monday morning. Sarah, James and Jim emerged from their apartments at the same moment, ready to go to school.

"How was Bursa this time?" Sarah asked.

"Simply fabulous!" James said. "We had such a good time!"

"We went to those hot mineral baths in Çekirge again."

"All men, right?" Sarah asked with a knowing smile.

"Of course!" The men looked at one another, their eyes bright. "It was so much fun! We're going to be regulars there."

"What about you? How was your weekend?"

Sarah smiled.

"I went to Edirne with Bruce. We had a nice time."

"Ho ho HO!" James grinned broadly. "Yet another weekend with Bruce! Sarah has found her beau!"

"Come on, boys, it was just a weekend. It was nice. Bruce is sweet. I like him."

She blushed.

"Ho ho HO!" the boys cheered in unison.

41

Mk-54

Dave Coughlin was at his desk reading freshly-decrypted top-secret signals. He picked up the page he was reading, read it again carefully, then pressed a button on his desk intercom.

"Mrs Nichols, I need to speak to the Consul-General right away."

After a few seconds, he heard "The Consul-General is waiting for you in his office, Mr Coughlin."

In Knowlton's office, the Consul-General frowned.

"What's up?"

"We've received a signal from the Incirlik base saying that something important has gone missing in Germany. At Ramstein. The Agency reports that it's an Mk-54, a nuke. From SAC."

"How could a nuclear weapon 'go missing'?" Knowlton asked.

"Well, the Mk-54 is an SADM…"

"No alphabet soup, Dave. What is it?"

"SADM: Special Atomic Demolition Munition. It's a battlefield tactical nuclear weapon developed for use on the Davy Crockett recoilless gun or to be deployed by special forces. Some people call it the 'backpack bomb' because it's small and light enough for a man to carry."

"How small? How light?"

"The nuclear core or warhead, called a W54, is about the size and shape of a soccer ball. The overall weapon, the Mk-54, is about 2-1/2 feet long, diameter eleven inches, weighs just over 50 pounds. That's not light, but it's light enough for a special-ops soldier to carry."

"What can it do?"

"There are versions with specifications from six tons of TNT to a kiloton—a thousand tons. If it's the latter, it can level two city blocks and leave a much larger area with a fatal level of radiation. For comparison, the nukes dropped on Hiroshima and Nagasaki were 16 to 21 kilotons."

"My god!" Knowlton said. "So the two-block destruction is the total, not-one-stone-on-another destruction, but the actual damage and death would be over a much larger area."

"Correct. A 1-kiloton weapon could effectively destroy a town or small city, certainly kill most of the people by blast, fire and radiation. But remember, we don't know this one's specification, at least not yet."

"Does it have to be fired from that Crockett gun?"

"No. One version is actually packed in a knapsack-type rig for deployment by Army Rangers and Navy SEALs. They parachute or swim in, position the device, set the timer, and get the hell out of there as fast and far as possible."

They were silent for a moment as the gravity of the situation sank in.

"What's Incirlik's interest?" Knowlton asked.

"You know they and our people at the Karamürsel base have got their ears trained on the Soviets, every transmission," Dave reminded him. "Even tanks in the field. Everything. They can hear the Russkis brushing their teeth."

"Well," Dave went on, "apparently something has changed in the patterns of radio traffic, which means reconfiguration of troops and weapons. The Soviets seem to know the weapon is missing from Ramstein. They may have something to do with its disappearance, and there's circumstantial evidence that the missing nuke may be heading our way."

"Don't the Sovs have their own small nukes?" the Consul-General asked. "Why would they want one of ours?"

"Sure, they have the RA-115, for example. Very similar small battlefield nuke. They have plenty of them. I don't know why they'd want one of ours."

"So…how easy is it to detonate one of these?" Knowlton asked.

"What are the risks? They can't just drop it or push a button and blow it up, can they?"

"The RA-115 is pretty sporty. The Swiss found one cached by the Russians near Bern. In a protected disposal area, they turned a high-power water gun on it and it detonated."

"Not theirs, ours! The Mk-54. The one that's missing."

"Well, since 1962 most of our nukes have PAL, Permissive Action Link. The weapon can't be armed without knowing and inputting an eight-digit numerical code, and if it's not armed, it can't be detonated."

"So it may not be usable by whoever stole it."

"Maybe, but Ramstein is a Strategic Air Command base, and on SAC bases in Europe the code is the same eight digits for all of these weapons. The idea was, if Command needed to use some of these quickly, they didn't want to have to go through the red tape of ascertaining and confirming lots of individual codes."

They stared at one another. It sank in. If a nuclear weapon could be stolen, so could the code.

"Don't tell me, Dave. I don't want to know the code. All I want is to find that weapon and get it back to where it belongs."

Dave Coughlin was in Knowlton's office again.

"I took a walk in Sultan Ahmet Square yesterday, checking on the hippies," Dave said.

"How's it look?" Knowlton asked.

"Same as usual, no problems that I could see. I stopped and talked with a neatly-dressed young man in a silver VW microbus. West German kid. Perfect English. Turns out his father is a local worker at Ramstein. I stayed on the Ramstein topic for a few minutes. He mentioned something about lockdowns on the base the last time he was there, around the time the device was discovered missing. He said that's all he knew."

"No surprise," Knowlton said. "Anything new from Karamürsel or Incirlik?"

"Not from them, but another source says something strange is going on among our friends in that big, well-guarded consulate on

İstiklal. You know about the Russian War Memorial that used to be in Yeşilköy? Ayastefanos? Has something to do with that. We've got some film. We're having it processed and assessed."

"What sort of 'strange'?"

"Well, it's strange that current official Russian documents are mentioning a memorial that was built 70 years ago and destroyed 55 years ago. Why would they care? Our source's report doesn't have all the details, but it could be the Russkis are planning something in commemoration of the monument. The source doesn't know exactly what, but thinks it might be pretty nasty."

"Nasty as in nuke-nasty?"

"Can't say. The source is working on it, but it's a tough nut to crack."

42

Midnight Express

"Halepli's goons have been particularly active recently, I can tell you that," Ralph said, sitting in Dave Coughlin's office at the consulate.

"Yılmaz's men have seen them all over the Hippodrome, Beyoğlu, even the islands. We think they're looking for Danny."

"And Danny?"

"That's another place they saw Halepli's goons. They trashed his apartment looking for clues. One's still there on stakeout. So I assume Danny got away."

"Flight?"

"I doubt it. Yılmaz's men would have got him."

"On the Posta?"

"Or a bus. Maybe. Probably."

"Well. He's out of our hair. He's some other consulate's problem now," Dave said.

"So what does that mean for Halepli?" he went on. "Danny was a loose cannon, loaded and primed, and he slipped overboard. He knows all about their operations. What if the cannon goes off? What happens to Halepli's organization? What will Kamanbay do to him?"

"Could be interesting," Ralph said. "Could be *loud* when the cannon goes off. Maybe Yılmaz will get enough evidence to shut them down."

"By the way," Dave said. "There's another situation developing. It's not strictly your beat, but you may be interested as it deals with

Bulgaria and the drug shipment routes. We're waiting for more details to come in."

"Any way I can help," Ralph said.

10:45 pm. Danny went up to the roof terrace of his hotel. At 10:50 he saw and heard the train approaching in the distance. He calculated the times and left the hotel. 10:57. Just as the departure whistle was sounding and the train beginning to move, he strode quickly through the station, wrenched open a train coach door and jumped in.

He felt he had made it. He had seen nothing suspicious even before he had been at Mustafa's, and nothing since. He checked Bruce's Timex and calculated when the train would reach the jumping-off point in Greece.

Danny stared out the train window. The ride from Halkalı toward Edirne was uneventful, even boring. He tried to sleep, but sleep came only fitfully. What if Halepli's men walked through the train looking for him?

6:30 am. Uzunköprü. Dawn was just starting to lighten the sky. By the time they crossed the border it would be light. Damn! Much better to jump in the depths of winter when the sun didn't rise until nearly eight o'clock. But he didn't have the choice.

6:43. The train pulled out of Uzunköprü and chugged toward Python in Greece. At the border, before Python, he knew Greek border guards would climb onto the last car of the train and keep watch for jumpers. He knew there was a good chance the border guards might see him jump and arrest him. They would take him to a police station where they would ask him a lot of questions, accuse him of entering Greece illegally, and quietly assume that he was escaping from a drug sentence in Turkey. They would scold him, perhaps rough him up just a little to scare him and discourage this sort of behavior. Then they would tell him to go to the US consulate in Thessaloniki and apply for a new passport.

Or maybe they'd just take a nap, or sit drinking tea and chatting with the train crew. It wasn't every day that people jumped from the train. The guard duty must be boring, routine. Lots of people had jumped and not been caught.

And so what if they caught him! If he stayed in Turkey, he was a dead man. If they didn't catch him, he would make his way to Thessaloniki anyway, without the unpleasantness in the police station.

He was at the door ready to jerk the handle and push it open. He felt a surge of adrenaline.

But...his mind raced. Halepli certainly would have concluded that he was trying to get out of the country. He would have his thugs cover the airport, the bus station, the train station. He might even expect Danny to take the Midnight Express and jump off in Greece.

What he wouldn't expect is for Danny to stay on the train and go all the way to Edirne.

He could lie low in Edirne for awhile. He spoke Turkish. He had money. Edirne was a way-station for all sorts of people going to and from the Balkans and Europe. Another foreigner would not be suspect in Edirne as he might be in some remote Anatolian village.

After a few weeks of no Danny in Istanbul, Halepli would probably think he was long gone.

So now that he had escaped the city and was presumed to have escaped the country, he didn't have to be in a hurry to leave. Maybe he could even get back into the business. The Greek and Bulgarian borders were right there. If he had to, he could even walk to the border. It was only 8 km—5 miles, an hour's fast walk—from the center of Edirne. A taxi would take just a few minutes. He could even take the *Posta* back toward Istanbul and jump off in Greece if it seemed the right thing to do—and the *Posta* from Edirne to Istanbul went through Greece in the middle of the night even at this time of year.

Danny went back into his compartment, stretched out on the seats and went to sleep. At 8:01 am he was startled awake as the train jerked to a halt.

43

Sema

Bruce and Sarah were back in Edirne. They stopped at the shop of Nur Baba to pay their respects.

"Welcome! Welcome!" Nur Baba said. "Please come in and sit down. We will talk!"

Nur Baba lifted his telephone handset and called for the extra chair, and tea.

Nur Baba looked intently into their faces as they talked and sipped their tea. Sometimes the talking would stop and he would just stare at their faces. Knowing now what it meant, Bruce and Sarah just smiled and waited.

"I will give you an invitation," Nur Baba said after a particularly long silence. "Will you remain in Edirne tonight?" he asked.

"Yes, we will be here tonight. We're staying overnight in Edirne," Sarah said.

"Good, good. Would you like to join us for our *sema,* our ritual? It is a Bektashi *zikr* in honor of the Key."

Bruce and Sarah looked at one another. Nur Baba smiled.

"No, no, you would not participate in the *sema,* only witness it. Hurufis and Bektashis welcome all visitors. You do not have to be one of us, or even a Muslim, to join us. We invite those whom we believe would benefit from it. I think I can see that you would benefit. We would welcome you."

They looked at one another again.

"Am I invited? Are women allowed?" Sarah asked.

"Of course!" Nur Baba smiled. "We are all children of Allah, made in His image, are we not?"

Nur Baba looked at Sarah. She was dressed modestly.

"But please, bring a head covering with you."

"Of course," Sarah said. "We would be honored to come."

"Good! Please come to my shop at 19.45."

At quarter to eight that night they arrived at Nur Baba's shop door. Only the desk lamp was on in the dark shop. When they knocked, the door was opened by a young man in a jacket and tie. He welcomed them in Turkish and asked them to follow him.

He reached for a gilded book on the shelves lining the back wall of the shop. He pulled on the book and the bookshelf-wall swung slowly out to reveal a long tunnel lit by small lamps. At the end of the tunnel their guide indicated they should remove their shoes. Sarah put on her headscarf.

They stepped onto Turkish carpets on the floor of a spacious circular chamber surrounded by a curved white wall. On the wall were huge calligraphic inscriptions in black paint. A simple unadorned *kıbla* on the southeast wall indicated the direction of Mecca.

Across the chamber from the *kıbla* were about two dozen men sitting cross-legged on the carpet. A few women in modest clothes and headscarves sat at one end of the group.

In the very center of the circular room, a *rahle*, a small Islamic lectern, held a large book.

When Bruce and Sarah entered, some of the men looked at them and smiled. They went to the left end of the semicircle and sat on the carpet. Several of the men looked their way and said *Hoş geldiniz!* Welcome!

The man next to them spoke in English.

"Welcome! We are glad to have you join us. My name is Mevlut. Do you know about our *sema?*"

"Not much," Bruce said. "I'm Bruce, this is Sarah. I know about the Mevlevi *sema*, where they whirl."

"Our *sema* is different though the goal is the same: mystic union with Allah. The *sema* will begin when our sheikh arrives."

The men sitting around the edge of the circular room chatted quietly for several minutes, but when the door through which they had all entered opened again, they all fell silent. As Nur Baba entered the room, bare-headed, all rose and bowed toward him. He smiled, bowed in return, and walked slowly across the room to a cushion at the center of the arc of men. A large white turban rested on the cushion. He picked it up and settled it carefully on his head. When he sat down, so did all the others.

Nur Baba looked from left to right and welcomed everyone to the *sema.* Then he looked to his right, to Bruce and Sarah, announced that two Americans had joined them to witness the *sema,* and he formally welcomed them. Everyone in the room looked toward them, smiled and nodded.

Nur Baba paused, then raised his eyes heavenward, his arms out in front of him, palms upward, and began to chant a prayer in a sonorous voice.

"Can you understand what he's saying?" Bruce whispered to Sarah.

"Only partly. He's using a lot of Arabic words. It's a prayer for all of us here, I think, for the country and the world."

After the prayer, twelve of the men rose and formed a circle around the book on the table in the center, facing it. Nur Baba began a chant-and-response: he would proclaim something and they would answer *Amin!* A man sitting by the wall of the room pressed a button on a tape player and slow, minor-chord music filled the room. The men began to move slowly around in a circle, slowly lowering and raising their arms and bowing toward the center. As the minutes passed they moved more quickly but steadily, in rhythm with the music. After about 15 minutes Nur Baba chanted something, the men stopped moving, crossed their arms across their chests with their hands below their shoulders, bowed, and were still.

The men in the circle repeated the ceremony three more times. After the fourth iteration, the music stopped and they stood with heads bowed toward the book in silence as Nur Baba chanted again. When they lifted their bodies from bowing, Nur Baba raised his arms again and offered a final prayer. All of the Muslims in the room held their arms out, palms up, in the attitude of prayer. When Nur Baba finished, they moved their palms over their faces to receive the blessing and the *sema* was ended.

Nur Baba looked from left to right, smiling. The men began chatting. Several rose, went to a rectangular basket and took out plates of dried fruit and nuts. They went along the arc of seated participants and offered the snacks along with glasses of water.

"This room is right beneath the Selimiye dome, isn't it?" Bruce asked Mevlut.

"Yes. And our *sema* room is designed according to the sacred numbers. For example, the circumference is 66 *arşın*. 66 is the number representing Allah because the values of the letters in the Name of God add up to 66: *alif, lam, lam* and *ha* equals 1, 30, 30 and 5, or 66. Every dimension and aspect of our *semahane* is in accord with the sacred letters and their numerical values."

"And, as you mention," Mevlut went on, "it is directly beneath the center of the mosque. The Selimiye is a special work of art, you know, the most harmonious of all mosques. This is not just *art*. The harmony of the Selimiye is a living symbol of Allah's presence in all things—and in all people. When we perform our *sema* here, we truly feel the presence of Allah."

"Are there other sacred numbers?" Sarah asked.

Mevlut chuckled. "Every number is a sacred number! It is so because each of the 28 Arabic letters and 32 Farsi letters has a numerical value, and these values correspond to the *Qur'an-i Kerim*, the Key."

"How do they correspond?" Bruce asked.

"For example, 7 is a sacred number because it is the number of verses in the *Fatiha,* the first *sura* of the *Qur'an-i Kerim. Cennet* and *Cehennem*—Heaven and Hell to you—have seven levels. Seven is also the number of times a pilgrim on *Hajj* must walk around the Kaaba in Mecca. A pilgrim performing the ritual of the *Hajj* must also run between Mount Safa and Mount Marwah seven times. But these are only a few examples. If one knows how to look, the sacred significance of letters and numbers can be seen in everything, in all of Allah's Creation."

As Nur Baba began to rise, all others in the room also stood. He bowed to left and right and received bows from all in return. He removed the turban that signified his office, placed it gently on the pillow at the center of the arc, and walked from the room.

As they were walking out, Sarah asked Mevlut about the significance of one of the painted symbols on the wall. It was a letter which looked somewhat like a '9' with a curved tail, entwined with a mirror image of itself. The symmetrical pairing almost appeared like a face, the two loops for the eyes, the crossing of tails for the nose, and the ends of the tails as a moustache, beard or smile.

Mevlut smiled. "Ah, the *Çifte Vav!* The letter *vav* and its reverse image. *Vav* is the first letter of *vahid*, "Unique," "the One," one of the names of Allah. *Vav*'s numerical value is 6. The *çifte vav* signifies Allah, the Divine because two *vav*s together makes 66 which, as I have mentioned, is the numerical value signifying 'Allah'."

44

Yergat Goes Shopping

After selling the drugs to Wolfgang in his van, Armen Bagratian
—Yergat—walked from the Hippodrome along Divan Yolu, came to
a mosque and went through the courtyard to the ablutions area. In a
toilet stall he pulled the wad of dollars out of his trouser pocket and
put all but a few of them inside his shirt. A hundred dollars should be
plenty to start. No need to draw attention.

He went over the chemistry in his mind, the five essential
ingredients: mercury, nitric acid and ethanol for the mercury-
fulminate detonator; ammonium nitrate and fuel oil for the main
explosive charge.

He made his way through the Mahmutpaşa and Tahtakale bazaars
asking questions and easily located a shop selling ammonium-nitrate
fertilizer. He could buy fuel oil at any gas station. Ethanol was the
simplest of all: he bought a bottle of vodka. But the mercury was a
problem. Shopkeepers showed him mercury thermometers or tiny
tubes of mercury—not nearly enough for a detonator. And for the
dangerous nitric acid, they told him to go to a chemical company,
something he could not do and remain anonymous.

Frustrated, he jumped to the last items on his list: after asking
only two men on the street, he found a shop where he could buy a
powerful pistol and ammunition, no questions asked.

He took his purchases to the drab basement room he had rented
for a week. A murky half-light filtered weakly through the two small
windows high up on the wall of the room. He plunked down into
the ugly stuffed chair and thought. Twisting the cap off the vodka

bottle, he sucked out a mouthful, swallowed it in one gulp, gasped from the burning in his throat, then sucked another mouthful.

He switched on the table lamp next to his chair and glanced at the old Russian alarm clock on the table. Three o'clock in the afternoon.

That was it! A clock! Electricity!

He would make a timed electric detonator.

But how to power it?

Cars use electricity. A car battery, of course. A car bomb! Perfect!

He knew chemistry, but he knew almost nothing about electricity. How difficult could it be to make an electric detonator? All a detonator had to do was to produce sufficient spark, flame, or heat. Would a car battery produce enough voltage or amperage to fire a detonator? And what would that detonator be? Could he jerry-build an electric detonator with sufficient activation energy to trigger the main explosive charge?

He reached for the bottle of vodka on the table. As he lifted it, the back of his hand touched the hot bulb in the table lamp. He cursed angrily from the burn on his skin, then caught his breath and was still. He began to laugh. Ignoring the sting of the burn on his hand, he lifted the bottle to his lips and took another gulp of vodka.

The flash point of fuel oil—the temperature at which there are enough vapors from the oil to be ignited by an external source—is 52°C. An electrified light bulb filament generates a temperature of... thousands of degrees! A light bulb filament would be his electric detonator!

Yergat left his dismal room and walked to Voyvoda Caddesi and the Ottoman Bank.

He saw an armed guard in front of the huge main doors of the bank building, which now belonged to the *Merkez Bankası*, the Central Bank of the Turkish Republic. Good! For his purposes, this was just as good as if it were still the treasury of the Ottoman Empire. It was a fitting symbol for his revenge. He went up to the guard, greeted him in Turkish and asked if the bank was open. Could he visit this historic building?

"If you have an appointment, I will notify the person you wish to see in the bank," the stone-faced guard told him.

"No rush," Yergat said. "I'll set up an appointment and return."

Yergat walked back to his basement room. Hmmm… He would have to steal a car. But first he worked on his escape plan, and his declaration.

Escape plan: he would walk from the bank down Voyvoda Caddesi to the corner of Billur Sokak, turn the corner, run down that side street almost to the bottom, then walk again unsuspiciously to the Tünel subway station where there were always crowds of people, and taxis waiting. He would take a taxi to the Halkalı main-line train station on the western outskirts of Istanbul, and from there a *mototren* to Edirne. If for some reason he missed the train, he would get in another taxi, give the driver a distant destination, and when they were out in the country force the driver out at gunpoint, steal the taxi and drive to Edirne. He would be across the border in Bulgaria in no time.

The Armenian revolutionaries' raid on the Ottoman Bank in 1896 had failed, but he would succeed! He sat down to write his declaration. He would write it in all the languages he knew.

The next day Yergat was walking by the ferry docks in Eminönü when he saw a car pull up to the docks and stop. Two people got out of the rear seat. The driver left the engine running when he got out, went around to the back and got two suitcases out of the trunk. Carrying the suitcases, he followed the two passengers to the turnstile on the dock. The car was unattended with the driver's door open and the engine running for at least 20 seconds. Long enough, Yergat thought, smiling.

45

Sarah's Next Step

Sarah was in love with Bruce. She was sure of it. She remembered her boyfriends in high school and college. They were fun, but this was different. She had met a man she might want for life: deep, thoughtful, together, concerned. It was still too early to know for sure, but those trips to Büyükada and Edirne had been wonderful. So where were they in their relationship?

She knew she must find out.

Living together was not a good idea right now. You could be married and join the Peace Corps as a couple. You could even get married during the three months of Peace Corps training in the US, then come to your work site in Turkey as a couple. But living together, unmarried, was probably illegal in Turkey, and if so, PCVs could not do it, even if others did.

Why are you even thinking about living together, she thought. It's way too early! But I want him. I'll be out of the Peace Corps at the end of this school year. Then what?

Edirne had been enjoyable, but since then she hadn't seen much of him and when she had, he'd been…different. He seemed to have something on his mind. Was it her? Their relationship? Or something else?

Had his interest in her cooled?

 She had to find out. Her future happiness depended on it.

What's the next step?

* * *

Bruce climbed the stairs to his apartment. He found a note stuck in the door.

"Dinner again? Last time was wonderful! This time I'm cooking. Sunday evening the 29th—*Cumhuriyet Bayramı*, Republic Day—at my place. Sunset's around 6, so come for drinks before & during, dinner after. Looking forward to it! xoxo —M."

What do I do with this? Bruce thought. Just us? Or is she inviting other people?

Bruce thought he knew the answer.

He knew, or he thought he knew, that it was dangerous. He had been firm in his resolve before the last dinner, and look what happened. The very memory of it excited him. If he went, would he —could he?—do what he wanted to do, what he knew was the right thing to do—*tell her about Sarah!*

And what about that time he had gone to her apartment, heard the voices, but she didn't answer the door bell? Who was in there? Why didn't she answer? They did not know it was him. They were not going to come to the door, whoever it might be. What was that all about?

It was Thursday. Bruce decided what to do. He didn't want to lose his friendship with Marina—if it was still only that—but he didn't want to do anything stupid either.

The thing to do was to strengthen his relationship with Sarah.

He called the school and left a message.

That night, when he went to sleep, his dream was of a tall woman with a commanding presence making passionate love to him.

Sarah called the grocery shop and replied. This was her next step.

Friday afternoon Sarah went home from school, packed a small bag, took the ferry across the Bosphorus to Galata, then a bus to Taksim Square. She walked down Gümüşsuyu Caddesi to Saray Arkası Sokak and into Bruce's apartment. She would spend the holiday weekend with him.

Saturday mid-morning, Sarah, in her nightgown, was making tea and arranging pastries she had bought for breakfast.

What a night! There could be no question now that they were deeply in love.

"I was just thinking about our last trip to Edirne," Sarah said.

"That was such a special trip," Bruce said. "Before that, I thought I loved you. After that, I knew I did."

Her heart leapt. She smiled.

"Maybe we should make Edirne a regular getaway," Sarah suggested. "I know it wouldn't be the same. We can't relive it. But the memory of our first trips would make the rest special. It's quieter than Istanbul. We could walk in the country, take it easy. Stay in a hotel room with one bed. Make love!"

He gave her a mischievous look.

"Let's do it!" he said.

The doorbell rang. Bruce went around the corner and opened the door. Marina was standing there with a large envelope.

"Good morning, Bruce. Sorry to drop in so early, and I have to rush off, but I'd like to ask a favor. Would you hold this envelope for me? It's important, and valuable. Photos and papers. Please put it in a safe place. I can't say for how long. I'll let you know."

Bruce took the envelope and said "Sure."

Marina took his head in her hands and gave him a fervent, meaningful, loud kiss. Then another one.

"See you Sunday night!" she said gaily.

Bruce pulled away gently, smiled at her and closed the door.

Oh shit!

"Who was that?" Sarah asked. She tried to sound nonchalant, but her body was shaking and her heart was pounding so loud she feared he could hear it.

"Nobody," Bruce mumbled.

"Nobody? It sounded like..." Sarah was shaking violently. "IT SOUNDED LIKE..." She couldn't go on.

"Sarah, I can explain!"

"Explain? Explain! No need to explain! I know what I heard!"

What a fool she had been!

She rushed to the bedroom, threw on her clothes, grabbed her bag, turned to him and shouted "Sunday night?" and stormed out the door, slamming it violently.

At the bottom of the stairs she burst into tears.

* * *

Sunday, Republic Day. Bruce bought a bottle of wine—a good Kavaklıdere white—and walked slowly to Marina's apartment. He was going to tell her about Sarah. It wasn't Marina's fault. She didn't know about Sarah. It was *his* fault. He hadn't told her. He would tell her tonight.

Or did he even still have a relationship with Sarah?

If Sarah would not take him back, should he continue his "friendship" with Marina?

He felt confused, defeated.

Bruce knocked on the door. Marina opened it with a weak smile. Bruce handed her the wine.

"Ah, this is a good one," Marina said.

She went to open it.

They sat on Marina's little balcony, sipping and nibbling olives and pistachios, and watching the setting sun light up the far shore of the Bosphorus.

"Dinner's all ready to go," she said. "Nothing fancy. Some *mezes* and a fish to fry. It'll only take 10 minutes when we decide we're hungry. How's the teaching going?"

Bruce gave her a half-hearted smile and said "Fine." He could see she didn't believe him.

"And you? The hospital? And what about those English lessons for the Russkis?"

She gave him a weak smile in return.

"Sometimes life gets complicated," she said.

"You bet it does!"

They sat in silence, enjoying the view. Was this the right time to bring up the topic of Sarah? Bruce wondered. Not yet, he thought, she looks too…glum. He was ashamed at his lack of courage, but he felt as though all the energy had been drained out of him—out of both of them.

Over dinner they talked about travels, good meals they'd had, where they'd travel in the future. They tried to get their minds onto happier subjects, but Marina seemed preoccupied—*was* preoccupied.

Bruce's mind was elsewhere much of the time. The conversation was forced and fake.

Around 9 o'clock Marina said "Well, I've got a big day tomorrow. Maybe you do too. 'Oh God It's Monday,' you know? Thanks for coming tonight. Next time maybe we'll both feel more like... celebrating."

They kissed on the lips at the door, a good kiss, but without passion. A good kiss, but what it left was sadness because in their minds—in their hearts—they couldn't help comparing it to the last time they had kissed, when time stood still.

They looked into one another's eyes and said goodnight.

46

Konya

The morning after the campfire, Ricky was up early making tea by the Love Bus. Denise came outside to wash her face and brush her teeth. Her hair was its usual cloud-of-fuzz and took care of itself. When she approached Ricky, he handed her a cup of tea. She waved him farther away from where the others were sleeping. They sat on a rock.

"So what about you, Mr Minnesota?" Denise asked. "I told everybody my story last night. Now tell me yours."

"I grew up on a farm. In Minnesota that's what you do. I went to the University of Minnesota and studied agricultural chemistry and biology, the kind of stuff farmers need to know: soil preparation, plant breeding, crop diseases, some of the economics. Maybe it sounds boring to a city girl, but I like it."

"Sounds like Outer Space," Denise said. "It took me years before I even realized that hamburgers were made out of cow. In South Philly we were lucky to have a geranium."

"If it's a *pelargonium*, it's edible," Ricky said.

"Eat flowers? Are you kidding? Is that what you do in Minnesota?"

"Not usually. Depends on how hungry you are," Ricky joked.

"So anyway," Denise went on, "with all those fine Midwestern farm smarts, what're you doing in Turkey?"

"In my World Agriculture course I learned that the Middle East is the oldest farming area in the world. Maybe it's even where agriculture began thousands of years ago. My professor said it may have started here and then spread to Europe and Asia. Y'know, first people were hunter-gatherers, then they started planting stuff and taking care of animals, then they learned how to cross-breed the crops, like they bred einkorn grass into wheat, things like that."

"Whatever works for you," Denise said. "That stuff'd make my head explode."

"With that hair, it looks like it already has," a sleepy Flora said in a saucy voice, walking up to them with a cup of tea in her hand. A sketch of the Cappadocia moonscape was on her T-shirt, with "I feel more like I do now than when I got here."

"Sorry, Denise, I had to say it."

"Tit for tat, honey. It's okay. In fact, you're right. But this bush has its uses. Scaring people is one of them."

"I'm not sure you need the hair for that," Ricky said.

Ricky passed around the tea as people came back from washing their faces and brushing their teeth.

Flora said it again: "I wish this place had a pool."

"Yes, it would be nice, a pool," Julien said. "But this Cappadocia is beautiful. They have vines. They make wine. It's like Provence."

"Provence shmovence!" Denise grumped. "Are we gonna go to Kathmandu or aren't we?"

"What about a ship?" Odie said. "Ships go all around the world from the Port of L.A. We put the van on those ferries from Istanbul, didn't we? Maybe there's a ship from Turkey to India or Nepal. We put the van on the ship, then drive again when we get off."

"Yeah, and some ships have pools!" Flora cheered. "We could get our pool, and we wouldn't have to drive all the way, so we wouldn't have to pay so much for gas!"

"Flora honey, we wouldn't have to pay so much for gas but we'd have to pay for the ride on the ship," Ricky said.

Flora frowned.

"I like the idea," Denise said. "I like it. We won't be cooped up in that rattletrap for weeks. No mean cops, no border crossings."

No tune-ups without Wolfgang, thought Ricky. He liked it.

"Would they have wine on this ship?" Julien asked.

"Of course they'd have wine on the ship! Ships always have

wine!" Flora said, based on no reliable information whatsoever.

"So where do we get this ship?" Denise asked.

"Well, I think Izmir is a big port," Ricky said.

"We could go to Izmir and ask. We could see where the ships go. Maybe they go to Iran or India, and from there we could drive to Nepal," Julien said.

"Which way is Izmir?" Odie asked.

"I don't know," Ricky said.

"There will be signs," Denise added.

After two more pleasant days among the rock towers of Cappadocia, the Love Bus crew decided it was time to head for Izmir and look for a ship. They loaded the microbus, climbed in, and Ricky turned the key.

Nothing.

"Shit."

Ricky got out of the van, went to the rear, opened the engine compartment and looked in. He saw a motor. Odie got out and joined him.

"Wolfie said something about the spark plug wires," Ricky said. "Jiggle the wires when I turn the key."

Ricky got back in the driver's seat and said "Okay, jiggle 'em."

Odie put his fingers on the wires and moved them around. Ricky turned the key. The motor started.

"Ah, good! Here we go!"

Odie closed the engine compartment door, got back into the van, and Ricky pulled away from their rock tower.

"Goodbye, little Rapunzel tower!" Flora said, waving to it.

"Goodbye, phallic condo!" Denise said, giving it the finger with a smile.

It was morning. Ricky drove with the rising sun in the Love Bus's rearview mirror. A sign read *Konya* and pointed to the left. Ricky went that way.

The psychedelic van putted along the ancient Silk Road over a dead-flat plain framed by low mountains in the far distance.

"Where the hell are we, Nevada?" Denise grumped.

They got to Konya in time for a late lunch. Driving into the city center they passed a hill with a big old building on top. Other old buildings were around the hill at its base.

"There's a restaurant over there," Julien said, pointing.

They went in, sat down, the waiter came, got them to stand up, and led them over to the steam tables where the food was. He signed that they should indicate what they wanted.

"What is all this stuff?" Denise wondered. "I see some kinda meatballs and maybe potato slices in this one, but that one is just a mishmash of stuff."

"There's meat in this one too, along with the soup," Flora said. "I see rice."

"This has gotta be fried eggs on top of tomatoes and stuff," Odie said.

"What are these little things? Ew, they look like those parasites. Little tapeworms!" Flora recoiled in horror.

"They're not tapeworms, Flora," Odie said. "That's okra, a kind of vegetable."

"Oh. You mean you can eat it? It doesn't eat you?"

"Flora, it's in a restaurant. It's food. Cooked vegetables. To be eaten."

"Oh."

"Do you have wine?" Julien asked the waiter.

The waiter stared at him, uncomprehending.

"Avez-vous du vin?"

Same reaction.

Julien pantomimed drinking from his thumb, then reeling about as though drunk.

The waiter frowned, almost sneered.

"Oops, not good." Ricky said. "No wine. Let it go, Julien."

"They don't serve wine," a man in a suit and tie said. He was sitting at a table drinking tea. "Konya is a conservative Muslim city. Muslims are prohibited from drinking alcohol."

"Sacré bleu!" Julien said. This meant a tragic lack of civilization.

"I'll have a glass of that milk," Flora said.

The waiter gave her a glass of the white liquid.

"Phew!" Flora spit it out. "It's sour!"

"It's not milk, it's *ayran,* the man at the table said. "It is made by mixing yogurt with spring water. Very healthy."

"Yogurt? What's yogurt?" Denise asked.

"Yogurt is a kind of soured milk, made by bacteria," Julien said. "We have it in France."

"Somebody had it in California I think," Flora said. "I never tried it. Sour milk with bugs in it. Yuck!" She spat.

They pointed their fingers at the identifiable dishes. The waiter took them to the table next to the man in a suit, then brought bottles of water.

"Konya is a very old city," the man said. "Lots of history and beautiful old buildings."

"What's that one on the hill back there—the big one?" Odie asked.

"A mosque. It's about 800 years old. Go see it."

The hippies looked at one another, then went back to eating their lunch.

"Have you visited the Mevlana Museum?" the man asked.

"No. We just got here," Ricky said. "I guess we're not very hot on museums."

"But this one you should see. Do you know about Jelaleddin Rumi? The mystic?"

"A mystic? Here? Can we visit him? Does he give lessons?" Flora was all ears. Om... Om....

"Well, no," the man said. "He died 800 years ago. But he wrote beautiful poems. He is buried here. You should visit his tomb."

After lunch they did.

The guard at the door of the Mevlana Museum indicated they must take off their shoes. Flora winked at him: she was barefoot.

Standing in awe in front of Rumi's gilded catafalque, Odie read a small sign.

"It says here this is a cenotaph. What's a cenotaph?"

"In London they have something called cellotape. Is that the same?" Julien asked.

"A cenotaph is a tomb with nobody in it," Ricky said. "They have one of those in London too. For the Unknown Soldier."

"But…" Flora gave them a quizzical look, "what's the point of having a tomb with nobody in it? Why all this fancy stuff if he's not even here? And where is he? When you die, you gotta be somewhere, right?"

Denise rolled her eyes. "'When you die, you gotta be somewhere.' 'Wherever you go, there you are.'"

"I don't feel any vibes," Flora said. "I thought, we go see this mystic, and we'd feel vibes. There aren't any vibes, just a lotta shiny gold and stuff. It's pretty, but it's not mystic vibes."

"Maybe we should head on," Ricky said.

But the sun was low in the sky, so they found a cheap hotel, separate rooms for boys and girls. Ricky noted the direction of the sunset, so he'd know in which direction to go in the morning.

Ready to leave Konya, the Love Bus's motor wouldn't start. Again.

Ricky said "Odie."

Odie got out, went to the rear, opened the engine compartment and jiggled the wires. Ricky turned the key and the motor started.

Konya receded in the rearview mirror as they drove away from the morning sun. Odie played his guitar, and the kilometers passed. They stopped for gas and to pee.

"Wait a minute," Denise said. "The sun doesn't always come up and go down in the same place, does it? I mean, it moves around depending on the time of year, no?"

"And where you are on the earth," Julien added. "In Paris, in the winter, the sun comes up very low and goes down quick. I see it at the end of the Rue de Rennes in the morning in winter, but it's in a different place in summer."

"So you're saying you think we're going in the wrong direction?" Ricky frowned.

"I'm just thinking that maybe we need to aim a little more south. Julien is right. I mean, there's that thing about the equator. The sun kinda goes around the equator, doesn't it? And we're not on the equator. I don't think."

"The equator. Sounds kinda communist to me. Everybody

equal?" Flora pondered. Her T-shirt bore a sketch of a tapeworm and the legend "You can never tell, so don't."

"So we'll turn a little south," Ricky said. "What can it hurt? We'll get to Izmir eventually."

At the next intersection Ricky turned left.

47

Yergat Acts

The day had come! All was ready.

Yergat went to the Eminönü ferry docks and waited for his opportunity. He only had to wait twelve minutes before an old Citroën Traction Avant, one of the most common old cars in Istanbul, rolled up. The driver and his male passenger got out and both walked toward the ferry dock, chatting and joking. As they hugged farewell, Yergat calmly sat in the driver's seat and drove away at normal speed. He was lost in the flood of traffic before the car owner turned around.

Yergat noticed to his satisfaction that the *Essence* gauge read full, and the *Amperes* meter signaled a strong flow of electricity from the generator and a fully-charged battery, all of which would make the car an excellent rolling bomb.

He drove to his basement room, brought up the boxes he had carefully packed, and put them in the back seat of the car, more or less above the fuel tank. Returning to his room, he ripped the wire out of the table lamp and took it to the car. He removed one of the tail light bulbs, taped the lamp wires to its contacts, then carefully broke away the glass to reveal the tungsten filament. He gently fitted the delicate filament into the receptacle he had prepared for it in the explosive charge.

Folding up the engine cover, he made the necessary connection to the car's electrical system and ran the wires back into the passenger compartment to the alarm clock. He would make the final connection to the detonator after he parked the car at the bank.

Finally, he stuck tape on three letters and numbers of the license plate and painted different figures on the tape.

All was now in order. He drove the car carefully along the streets of Old Istanbul, across the Galata Bridge and up Voyvoda Caddesi to the Ottoman Bank. Parking the Citroën in front of the bank, he walked up to the armed guard at the door and handed him an envelope.

"Would you please see that the director of the bank receives this important envelope?" he asked in Turkish.

"Yes, sir. I will see that he gets it."

The guard pressed a button in his shelter and gave the news over the intercom that there was an important envelope for the bank director waiting at the front door.

Checking his watch as though pressed for time, Yergat said "I'll return in a few minutes."

He got in the car, connected the wire from the clock to the detonator, took the briefcase that held his pistol, closed the car door and walked down Voyvoda Caddesi, turning right onto Billur Sokak.

A messenger appeared at the front door of the bank. The guard handed him the envelope. The messenger disappeared back into the bank building.

Nine minutes later alarm bells clanged throughout the Ottoman Bank as the intercom blared "Take cover! Emergency positions! Take cover! Emergency positions! Exit immediately via the Golden Horn doors!"

The guard at the front door rushed inside and swung the huge, thick wooden doors closed, then the secondary glass-and-metal doors inside.

"The car out front is a bomb!" another guard shouted to him. "Run for cover!"

Yergat had calculated the time necessary for the message to make its way from the guard at the street door to the office of the bank's director.

He wanted the Turks to have time to read his declaration. He had set the bomb's clock accordingly. He wanted them to know why he was doing what he did.

Riding toward Halkalı train station in a taxi, Yergat smiled. He pictured the Ottoman Bank building as it was now: a huge hole blown in its façade, corpses littering the interior, and his message, which he had also sent to the offices of *Cumhuriyet,* Istanbul's foremost newspaper, being nervously set in type for an extra edition.

The train was right on time. Hours later, arriving in Edirne, he left the station, got in a taxi and said "*Kapıkule*" to the driver.

He would be over the border and safe in Bulgaria within 15 minutes.

The triumph of his Ottoman Bank bombing lifting his spirits, Yergat left the taxi, breezed through the Turkish border post and walked quickly to the Bulgarian border post.

He handed his French passport to the Bulgarian Immigration officer who looked at it, then at Yergat. The officer turned around and pushed the passport into a narrow slot in the wooden wall behind his desk. Yergat knew there were clerks behind the wall who would examine his passport in detail, photograph its pages, and look him up in typewritten lists of names. Then his passport would be passed back through the slot, handed to him, and he'd be on his way to celebrate his triumph.

Yergat waited.

Another officer approached the first and whispered in his ear as he glanced at Yergat. They both glanced at Yergat, then looked fixedly at him and one said in Russian, "Come with me. You will answer some questions."

The officer took Yergat to a small room at the back of the border post. Another officer entered and they began the interrogation. What was his name? Where was he born? What were his parents' names? Where did they live? He was not really French, why did he have a French passport? What was he doing in Turkey?

Yergat answered with truths, half-truths and lies as appropriate.

"You will be taken to Sofia for further interrogation," the officer told him.

"I am a French citizen! I demand the return of my passport! I demand to notify the French consulate of my detention!" Yergat said firmly.

"You can do it in Sofia!" the officer answered, smirking. "That is where the consulate is!" The two officers laughed at their little joke.

This Armen Bagratian, a Soviet citizen, they thought, was in for a surprise.

They handcuffed Yergat, gripped him by the arms and shoved him into an official car.

The messenger at the Central Bank had done his duty. The bank director's secretary had immediately opened Yergat's "urgent" envelope, then rushed into the director's office. He looked out his window, saw the Citroën parked directly in front, and triggered the bank's elaborate alarm system. The building was evacuated through the Golden Horn side of the building, away from Voyvoda Caddesi and the bomb-car, in less than ten minutes.

An hour after Yergat had walked away from the Ottoman Bank, the rotor blades of a huge Huey helicopter blew up the dust on Voyvoda Caddesi and deafened the Army sappers in protective gear who were positioning broad canvas straps under the Citroën. A hook descended on a long cable from the hovering helicopter. The sappers attached it to the straps cradling the car, and it was slowly lifted up and clear of the buildings. After gaining height, the helicopter slowly banked southward, headed for the Sea of Marmara, the bomb car swaying like a pendulum on its cable far below.

Before the car was even dropped into the sea, the editor-in-chief's secretary at *Cumhuriyet* received Yergat's envelope, opened it, scanned the contents and rushed into her boss's office. He told her to connect him immediately to the director of the Central Bank.

The director's secretary answered the call and, in a calm voice, asked the editor to hold while she notified the director of his call.

In a moment the bank director was on the line. He greeted the editor cordially and asked how he might help.

"We received a declaration saying that the bank would be attacked today! Bombed!" the editor said urgently.

"Oh, that," the director interrupted. He took a deep breath and exhaled. "Nothing but a hoax! All is well here, I can assure you. You may ignore that nonsense."

PART THREE

NOVEMBER

48

Pamukkale

The hours passed, the Love Bus hummed along, eventually passing a highway sign that read *Denizli*.

"That's a cool name," Flora said. "Denizli. Denizli! I like it. Let's go there."

Ricky steered toward Denizli. When they got there, they saw a building surrounded by buses. Ricky pulled up to it.

"This looks like a bus station," Julien said.

"Points for noticing the obvious," Denise said. "Ricky, why are we stopping at a bus station?"

"Yeah," Flora chimed in. "We're already in a bus—the Love Bus! Ha, ha!" Today her T-shirt was of a puffy blue cloud and read "The sky is made of air. Air is not blue. Go figure!"

"We're looking for a hotel," Ricky said matter-of-factly. "Travelers arrive here by bus. They need hotels. They ask the people at the bus station where there are hotels. The people at the bus station tell them, 'cause they know, 'cause they live here."

"Ask for one with a swimming pool. For Flora!" Julien joked.

"Yeah, get one with a pool, like the Hilton!" Flora laughed.

Ricky went into the bus station, and came back smiling.

"Lots of hotels at a place called Pamukkale not far from here. They're not expensive on weekdays, and they all have pools!"

"Whooo-wee! Far out!" Flora shouted. "People in bathing suits! Turkish cops! Look out! Here we come!"

"Follow the signs," Denise said.

They drove north from Denizli following signs for Pamukkale. Flora was riding shotgun.

"What's that big white thing?" she asked, pointing through the windshield.

"I dunno," Ricky said. "We'll see."

"What big white thing?" Julien asked.

"It's a big white thing," Flora said.

Soon they reached the big white thing.

"Oh, wow! Look at that! The big white thing is all…it looks like clouds, or cotton. What is it?"

"It's a big white thing, Flora. You said so yourself." Denise couldn't resist.

They drove into the big white thing, a huge band of white spread across the grey side of a mountain. The white turned out to be travertine, hard pure-white rock deposits of calcium. Hot calcium-saturated mineral water burst from the earth atop the cliff and cascaded over the side. As the water cooled, the calcium cooled, precipitated from the water, and formed calcium rock, a huge horizontal cliff of it a quarter-mile long. Over millennia, the white calcium rock mass had grown to cover the entire cliffside across the mountain, like a gleaming white waterfall, but of hard calcium rock.

"There's a sign for a motel," Denise said. "Let's go."

The İş-Tur Motel was built at the edge of the cliff. Ricky went in and asked about rooms.

"It's cheap, and highly moral," he said when he came out. "Two rooms again, one with three beds for the boys, one with a big bed for the girls."

"Damn!" Denise spit. "Flora, I love you, but I want to sleep with my sweet Odie, not you."

"Yeah, I get it, Denise! I want to sleep with my sweet Julien. He cuddles so nice!" Flora looked at Julien, put on a lascivious grin and fluttered her eyelashes.

"Not tonight, ladies. The guy was no-nonsense. No sin in his hotel."

"Sin, shmin!" Denise said. "We're in a hotel! With real beds! Not a stone floor in a stone phallic condo! I want to get it on!"

"That's sin in Turkey, Denise," Ricky said. "The Turks think sex is sin."

"SO HOW DID THEY ALL GET HERE??" Denise shouted.

"*Soyez calme*, Denise," Julien said, putting his arm around her. "Soon we will be on the ship. Ships are international. You can do whatever you like on a ship. Like drink wine."

They took their backpacks into the hotel and found the rooms.

"Oh wow! Far out! Unbelievable!" Flora shouted as they entered the rooms. The far wall of each room was all glass and opened right onto the swimming pool, a long rectangle that ran all the way across the back of the hotel right by all the rooms. Every room had its own section of pool. The rooms and the pool were right at the edge of the white cliffs, overlooking the entire valley, a panorama for many kilometers.

Flora stripped off her clothes, stepped out through the sliding glass door and jumped in the pool. In less than two minutes, they were all in.

With heads above water, they could see the 10-kilometer view. The water was warm and mineral-rich from the hot springs, silky on the skin, almost like soap. Sensuous.

Flora swam up to Julien, wrapped her arms and legs around him tight as a leech and gave him a big, deep, wet kiss. Odie was gazing at the view. Denise snuck up to him, pressed herself against his back and reached around to his crotch.

Ricky lay back in the water, closed his eyes and smiled.

"This is too good," Ricky said, getting out of the warm water. "We don't want to get thrown out, or have the hotel call the police. Let's stick to the boys-and-girls-separate policy, at least for tonight."

After some bread, cheese, eggs, tomatoes, cucumbers and two bottles of Güzel Marmara on the terrace by the pool, Flora and Denise went to one room, Ricky, Julien and Odie to another.

"What if we were homos?" Denise asked. "It's all right for homos to have sex but not heteros? Shit!"

"Homos can't have babies," Flora said. "At least I don't think so. In California people don't want you to have a baby if you're not married. It's the same here."

"Yeah, but we can ignore them at home," Denise said. "And

we're not gonna have babies anyway. Don't they have diaphragms and The Pill here?"

The two women put on long drapy nightshirts and got into bed. As soon as they did Denise sank into the middle of the bed and Flora rolled on top of her.

"Damn!" Denise raged. "This sucks! Goddam bed is a disaster!"

"Why is it this way?" Flora asked.

"It's worn out! Too many big fat people sleeping in the middle. The springs are shot. If it's only one person, you sleep in the middle in a V. If it's two, they're on top of one another in the V."

"I'm not doin' this!" Denise said and climbed from underneath Flora and out of the V-bed. She walked out the pool door and banged on the window of the men's bedroom.

"Guys, I can't do it. The bed sucks! It'd be okay with Odie, so I'm sleeping with my sweetie. Come on, Odie. Flora and Julien can have this room. Ricky, sorry, but you sleep in the van."

"No problem," Ricky said. "It'll be quiet."

The next morning, Flora and Julien went out for a walk. Flora took her big drawing pad and pastels. Ricky drove down into the valley below to look at the farms. Denise and Odie slept late, ate some bread and cheese, swam in the pool, then went back to bed.

Sitting on their terrace in the afternoon, sipping Güzel Marmara, they compared notes.

"There's lots of cool stuff to draw here!" Flora enthused. "Those old Roman buildings and stuff—Julien says they're Roman—and The Big White Thing. A bunch of Germans saw me drawing, so I showed them my sketches…and they bought them! For money! Outta sight!"

"*Oui!*" Julien said. "There is a very fine Roman theater, and a Sacred Pool temple. And they do this marvelous thing with wine bottles: they put them in one of the little channels of hot water coming out of the mountain, and after a few days the bottles are completely white! They're covered with this *calcaire*. We used some of the money from the Germans to buy a bottle!"

He held it up proudly.

"Heat isn't good for wine," Ricky said. "It over-develops tannins, kills the fruit and raises acidity."

Julien looked doubtfully at his treasured pure-white bottle.

"It's a good souvenir, though," Ricky added charitably. "Keep it just as it is. Have some Guzzle Marmara instead."

Julien poured himself a large glass.

49

Seven Sleepers

The Love Bus hippies had the Iş-Tur Motel in Pamukkale almost to themselves now, but the weekend was coming and the desk clerk told them that on the weekend the motel would be full.

"No more nude swim?" Flora said. "Bummer!"

"It's time to leave anyway," Ricky said. "It's been great here, but we should move on."

"One more swim!" Flora said. "I'm really gonna miss this pool."

They all slipped off their clothes and slid into the warm, silky water.

A knock on the door.

"Uh-oh. Everybody under water when I say 'now'," Ricky said. He lifted himself out of the pool, wrapped a towel around his waist and padded to the door.

"Now!"

Glug. Four heads submerged themselves next to the pool wall, out of sight.

Ricky opened the door. A bell boy.

"Please you leave one hour... Other tourist come."

"Okay, okay."

Door closes. All clear. Splashing water, gasps for air.

Ricky slides back into the pool.

"There are restaurants at that bus station," Ricky told the others as they drove away from the Big White Thing. "We'll stop there for lunch and ask directions to Izmir."

The men in the bus station pointed west, down the Meander River valley.

The Love Bus rumbled westward along the road past low hills, cotton fields, fruit orchards and vineyards. After a few hours, a sign pointed to the right, north to Izmir.

Julien was sitting on the rear-facing seat behind the driver's seat. Going around the corner he slipped off the seat and the seat cushion came off as well. Beneath it was a storage area. He peered in and saw a small, tattered book.

"Oh la la! C'est un guide—a guidebook...*en français!"*

He started to read.

It was getting late in the day, the sun low in the western sky.

"Let's find a place to camp," Ricky suggested.

At the edge of a place named Selçuk he turned left off the highway. A short way down the country road a dirt track went off to the right through a field of poppies.

Ricky stopped in front of a weird cave in the side of a hill.

"Looks like we won't have to sleep out in the open," he said. "This is our new stone home."

Taking their stuff into the cave they noticed a small sign: *7 Uyuyanlar*/Seven Sleepers.

"Seven sleepers? But we're only five people who want to sleep," Flora said. "Will they let us stay here?"

"Sure, Flora. Maybe two more people will wander in and sleep with us during the night," Denise said. "Or maybe not people. It says 'sleepers,' right? The sleepers don't have to be people. Maybe it'll be animals. Cows, pigs, sheep, dinosaurs. So long as they sleep."

Flora looked uncertain. On her T-shirt, two large painted eyes with Xs through them, and "If you never notice, then you're still that way."

Julien read the French guidebook.

"It is named for a legend," he said. "Seven young Christian men were persecuted for their faith by the Roman Emperor Decius. They took refuge in this cave and slept for two hundred years."

"Two hundred years?!" Flora exclaimed. "We can't stay here two hundred years! I'll be SO OLD then! We'll never get to Kathmandu and I'll miss *everything!*"

Julien calmed her down.

After some bread and cheese and Güzel Marmara in the van they spread their sleeping bags on the dirt floor of the cave and settled in for the night.

Like a good farmer, Ricky was up with the sun. He crept out of the cave quietly so as not to disturb the others, intent on looking at the farmers' fields and the lie of the land. Odie followed him out. They made tea in the van, then climbed the hill above the cave.

They reached the top of the hill. On the other side they saw ruined marble buildings, dozens of them, some of them huge. Marble-paved streets extended through what had obviously been a big ancient city. Beyond the end of the main street, in the distance, they saw the sea.

"Wow!" Odie said. "What *is* this place?"

"Dunno," Ricky answered. "Sure is impressive."

They went back down to the van. The others were coming out of the cave to the van, looking for tea.

After breakfast, Ricky and Odie said "Follow us!" and started up the hill.

"Mon dieu!" Julien said as they came over the top. "Look at all of the buildings! They are all of marble! And sculptures!"

He raced down the side of the hill to the marble street. The others followed.

Julien couldn't believe his eyes. Marble statues, reliefs, columns, capitals, inscriptions. It was all sculpture.

"We have Roman buildings in France, but nothing like this!" he said. This is incredible! I wonder if it is *Éphèse.*"

"A fez?" Flora asked, quizzically. "Isn't that the funny red hat those old Turks wear?"

"Not 'a fez,' Flora, *Éphèse.* I think it is 'Ephesus' in English."

Flora still wore a blank look.

"It's nice," she said. "But somebody knocked all the buildings down. Why would they do that?"

"Those old Romans," Ricky said with a smile. "You never can figure 'em out, Flora dear."

"They didn't need 'em anymore, Flora," Denise added. "One night they all tanked up on Guzzle Marmara, ran around pushing buildings down, then they left and took the ferry to Istanbul. That's where they live now. And, like Julien says, this is where they got the name for that hat."

"Oh."

"*Non!*" Julien said, excited. "It is *Éphèse*. I read about it in the *guide*. There was a great Temple of Artemis here, and Saint Paul, and even *La Sainte Vierge*, uh, the Virgin Mary! She was here too!"

"I don't believe it," Denise said. "It's gonna be like that mystic guru guy in Konya: there'll be some fancy place, but he won't be there."

They wandered through the marble streets. Julien subjected each chunk of marble to elaborate examination. Flora ran back to the Love Bus for her drawing pad and pastels.

They woke after another night in the Cave of the Seven Sleepers.

"Enough marble buildings! I don't care if they're standing up or falling down, hanging around some old Roman city doesn't get us any closer to Kathmandu," Denise grumped. "Right now we're farther away than we were before. I wanna get that ship!"

They packed their stuff out of the cave into the van and headed north following the signs to Izmir.

"Those two other sleepers never showed up," Flora mused. "I wonder what happened to them."

Denise, for once, refrained.

They drove due north. After a few hours they came over the crest of a hill.

"Wow, that's a big city!" Flora said. "It looks kinda like San Francisco, with the water and all, but no Golden Gate Bridge."

"I like the palm trees," Odie said. "Looks like L.A."

They drove down into Izmir and along the waterfront. Big old wooden *kayıks*, the traditional coastal freight boats, were tied up by the sea wall north of Konak Square. Around the curve of the seawall they saw big ships in the port. Along the docks were shipping offices.

"Julien, you go find out. If they don't speak English, try your French," Denise said.

Julien got out of the van, entered the port and walked around looking for someone to speak French or English to. The ships in port looked like freighters except for a few Turkish Navy and Coast Guard vessels. None looked like it would take passengers, especially not to India.

After an hour, Julien returned to the Love Bus. The others were having a picnic under a palm tree.

"Nothing," he said. "No one knows of ships to India. One man laughed when I asked. They say there are ferries to Greece, to the Greek Islands, from towns on the coast, but there are no ships to India. Only a ferry to Istanbul once a week."

"We've been on a ferry to Istanbul—twice!" Denise said. "We want Kathmandu!"

"I don't think this ship thing is gonna work," Ricky said. "Too bad. It was a good idea."

They were silent for awhile. Then Odie asked the question that everyone was already asking silently in their minds.

"So…what now? Are we really sure we want to go all the way to Kathmandu? What's there, anyway?"

Nobody seemed to know, except that it was a cool place to which, if you were a hippy, you wanted to go.

"There's gurus and cool stuff like that," Flora said, "and lots of sweet drugs."

"The last guru guy we saw was dead! He'd been dead for 800 years!—and we didn't even see him! He wasn't even there!" Denise said. "I'm finished with gurus, dead or alive. I'm thinking maybe I want to go back to the US of A."

Odie thought for a minute.

"Well, if we went back to Philly maybe we could get a van and make a road trip to L.A. It's got palm trees like this, but nicer."

"This port here is too serious," Flora said. "All people do in places like this is work! At least in San Francisco we have the Haight and Berkeley and lots of other cool stuff."

"So Julien," Ricky said, "now you're gonna say you want to go back to Paris so you can drink proper wine."

"How did you know? Ricky, you read my mind."

"I guess that answers it," Ricky said. "We forget about Kathmandu. It's probably a dump anyway. I'm not interested in how they farm there. I bet it's too different from where I come from. Now I've seen some of these Turkish farms. I guess I got what I came for."

"Let's do something hippies don't do," Odie said.

"Like what?"

"Go home."

"Which way?"

"Back through Europe."

"Which way is Europe?"

"Look for signs."

50

Sofia

Yergat looked at his watch. The ride from the border post at Kapitan Andreevo to Sofia took nearly four hours. The official car carrying him drove into the courtyard of a large Soviet-style cement-block building on the city's outskirts. It was now nighttime, but the building was active with uniformed men and women. Yergat was taken to a prison section in the building and shoved into a cell.

Several days later—Yergat lost track of the days—guards took him to a fluorescent-lit room and sat him at a table. Two men dressed in business suits entered the room, sat down opposite him and spoke to him in Russian.

"You are Armen Bagratian," the first man said. "You were born in the Armenian Soviet Socialist Republic. You served in the Red Army during the Great Patriotic War. You participated in the conquest of Berlin. You then deserted the Red Army and went to France. You traveled on the Orient Express through Bulgaria recently."

"You are a deserter from the Red Army!" the second man said. "The penalty for desertion is death. You will be taken to the Soviet Union, tried in a court martial, and executed."

The men were silent.

Yergat was astonished! It was 23 years since he had walked away from the 89th Rifle Division in Wittenberg. Through the chaos of war, the death of Stalin, and decades of political purges in the Soviet Union, they had kept his military record alive as Missing in Action. But now they knew he was a deserter.

"Do you have anything to say?"

Yergat told them of the heroism of the 89th Rifle Division, and then of his attack on the Ottoman Bank building and added, unnecessarily, that this was a serious blow against a NATO country, which could only help Bulgaria and the Soviet Union. He hoped this would change his fate.

The two interrogators looked at one another, then back at Yergat.

"You are lying! No such attack has taken place! You tell us that you attacked the Central Bank in Istanbul recently, but we have received no report of any attack anywhere in Istanbul. We are in constant contact with our consulate there. They would have reported any such incident at once. We received no such report!"

One of the men whispered something to the other. The first man nodded.

"You will be held here until arrangements can be made for your extradition to the Soviet Union."

The next morning the guards took him back to the interrogation room. The two suited interrogators—Russians, he guessed from their accents—entered and sat down.

"Our consulate in Istanbul tells us that there was in fact an attempt to destroy the Central Bank building. A car, a Citroën filled with explosives, was parked in front of the bank, but it did not explode."

Yergat's eyes opened wide. His jaw dropped. That lousy electric detonator. He had failed!

"The car was removed and sunk in the Marmara Sea. If it was you who planned this attack, you are a failure."

They sat in silence. Yergat saw that he had failed in more than the attack. He was now facing execution by a Red Army firing squad.

51

Oğuz

Oğuz Kubratov had a significant name. His first name hinted at a history of Turkic ancestors resident in Bulgaria even before the Slavic invasions of the 500s CE. His last name hinted at being a descendant of Kubrat, Turkic ruler of Great Bulgaria in the 600s.

But Oğuz knew that Slavs, not Turks, controlled Bulgaria since its liberation in 1878 by the terms of the Treaty of San Stefano—Ayastefanos—which ended the Russo-Turkish War. And even though Bulgaria's constitution declares that all ethnic groups are equal, it did matter. Slavs were in control, Turks were an ethnic minority and treated as such. When the communists took control of the government in 1948 they continued the Slav domination.

Oğuz discovered that the way to rise in the Slavic communist hierarchy was to be more Soviet than the Soviets, to be a hyper-communist. He could quote chapter and verse of Marx, Engels, Lenin and Stalin. Whenever the embassy of the USSR, which wielded controlling influence in Bulgaria, wanted a local volunteer for a dangerous undercover operation, Oğuz Kubratov was the first to step forward.

These days the Soviet embassy in Sofia was intent on destabilizing Turkey, a crucial NATO ally. Bulgaria made it easy for drugs to come out of Turkey and pass through to Europe and America. Bulgaria made it easy to smuggle Russian handguns and other weapons into Turkey, to be distributed to dissident groups that would then cause mayhem and weaken Turkish society and the government.

Just as Imperial Russia had once sought to exploit Ottoman Armenians to act as a Fifth Column vanguard for a Russian invasion of northeastern Turkey, now Soviet Russia used Bulgarians to weaken Turkey, this NATO bastion with armed forces second only to those of the USA itself.

Oğuz was ready to serve. He could speak Bulgarian, Russian and Turkish. As an ethnic Turk, it was easy for him to cross the border into Turkey for shopping and to meet with the ever-growing community of exiled Bulgarian Turks living in Edirne. When the Bulgarian Committee for State Security requested his help organizing a smuggling route to bring small arms into Turkey, he readily accepted.

"What do I do with the small arms after they have been smuggled into Turkey?" he asked.

"Our consulate in Istanbul will tell you. They will supply men and transport to take the shipments to revolutionary groups within Turkey to be used against the Turkish government. This will help to destabilize the capitalist Turkish regime."

Oğuz developed a brilliant plan. Whenever a Bulgarian Turk died and the family wanted the deceased buried next to relatives in Turkey, a hearse was driven from Edirne into Bulgaria to pick up the corpse, with which it returned to Edirne, dropping the coffin at an Edirne mosque for the funeral service. This happened at least once a week.

Oğuz went to Edirne and talked to the staff at Gündem Transport, the company that owned and operated the hearse. They connected him with Mr Devin Halepli, the company director. In a private meeting, Oğuz delicately explored the possibility of having the hearse bring contraband cargo in return for a substantial payment. Devin listened to his proposal and agreed. He told Oğuz about the special space beneath the coffin platform in the hearse.

"This is just between the two of us," Devin said. "No one else, including employees of Gündem Transport, can know about these shipments. This is a very sensitive matter!"

Devin Halepli knew that if Ahmet Kamanbay ever heard about the small-arms-smuggling business, Kamanbay would explode, and Devin Halepli would be in mortal danger. The hearse was meant to be only for Gündem Transport drug shipments, not for anything else. But Halepli wanted more money.

"I understand. I agree," Oğuz told him. "It is sensitive to me as well! I do not want to be caught by Turkish Customs smuggling arms!"

"After I drop the coffin at the mosque," Oğuz went on, "I will have the arms unloaded in secret by my own men before I return the hearse to its garage."

Oğuz was as invested in this operation as Devin Halepli. There would be no slips.

Several times each week Oğuz drove the hearse from Edirne to Bulgaria, had it loaded with small arms, picked up a corpse in a coffin, then drove across the border back to Edirne where he unloaded the coffin first and then, secretly, the small arms.

After several months during which everything operated flawlessly, Oğuz had an idea. Bulgaria grew a lot of tobacco and turned much of it into counterfeit Winston and Marlboro cigarettes for smuggling. The Turkish government maintained a monopoly on cigarette manufacturing and marketing within Turkey, and kept the prices of imported cigarettes extremely high to protect sales of the government-manufactured Turkish smokes. If he could smuggle counterfeit American cigarettes into Turkey, he knew black market dealers who would sell them in Istanbul for a huge profit. Smuggling fake Marlboros from Bulgaria to Turkey could provide Oğuz with a tidy little extra revenue stream.

Oğuz smiled at the thought: he was paid by the Committee for State Security to drive the hearse and smuggle small arms. Now he would start his own little cigarette-smuggling business, earning even more money, at no additional expense.

Capitalism is wonderful!

52

Hearse

Every morning, a prison guard slid a bowl of slop and a mug of weak tea into Yergat's dank cell in Sofia. Yergat drank the tea, mostly for hydration. The slop was inedible. He had lived in Paris for too many years to stomach it.

But this morning's breakfast was different: tomatoes and cucumbers, bread, margarine, an egg, and real coffee. Something had changed.

Mid-morning, the guards came, unlocked his cell, and led Yergat to the interrogation room where three men were waiting: his two original Russian interrogators and another man he had not seen before.

There were no introductions. The first interrogator began.

"You said that your action in attempting to destroy the Central Bank building in Istanbul was to be a blow against a NATO country, an enemy of Bulgaria and the Soviet Union. That is true. Of this we approve. But you are a deserter. You fled from your post and your army in battle when your comrade soldiers were fighting and dying for the fatherland and the Soviet future. You deserve to be executed, but we have come to a different decision."

"You have demonstrated that you may be useful in the service of the Soviet Union," the Russian went on. "If you agree to go on another mission similar to the one that you planned yourself, and if you perform your duties to our satisfaction, your sentence of death may be commuted and you may even be given the opportunity to work with us in the future."

"You have seen that my goal is to inflict damage on Turkey and the Turks," Yergat answered. "I will admit that I did it in revenge for the genocide of my people. I failed. If you send me on a mission by which I can express my revenge and succeed, I will complete the mission whatever the cost. It may serve the Soviet Union. And yes, it is important to me to get my revenge."

"Our reasons are different, but our goal is the same, so we are allies," the Russian said. "Our colleague here, Mr Petrovsky," indicating the third Russian, "will instruct you soon in the details of the mission."

Vladimir Petrovsky sat with Yergat in a hotel room in Plovdiv as they reviewed the mission plan using maps and photographs.

"You failed to properly arm the car bomb you parked in front of the Central Bank. You must not fail to arm this weapon correctly!"

"I will not fail! Tell me what to do."

"Tomorrow we will take you to Edirne so that you can rehearse the operation in place. You will then return here to Plovdiv. In five days, on Thursday, 14 November, at 12:00 noon, a car will take you from here to Svilengrad, fifteen kilometers west of the Kapitan Andreevo border post. That is where you will meet the Turkish hearse. It will be parked behind the Jisri Mustafa Pasha Mosque. It will have a coffin in the back. The coffin will contain the bomb. You know something about armaments, yes?" Vladimir asked.

"Yes. I learned about them in the Red Army."

"This is a very different kind of bomb than any used in the Great Patriotic War. It is a very powerful bomb, so listen carefully! The weapon is detonated by a timing device. Once armed, the timing device allows you thirty minutes to escape from the blast zone."

"Thirty minutes?! That's not enough time! I want hours!"

"Hours? Hours would allow a much higher probability of discovery of you, or the device, or disruption of the plan, and thus its failure. No! You have already failed once by leaving the site of the event too early. Thirty minutes is fully sufficient time for you to return to Bulgaria. It is plenty! Immigration personnel at the border will be instructed to let you through quickly. This short time between arming and detonation is an essential part of the plan."

"If you perform your duties according to the plan, you will be safe, your court-martial sentence will be commuted...and you will be a hero!—but secretly, only to us. You may have a brilliant career ahead of you in our service."

"You have been shown photographs of the weapon and its arming panel. To arm the weapon and start the timing detonator," Vladimir continued, "you input the arming code. It is eight zeros."

"What? That can't be correct. That's stupid! It must be a mistake!"

Vladimir laughed out loud.

"No! It is correct! The Americans are idiots! The arming code is supposed to be different on every weapon and known only to the few officers in charge of nuclear-action orders, but at NATO bases in Europe all of the weapons have the same code. It is eight zeros. We have confirmed it."

"Fools! You are telling me that not only is the code always the same, but it is not even a number? Eight zeros? That is like having no code at all!"

They both laughed and laughed.

"They are idiots! They have bad memories," Vladimir joked. His smile faded. "They tell me that it was actually easier to steal the weapon than to learn the code, but we discovered what it was—and we laughed then too!"

They both laughed again. Then Vladimir's laugh stopped and he was serious.

"So, repeat to me the plan for transporting, positioning and arming the weapon!"

"On 14 November I am taken to Svilengrad. I meet the Turkish hearse behind the Jisri Mustafa Pasha Mosque. I accompany the driver across the border to Edirne."

"The hearse has supposedly come to the border to transport the corpse of a Bulgarian Turk for burial next to relatives in Edirne," Vladimir explained. "The driver of the hearse is a Bulgarian Turk using a Turkish passport. He is an agent for the Committee for State Security, and he is armed. In the coffin, the bomb will be covered with cartons of American cigarettes being smuggled into Turkey. Certain Turkish Customs officials at Kapıkule have been persuaded not to look too closely when the hearse comes through. The driver knows who. In return for presents, they always allow the hearse to pass."

"It is routine," Vladimir concluded. "The hearse has been passing in this way for months."

"We drive into Edirne and park by the stone retaining wall of the Selimiye so that the rear door of the hearse opens to the entrance of the arasta, the row of shops," Yergat continues. "We remove the coffin from the hearse, carry it into the arasta and enter Shop 66. The owner of the shop, Nur Baba, will not be present. He will have been invited away by the shopkeeper who normally receives the contraband cigarette shipments. We pull out the *Hurufilik* book in the bookcase on the rear wall. This opens the entrance to the passage which leads to the dervish hall beneath the center of the mosque. After we set the coffin on the floor I instruct the driver to open it. When he bends over to do so, I strangle him with the garrote. I open the coffin, set the arming code, switch on the timer control, cover the coffin, exit the shop, and drive the hearse back across the border. I meet your contacts here in Plovdiv as soon as possible."

"Correct! You also have instructions of what to do if something does not go according to plan. If the shopkeeper is in the shop when you arrive, kill him. He is an old man, and unsuspecting. Push the body under the desk. If the bookcase does not open, you have a steel tool. Force it! If for some reason you cannot use the garrote on the driver, you have the syringe. You stab it in any bare flesh—his neck, if possible, but anywhere will do. The poison acts in seconds. You also have a knife. Do not use your pistol! Even though the dervish hall is subterranean, we do not know if the shot of a pistol—even one with a silencer—can be heard in the arasta or in the mosque above. The mosque is quiet! Perhaps it cannot be heard, but we must not take any chances. If you are detected after the bomb is armed and the timer triggered, you may not be able to escape the blast, so *do everything according to plan!*"

Vladimir stared intently into Yergat's eyes.

"Are you ready?"

"Yes!" Yergat barked.

This time, I will not fail to get my revenge, he thought.

Nur Baba was sitting in his shop when a man came in. The man greeted him in Turkish and looked around the shop. Two other men waited outside. The man who entered scanned the books on the back shelf. Nur Baba followed the man with his eyes.

"Do you have General Kazım Karabekir's *Edirne Memoir?*"

"No. I do not sell any modern, secular books. My shop has only books on Islam, Islamic mysticism and similar subjects."

This man has a strange accent, Nur Baba thought. He is not a Bulgarian Turk, or a Turk who lives in Germany. He is not from Istanbul. Is he from the East?

As the man was speaking to him, Nur Baba looked into his face. What he saw caused his heart to beat faster, and faster yet. This man's purpose and destiny were not clear, but still frightening. Nur Baba was greatly alarmed.

The man left his shop, and he and the other two men walked away. Nur Baba sighed with relief and patted his brow with his handkerchief. But what did these men really want? The man who came in was not a normal customer. Why would they think Nur Baba would have such a book?

53

The Message

Tuesday, November 12th, midnight. Lights were on in the Soviet consulate. Vladimir entered Boryana Ermolayevna's office without knocking. She looked at him. He smiled.

"Report!" she barked.

"All is ready according to plan. He is instructed and armed—and eager!"

"You told him that he would have thirty minutes from the activation of the timer to return to Bulgaria?"

"Yes."

"Good!"

She did not tell Vladimir that the device was set to detonate the instant the code was entered and the timer triggered. All evidence of the mission must be obliterated, with no loose ends.

"Now we wait," she said, and looked up at the photograph of the Ayastefanos Monument.

Wednesday, November 13th. Marina was on the Kadıköy ferryboat, sitting alone. Behind her, with his back to her, was a man in a hat. They were the only passengers in the ferry's rear salon. They both had their faces turned to the window, looking at the view, so they could talk in low voices without being observed.

"We need the precise information. We *must* have it *now*."

"It will be the end of the source, and it might blow my cover!"

"We'll have to take the chance. This is big. Just too important. If the source goes, he goes—as long as we get what we need. I cannot emphasize enough how important this is."

"The next contact is on November 18th."

"NO! It must be as soon as possible! Tomorrow if not today!"

"You are asking the impossible! What if he's suspicious? What if he doesn't agree to a meeting? Do you realize how dangerous this is?"

"I do! You do! We're ready. Do it *immediately*. Believe me, this is a matter of life and death...*big* death, if it comes to that. We *must* have more information—immediately!"

When the ferry docked, Marina went directly to the German Hospital and wrote a message:

Dear Mr Petrovsky,

The results of your medical tests have been returned. They contain indications of a potentially serious condition which must be assessed immediately. We urge you to come to the hospital tomorrow morning, November 14th, at 08:00 for an examination and further testing.

Marina Schiller, RN

"Please telephone this message to Mr Petrovsky at the Soviet Consulate immediately," Marina said to her assistant. "It's urgent!"

This is not the time, Vladimir Petrovsky thought as he approached the German Hospital the next morning in answer to Marina's message. What is going on? I don't have time for this! I will reprimand her!

He was torn between his urgent duty and the intense pleasure he would experience from her. But everything for the Edirne operation was properly arranged! It was already under way, out of his hands. He must not be seen to have any part in it, so what better alibi than to say, "I was at the hospital." Besides, Marina would dispel the extreme stress he was under.

Marina welcomed him into the examination room in the usual way. Vladimir frowned at her.

"This is not our usual appointment!" he whispered. "Why are you taking such a risk? I do not have time to do this!"

"Darling, it is not a big risk. Sometimes a patient needs a 'special examination."' She smiled and winked at him. "I couldn't bear being without you so long."

He submitted to her, uneasily at first, then with a flush of ecstasy.

Afterwards, when he was lying sated on the table with his eyes closed, the door to the examination room opened quietly. Three orderlies, shoes off, came in. One handed Marina a syringe and clapped his hand over Vladimir's mouth. Another pinned Vladimir's arms to the table. The third pinned the patient's knees. Marina quickly took Vladimir's arm, found a vein, stabbed in the needle and emptied the contents of the syringe into his bloodstream. Within seconds, Vladimir's struggles weakened. Within a minute he did not move at all.

Marina whispered into his ear. Somewhere deep within his sodium pentathol-addled brain her questions resonated and Vladimir, his tongue loosened by the "truth serum," slurred some answers.

54

Troy

Ricky was driving north along the Aegean coast road. It was getting dark but they didn't see any town with hotels. They kept driving. It got darker, and later, and darker. There was no moon.

Ricky said "It's late. It's pitch black. I'm gonna turn off the highway here and go down this side road. We'll find a place to camp, like last night."

"Find a cave for five sleepers," Flora said.

A few kilometers down the road they came to a small parking lot with a fenced area beyond. There was nobody around.

"Can't see much, but this'll do," Ricky said.

"It's a beautiful night, not even so cold. The stars are so bright! I want to sleep out under the stars," Odie said.

"Like your Mexican ancestors did," Denise joked.

"My Mexican ancestors lived in a house, Denise." But then he got with the joke, picked up his guitar and started singing "Ay, Yay Yay Yay! Oh, my sombrero!"

This triggered a laughing fit in the others. They laughed until their faces were soaked with tears and their stomach muscles ached. Exhausted, the laughter would subside in one of them, but another would start again, and then another laughing fit would seize them all. It went on and on until they had all collapsed.

Odie was the first to recover. He grabbed his sleeping bag.

"I'm going up on that little hill there."

"To be closer to the stars like the Aztecs!" Denise shouted. This triggered another fit. Odie couldn't move. He stood there helpless, laughing and gasping for air. They were all imprisoned by mirth.

Exhausted, they were finally quiet. They went slowly up on the little hill, wiping the tears from their faces, and bedded down.

In the middle of the night, when a half moon finally rose, it woke Odie and he began laughing at the memory. That woke the others, and the little hill rang to the sound of their laughter again.

The sun woke them before 8 o'clock. Julien sat up first and looked around. Bushes, grass, stone walls, signboards. Signboards?

He rubbed his eyes, got up and went to wash his face and brush his teeth at the Love Bus.

Denise woke next, then Flora and Odie.

"Let Ricky sleep," Denise said. "He drove for so long."

Julien stood up and looked around.

"We are at Troy," he said.

"Troy? What's Troy?" Flora asked.

"Troy! It's an ancient city," Julien said. "You know, the Trojan War and all."

"Trojan War?" Flora looked surprised. "Trojans are a kinda safe, you know, a rubber. How can they go to war?"

"Trojans is what they call the people who lived in Troy," Denise explained. "They're not just condoms."

"Condom is a town in France," Julien said. "They make armagnac there."

"Okay, but they're also a kinda rubber."

"Sure, Flora. You would know."

"What?? We all would know! Who here doesn't know what a Trojan rubber is? It says 'Trojan' right on the package in big letters."

"So..." Flora went on, "so...were the rubbers named after the guys who lived here? Did they invent them? Maybe they used a lot of them here and then they exported them to America?"

"Archeology and commercial history à la Flora," Denise deadpanned.

"No, really," Flora said, "maybe the guys here were famous for... well, you know. And they invented these things and called them

Trojans, and other guys got jealous and wanted them too. The Turks don't want babies, right? *That's why you use a rubber!* So now there are Trojans everywhere, in every drugstore. I've seen them."

"But no Trojans. The guys I mean. Do you see a Trojan here? A single Trojan?" Denise asked. She couldn't help herself when it came to Flora's fits of pseudo-logic. She had to milk them. It was just so easy, and such a hoot.

"I see one over there!" Flora said and pointed over their heads.

Along a path came an old Turk in an official-looking cap. He had a nameplate pinned to his shirt—some sort of official. He came up the hill to them.

"Kamp—no!" he said. With sign language he indicated they should pick their stuff and take it back to the van. That woke Ricky, who got up.

When they got to the van the guy in the cap said "TEE-kett?" and held out a pack of tickets.

"No thanks," Denise said. "We've got to hit the road. Say, Flora, if the guy sells you a ticket do you think he'll give you a rubber for the same price?"

"Why would he?" Flora answered, miffed. "Maybe tickets and rubbers don't cost the same. Besides, I don't NEED a rubber. The men do."

"Sure enough," Ricky said, and swung into the driver's seat. Odie was ready at the rear to jiggle the wires. Off they went.

"Another ferry," Denise said. "Ricky, are you sure this thing goes to the right place? We don't want to sail back to goddam Istanbul again."

"This is Çanakkale, Denise, and that over there is Gallipoli. Look, you can see the other shore over there, and it doesn't look like Istanbul."

It didn't.

"What's that say up on the hill over there? What does 'DUR YOLCU' mean?" Flora asked. On the hillside, picked out in white stones, was a huge outline of a soldier and an inscription in Turkish. It was enormous.

"Who knows?" Odie said. "Something about war. It's a soldier."

Julien asked one of the ferry mates what "Dur Yolcu" means.

"He says it means 'Stop, Traveler!'"

"Wait!" Flora said, alarmed. "You mean we have to stop when we get over there? We can't go to Europe? We can't go home? Are soldiers gonna stop us?"

"I do not believe so," Julien said. "It is just a monument."

Flora was still upset. It was big. She was a traveler. It said STOP! It seemed clear to her. On her T-shirt, the buildings of Ephesus were pictured before they were ruined and "You can't get over something bad that hasn't happened."

Julien consulted the old guidebook he had discovered in the van.

"It is from a Turkish poem. It means stop here and remember the war," he told them.

"What war?" Odie asked.

"The Gallipoli War."

"When was that?"

"I don't know. A long time ago."

"Like that Trojan War?" Flora giggled at the thought of soldiers wearing condoms and whacking one another with their...

"I think there were Australians fighting here, at least that's what the book says."

"Australians? WHAT the HELL?! Australia is all the way on the other side of the world! It's farther than Kathmandu! What the hell are Australians doing fighting Turks in their own country?" Denise was outraged at the stupidity of war, which seemed obvious.

"I think the Australians lost," Julien said. "They sailed away."

"You bet they did! What asshole thought that one up, I wonder —Australians fighting here."

"So we really don't have to stop here?" Flora asked, seeking reassurance.

"Never you mind, Flora dear," Ricky said. "We'll sail away home just like the Australians."

Ricky drove off the ferry and knew that to get to Europe you wanted to go away from the water, so that's how he drove: north. Soon they saw signs that read "Edirne" and "Bulgaristan."

"Bulgaristan! Bulgaristan!" Flora chortled. "I love it! Like Afghanistan, only fulla Bulgars! We gotta go there!"

"We will," Ricky said. "Bulgaria's connected to Europe. We go through it to get to Europe."

By mid-afternoon they had driven through Edirne and on to the Turkish-Bulgarian border at Kapıkule. Ricky stopped at the Turkish border post and took the car papers from the glove compartment into the office.

"Pasaport!" the Customs officer demanded. Ricky hauled up his neck pouch and handed over his US passport. The officer examined the passport, thumbing through page after page.

"No goot," the Customs officer said. "Car not you!" He summoned another officer and said something to him in Turkish.

"Car not write in passport. Your name not car owner name. *Carnet de passage* end. You must pay duty import tax for car, t'ousan dollar."

"A thousand dollars?" Ricky went ballistic. "For that piece of shit? It's hardly worth… We're not paying anything!"

"No! Car now import in Turkey. Duty import tax t'ousan dollar."

Ricky and the two Customs officers glared at one another in silence for a tense minute. The Customs officer looked down, took a pen and slip of paper.

"Bulgarya….no! Drive car, go Gümrük Edirne, Custom office," the officer said, writing down an address. "Office tell you."

Ricky went out to the Love Bus and told them.

"Shit!" Denise raged. "Let's just shoot across the border when they're not looking!"

"Denise," Ricky said, *"shoot* is the operative term! Look at those machine guns! They have lots more in Bulgaristan! You're gonna mess with Turkish border guards? Or Bulgarian? They're always looking! Shoot? No way! Not with me in the van."

"What about hitchhiking?" Odie suggested.

"Through those weird communist countries?" Denise responded. "I don't think so! Maybe in Italy or France, but not here."

"Listen," Ricky said, "we'll go into Edirne and see what we can do. Maybe a bribe or something."

"Perhaps we can sell the car and take a train?" Julien asked.

"Trains cost money, Julien," Denise spat. "What would we get for this piece of shit? Fifty bucks? We didn't pay anything for it, it's not even officially ours, and its papers are expired. All we could do with it is go back where we've already been. They want us to pay a thousand bucks for it! It's just a huge liability."

"So then…are we grounded here?" Odie wondered.

"Tomorrow we go to this office and see what the situation is," Ricky said, and swung into the driver's seat.

He forgot to tell Odie to jiggle the spark plug wires, but the motor started anyway.

Part Four

November 14, 1968

55

Anger

The Love Bus crew slept late. After they woke up in Edirne's cheapest hotel, they found the breakfast room, sipped tea, and looked glum. Only Flora was smiling.

Flora was painting her T-shirt: "Today is *not* the first day of the rest of your life—that's *tomorrow!*"

"Leave all your stuff here," Ricky said. "They might impound the van."

"Impound?" Julien asked. "What is impound?"

"It means they take the van away from us and keep it until we pay the import tax on it."

"Then we're really grounded!" Odie grumbled.

They finished their breakfast and, glum, climbed into the Love Bus. Ricky drove into town and showed the slip of paper bearing the address to three people one after another. He finally found the Customs office up the hill right across the street from the Selimiye Mosque.

Gümrük it read on the office sign. He parked across the street, next to the mosque.

"Wow! That's a big mosque!" Flora said. "I wanna go see it."

"Me also," Julien said.

They got out.

Ricky went into the Customs office, ready to do battle.

* * *

With the help of Jim and James, Bruce had finally persuaded Sarah to try for a reconciliation. Thursday, November 14th, was a teacher training day for the Turkish faculty at the school, but not for PCVs, so it was a free day for her. Come to Edirne, Bruce said in his letter. We'll ask Nur Baba for advice. He can see our destiny.

But would she come?

Thursday morning, Bruce knew this could be one of the most important days of his life. He would catch an early bus to Edirne to be there all day. On the way to the grocery shop for his breakfast eggs, he saw Marina running toward him.

"Marina...."

"Bruce, *listen!*" she said. "You must trust me! Don't ask, I can't tell you, but you *must* take this envelope and the one I gave you earlier to Dave Coughlin at the American Consulate *right now*. Take a taxi from the end of the street. Don't let anything stop you! I've left a message. They're expecting them."

She turned to go, but then turned back and gave him a fast, hard kiss and stared in his eyes like a stab. Bruce saw tears and terror in hers.

"Goodbye, Bruce," she said.

She turned, ran, and was gone.

He did as she ordered: returned quickly to his apartment, grabbed the other envelope and a few things for the trip to Edirne, took a taxi to the consulate and handed the envelopes to the Marine guard, then took a taxi to the bus station. An Edirne bus was just leaving.

He'd ask Marina what all this was about later.

Or was that really "Goodbye?"

Ahmet Kamanbay, sitting at his desk sipping his first Turkish coffee of the morning, listened to the informer.

Halepli was using the drug export channel to smuggle weapons from Bulgaria into Turkey. The informer, an employee of Kamanbay's, didn't know the exact details, but she confirmed that the hearse crossing the border from Bulgaria to Turkey was carrying small arms. She had heard it from the wife of a relative who was sympathetic to revolutionary causes.

Kamanbay looked at the informer calmly.

"Teşekkür ederim," he said. Thank you. He told her that she would be kept safe and rewarded for her loyalty. She left his office.

He opened his desk drawer. Beneath his pistol was a piece of paper. He glanced at the shipment dates on it. Shipment to Bulgaria November 13, return to Edirne November 14. Today!

The hearse would arrive mid-afternoon. He lifted the handset of his telephone. He would be there with a team to welcome the hearse and to confirm what the informer had told him. If true, he would deal with Halepli quickly.

"Eşek oğul eşek!" That bastard!

Devin Halepli was furious. The fools were sneaking cigarettes into Turkey along with the weapons smuggling for which the Bulgarians paid him so richly. Somebody—that Bulgarian-Turkish driver of the hearse, Oğuz?—was jeopardizing both Ahmet Kamanbay's priceless drug export channel and Halepli's own lucrative secret small-arms import channel just to smuggle in fake cigarettes worth a few thousand liras!

If Kamanbay found out about the cigarette smuggling, he would be angry. He would blame Halepli for sloppy oversight, and he would demand extreme measures from Halepli to deal with the cigarette idiots. But if Kamanbay found out that Halepli had his own private weapons-smuggling business piggybacking on the drug export business, Kamanbay would send his hit-men and Halepli would have to flee for his life—immediately.

His anger increased, mixed with dread. He would get to the bottom of this. He would go to Edirne himself immediately and teach the cigarette fools a lesson. Whoever was in charge of this nonsense would die. Whoever else was involved would learn their lesson, the last lesson they would ever learn. But he must be prepared for the worst. Maybe Kamanbay had already heard about the cigarettes and guns, or would find out before Halepli could get to Edirne, crush the fools, and get rid of the evidence.

He wondered if he could take Astrid with him. He would miss her if he didn't. He took his passport and Astrid's from a drawer, stuffed wads of hundred-dollar bills and an extra pistol into his suitcase with his clothes, made a phone call to Bulut, then called for his driver.

* * *

"Go in car!" Bulut shouted at Astrid. He grabbed her arm.

"Don't touch me!" She was strong, but he was stronger, and Halim, the porter, was standing right there to help him. Seething with anger, she got in the back seat of the Mercedes.

"Where are we going?"

"To Mr Halepli. He tell."

I don't want to go to Mr Halepli, Astrid thought. I never want to see him again! He tricked me. He lured me into a trap with his jokes and his flashy style, with the chauffeured Mercedes and luxury apartment. He acted like he wanted a colleague, then a "girlfriend," but he really wanted a harem concubine! Yes, it was romantic at first. He was a good lover, but he is married, with children, and he is a cruel, brutal man! He took my passport and kept it, he had his guards —Bulut, Halim, Ali—to guard me, to never let me out of their sight.

She began to fear that this might be her last ride anywhere. Did he suspect that she knew she was a prisoner and did not want to be his mistress? Had he decided to "dispose" of her? She was pretty sure that his *real* business was not Club Casablanca, but…drugs! Drug dealers kill people. Would she be next?

She must find out.

"Bulut Bey, I am sorry that I was difficult back there. I was worrying about other things. I am not myself today. I hope you will not mention it to Devin Bey."

"I wonder why we are driving so far," Astrid added. "This is a long trip!"

Bulut said nothing.

"Are we going to a special place? Devin Bey likes to surprise me."

"Maybe he take you to holiday, Aslı Hanım."

"On holiday? A trip? But we passed the airport long ago."

"This car trip," Bulut said.

"Oh, wonderful!" She smiled into the rear view mirror. I will be all sweetness until I find out what they have planned. I must wait for the moment when I can escape.

56

Love...or Not

Bruce was sitting with Nur Baba in his shop when Sarah walked in. She glanced at him, then looked down. He looked at her, waiting, hoping for recognition. She gave none.

Nur Baba could tell something was wrong. This saddened him. He knew they were meant for each other, but for some reason there was now a cloud over their future. It must be removed. They must be reconciled!

"Good morning, Sarah Hanım!" he said gaily. "I am delighted that you both could visit today! I humbly hope that our time together will be worth the trouble you have experienced to come here."

The young Americans stood silently, looking at him, not at one another.

"Ahem...I have spoken with the *müezzin* and he has given us permission to mount to the *müezzin mahfili*, the platform in the center of the mosque. Let us meet in the Selimiye at the fountain beneath the *mahfil* at 14.00. We will then go up the stairs together."

Sarah left the shop with Bruce behind her.

"Sarah..." Bruce called.

She kept walking. He caught up to her.

"Sarah! Let me explain!"

She looked at him.

"Explain what? There's nothing to explain. I understand!"

"But you don't! I swear! Please! Let's sit down and talk."

Sarah kept walking. They were out of the arasta now and walking down the hill into the city.

"Give me five minutes!" Bruce pleaded.

Sarah stared at him grimly.

"Five minutes!" she said. "Okay, but I don't want to see you any more than that. I don't want to see you at all! I don't know why I came today! I guess I couldn't stand the thought of disappointing Nur Baba. I will stay for his sake. I'm here for him, not you!"

She paused.

"I don't want him to know that…that we're not…"

"Know?! He can read our faces! He knows already! We're standing in there not saying a word, not looking at one another. He knows! I want to talk to you so we can go into the Selimiye, sit with him, and he will know that I love you and that there's no longer any misunderstanding between us."

"Misunderstanding?! I know what I heard!"

"Yes. You heard. But what you heard is not what matters."

"It matters to *ME!*" she shouted at him. "It matters a *lot!* It *totally* matters!"

Bruce guided her into a tea garden and they sat down. Bruce signaled the waiter for two teas.

"That woman, Marina, is my neighbor. I met her in the grocery shop. She helped me buy something. She took an interest in me. She initiated it. You and I were not…well, we were not an *item* when she took an interest. I guess I was flattered, an older woman, accomplished, multilingual, taking an interest in me. I was going to tell her about you, but…"

"*But what?!*" Sarah exploded. "This is the same bullshit every man tells a woman every time he cheats on her! 'Oh, I was going to tell her!' 'Oh, I was going to tell *you.*' 'Oh, those other girls don't mean anything to me!' 'Oh, I'm going to divorce my wife and marry you!' It's bullshit, Bruce, bullshit! And you know it!"

"Sarah," Bruce said calmly, "it's not. I love you. Yes, Marina turned my head. I was in a strange country, she was a neighbor, and an attractive, accomplished woman. She came on to me. I should have set her straight…but I didn't know you well then! How did I know I'd fall in love with you?"

Sarah softened. "You should have," she said in a gentler voice.

"You bet I should have!" Bruce said in return. "I knew after our picnic on Büyükada, but—Sarah! Men are stupid! *I'm* stupid! Had I done a reality check then, I would have realized I loved you and that I *had* to tell her. I just didn't get the chance to tell her. I should have been decisive."

"I am now!" he went on, his voice rising. "Sarah! Tell me what I have to do to get you back. I'll do it! I don't care what it is. Just tell me! Do you even want me?"

That got her. She knew she wanted him. That was not the question. The question was… could she believe him? Or would he break her heart?

She made her decision but she didn't look at him.

Head down, speaking calmly to her tea glass, she said, "We will go with Nur Baba and experience the Selimiye again. We'll sit together. Afterwards, I think we'll know what we should do."

At the door of the mosque, Sarah put on her headscarf, they removed their shoes and walked into the prayer hall together. Nur Baba examined their faces. There was reason for hope.

He smiled at them. They smiled in return. Their smiles added up to a much more felicitous formula. Or was he misinterpreting, letting his heart see instead of his eyes?

"Please come with me," he said and walked around to the steps leading up to the müezzin's platform.

The platform was covered in rich Turkish carpets. Nur Baba sat facing the prayer niche.

"Bruce, please sit on my right. Sarah, please sit there, on my left. Over a little more this way, closer to Bruce. The proportions, the distances, must be correct."

"I will say a prayer for your well-being," Nur Baba told them. "Nothing is required of you. Rather, it is an opportunity for you to look into your hearts, to look deeply, and to see your destiny. The sacred place in which we sit may help us, but the Selimiye alone is just a collection of stones. It is not the stones that make the Selimiye what it is. Stone is nothing by itself! It is the genius, the love, the spirit, the gifts of God to us, that have transformed it from stone to a place where we can experience the peace of God."

Nur Baba held his arms in front of him, palms up, raised his eyes to heaven and began to chant. Bruce could understand nothing of the words, and Sarah just a little, but the tone of his voice, its passion and music, its pleading and exultation, told them everything they needed to know. Then he was silent. Wiping his hands to his face, he lowered his arms and closed his eyes in meditation.

Bruce closed his eyes. His brain was a chaos of shouts, fears, bad dreams, silent noises, flashes of light. He concentrated on the silence in the sacred space and that calmed him. His mind slowed down and began a disordered but rough chronology of the last months: graduate school, war protests, unhappiness, the flight to Turkey, Mustafa's café, the people he met there, and finally Sarah. Forget the tension, he thought. She's sitting right next to me now. I truly believe I will have her next to me the rest of my life.

Peace came to him.

The silence in the vast space was somehow the sweetest music. It was not total. Water from the fountain beneath the platform made soft, jewel-like sounds as it fell. A faint, indistinct low hum came from the city outside. Sarah, Bruce thought. Sarah....

Sarah sat and thought. Her outburst at Bruce, her telling him off, had helped. Her anger was past. Anger is not good, she thought. Anger doesn't help, it harms. Defeat the anger! Concentrate on love. She thought of Bruce. She had never loved anyone like she loved Bruce. She didn't know why, but she didn't have to know. The love was enough. Love is not to be understood, it is to be treasured. I love him, she knew. I hope we can be together. With that, her mind stopped moving. It was blank. The peace of the Selimiye had claimed her. It was bliss not to worry, not to feel tension or bitterness. Bliss.

Nur Baba raised his head, opened his eyes and looked at Bruce and Sarah. He examined their faces. Yes! There it was! This was their destiny.

It was time. He moved slightly. They opened their eyes. Their faces were completely at rest, and so beautiful! He looked at each in turn. Long, benign looks, communicating with his eyes. Then he smiled. They smiled in return.

He began to rise.

They stood with him and followed him silently down the steps of the platform and toward the main door.

57

The Race

November 14, 13:00. Oğuz drove the hearse along the highway from Svilengrad toward the Turkish border. Yergat sat beside him. They rehearsed the mission.

"At the border," Oğuz said, "the Bulgarian Immigration officers will make a show of examining our passports, papers and cargo, but they have been instructed not to detain us. You have your new passport and new name. Our friends at the border will be paid later in cartons of *real* Winstons and Marlboros. The fakes only go to the Turks in Istanbul!" he laughed.

"On the Turkish side, I have promised the same cigarette *bakshish* to the Turkish officers," Oğuz smiled. "They will get the real cigarettes as well, and we will have no problems."

"The Customs declaration for the coffin bears the name of a Bulgarian Turk who died in Bulgaria but who wants to be buried next to his relatives in Edirne—our usual story. The Bulgarian consulate has made the necessary official arrangements for the import of the corpse, for the funeral at the Selimiye, and for the 'burial,'" Oğuz said. "Of course, the funeral will never take place—nobody cares about an old, dead Bulgarian Turk nobody knew—and the 'burial' is in a shop of the Selimiye arasta, where the cigarettes are hidden and we receive our pay."

"But this time it's a different shop, and we are to leave the cigarettes in a different place. I'm sure you remember," Yergat reminded him.

"Of course! I understand. I'm glad we're not transporting

hundreds of weapons this time. That always makes me nervous," Oğuz admitted. "Getting caught with cigarettes means I'm a smuggler," Oğuz went on. "This is not a big problem. Getting caught by Turkish Customs with guns means I'm a traitor."

Yergat smiled. Oğuz, the fool, really believes that this trip is like all the others—a load of fake cigarettes with a payoff of a handful of dollars—probably Bulgarian counterfeit dollars!—from a shop owner in the arasta. However, this time the delivery is unique. Oğuz was worried about being discovered shipping handguns? If he only knew what this weapon will do! And the delivery will be to a different shop—a bookshop. Oğuz will remain with the shipment whether he wants to or not, his payoff will be the forty virgins in heaven, the funeral will be that of the Selimiye itself, and the whole world will notice! It is a brilliant plan. I will get my revenge at last!

"When we reach the Selimiye, we are taking the cargo to a different shop, but we must park the hearse in the usual place for the delivery. This is what we have arranged with our contacts so as not to cause any suspicion. It must be done, nothing must be changed, or the channel for shipments may be compromised."

They drove on. The Bulgarian border post at Kapitan Andreevo was only a few kilometers ahead.

"Where's Ralph?" Dave nearly shouted as he emerged from his office. He had just seen the report on the new documents that had been given to the Marine guard.

"He said he was going to the Hippodrome to check on something," a staffer answered.

"Is there a car available?"

"One should be available in about 15 minutes."

"Keep it here for me. I'll need it all day."

Dave rushed out of the consulate, turned left and sprinted to the taxi rank in front of the Pera Palas Oteli.

"Sultan Ahmet," he said loudly to the driver. *"Çabuk ol!"*

The driver pressed on the accelerator and sped down Meşrutiyet Caddesi, across the Atatürk Bridge, turned left along the shore of the Golden Horn and sped to the Hippodrome.

Dave saw Ralph at the far end next to a silver VW microbus.

"Ralph, we've got to get to Edirne *now*. I'll explain on the way. A car's waiting at the consulate."

"I can get you there faster, and we can leave immediately," the microbus's driver said.

"He can," Ralph said. "I'll explain that later, too."

Dave and Ralph climbed into the back of Wolfgang's VW van.

"All I can tell you now is that it's a matter of life and death," Dave told Wolfgang.

"Good enough for me," Wolfgang answered.

Wolfgang used the horn liberally as he descended the hill to the Sea of Marmara shore, turned right and shot westward along the seaside highway. Soon the city walls were behind them and they were on the D100 highway toward Edirne.

"Wow! This thing *does* move!" Dave said in awe. Ralph explained about the Porsche engine.

"If I didn't know better," Ralph joked to Wolfgang, "I might suspect you'd use this for moving…illegal substances."

"Just carpets," Wolfgang said, but he didn't smile at the joke.

As they raced toward Edirne, Dave told Ralph what he knew, his voice concealed by the noise from the powerful engine.

"We received intelligence this morning. We don't have all the pieces, but what we do have points to our Sov friends doing something big in Edirne today—we don't know exactly when or where, but we're guessing an explosion near the Selimiye."

Dave did not say what type of explosion. No need to alarm his friend. Either they would live through the day or not. They had to risk it. It was their only chance. Minutes mattered, even seconds.

"Yılmaz's people have been alerted, but…" Dave went on, lowering his voice even more, "besides the drug-smuggling route, there may be top secret material involved, so what we can tell them now is limited."

Half way to Edirne the silver VW shot past a police cruiser idling by the highway.

"*Scheiss!*" Wolfgang swore. He looked in the rearview mirror and saw the cruiser pull onto the highway and accelerate. "*Polizei,*" he said. "Police. Behind us."

Dave and Ralph looked through the back windows of the van and saw the cruiser.

"Look," Dave said to Wolfgang. "This is too important! You'll understand later, but now you've got to lose them."

"Easy!" Wolfgang said, tromped on the gas, and the van shot away from the cruiser.

"But what if they radio ahead to others?" Ralph asked.

Wolfgang glanced at Ralph, then returned his eyes to the road.

"I think I can take care of it," he said.

His face was grim. Well, there goes my dream of riches, he thought. Maybe it's just as well.

He eased back on the accelerator until the cruiser was gaining on them. Soon it was close behind, lights flashing, siren blaring.

Wolfgang reached under the dashboard and pulled the heater control knob all the way out. The doors on the heater boxes underneath opened and a cloud of white dust spewed from the back of the speeding van, spreading over the cruiser and through its air intakes. A few minutes later the cruiser began to slow, drop back, and wobble erratically on the road. Then it pulled off the road and stopped.

"What did you do? What *was* that?" Ralph asked.

"Secret German smokescreen!" Wolfgang laughed. "Another special adaptation!"

The guys in the cruiser are feeling pretty good right now, Wolfgang thought, ... at the cost to me of my hundred-thousand-dollar dream.

They all turned forward again to watch the road ahead as the van careened toward Edirne. As they approached the foot of the Selimiye hill, Dave told Ralph about the bomb just before Wolfgang slammed on the brakes in terror.

58

Apocalypse

Denise and Odie sat in the back of the Love Bus. Through the windows of the Customs office across the street, they saw Ricky arguing with the officers.

Denise fidgeted. Odie could tell she was furious. Now that they weren't going to Kathmandu, her mind was already racing ahead to Europe and home. But they were trapped here.

Bang bang bang bang!

Someone was banging on the side of the Love Bus. They looked up and saw a man peering in. Odie opened the side door.

"*Çık buradan!*" he yelled at them and waved his arm. "*Çık! Çık!*"

"What's he want?" Odie asked.

"*Çık hemen!*" he said, and kicked the van hard, denting the door.

"He wants us to move the van," Denise said. "He wants to park where we're parked. He thinks he owns this spot."

She glared at him and started to get out. Odie knew what might happen. He grabbed her and pulled her back in.

"Denise, take it easy. We don't need trouble. Let's just move the van."

Denise glared at him fiercely, went limp for a moment, then looked up and said, "Okay, Odie, I'll move it."

She climbed out the side door, walked around to the driver's door and climbed into the driver's seat.

Looking straight ahead she said "Odie. Get out of the van."

"Denise…"

"Get out!" she shouted.

"Denise, I…"

"GET! OUT!!"

Odie scrambled out.

Denise slowly pulled the van away from the stone wall. The man who had yelled at them walked back to his long, odd-looking black vehicle, got back in with another man, and slowly pulled it into the space where the van had been parked.

Odie looked at the unusual vehicle. It was larger than an American station wagon. Glass windows in the rear were etched with decorations, something ceremonial. On top was a small dome topped by a little crescent. Inside, in the back, through the glass, he could see a long wooden box, like a coffin.

Both men got out of the hearse, walked to the back, and began to open the rear door.

Denise turned and maneuvered the Love Bus until it was perpendicular to the hearse, facing away from it, about ten yards away. She took a deep breath, tromped on the clutch, jammed the gearshift into reverse, clicked open the driver's side door and braced herself.

"DICKHEADS!"

She stomped on the accelerator and popped the clutch.

The van shot backwards and smashed full force into the side of the hearse, pinning it against the stone wall. Denise was slammed back in the driver's seat by the impact. It knocked the breath out of her, but in fifteen seconds she recovered, swung open the driver's door, climbed out unsteadily and started to walk toward the Customs office.

Odie recovered from shock and ran toward her.

The impact drove the metal step on the side of the hearse into the engine compartment of the VW, where it ruptured the failing fuel pump which spurted gas into the engine compartment. At the same moment, the damaged ignition coil discharged 10,000 volts into the frayed spark wires.

* * *

"WHAT WAS *THAT?*" Flora shouted. "Oh wow! Look!" She and Julien looked to their left to see a giant ball of flame rise from the side of the mosque, right from where they had just been. In a second, the heat was intense.

"Mon dieu!" Julien shouted. *"Nos amis!"*

At the door of the Selimiye, Nur Baba looked at the flames in horror.

Bruce and Sarah stood transfixed, open-mouthed, staring at the inferno.

Dave Coughlin and Ralph Graves came running up the hill toward the explosion. They ran to the front of the Customs office.

"That's gas," Ralph said to Dave.

They heard sirens.

"Yes," Dave said. "Gas. The device wasn't triggered."

"Will the heat affect it? Is it gonna blow?"

"No. Heat won't do it," Dave said. "In fact, I'm sure all the weapon's circuit boards are now fried. Melted. It'll never blow." He smiled. "Ralph," he said grimly, "if heat would do it, none of us would be here now. Neither would the Selimiye."

"Denise!"

Ricky and Odie saw her running toward the Customs office. Her hair was on fire. Odie caught up to her, tore off his jacket and threw it over her head to smother the flames.

"Denise! What happened? Are you all right?"

"Dickheads!" she yelled and started to sob. Her scalp was stinging, her ears ringing. She put her hands up to her aching head. Nothing. Her nimbus of frizzy hair was gone. All of it.

"Are you all right?"

She sobbed for a moment, then took a deep breath and let it out.

'Yeah, sure, I think I'm okay. Jesus! Look at that!"

They shielded their faces with their arms from the blast of heat. The Customs officers came running out, but the heat was so intense they all retreated into the office.

Just then the heat and flames from the VW reached the fuel tank of the hearse. The second explosion was even louder, the fireball enormous. The windows in the Customs office blasted inwards in a blizzard of glass shards.

The vehicles burned furiously, giving off a strong odor of gasoline and burning automobile with a faint top note of 500,000 freshly-lit cigarettes.

The Customs officers got up from the floor. They looked at Ricky, then at Denise—bald, her scalp black.

Her mind raced. She looked at Ricky.

"I'm not used to that shift pattern," she said. "I went backwards instead of forwards."

She lowered her head and smiled to herself.

Ricky looked at her.

"Solved two problems at once," she murmured.

Ahmet Kamanbay's limousine had pulled up to the Customs office. He got out. His driver remained in the huge car. His bodyguards began to get out.

Three police cruisers rushed up and squealed to a stop in front of the Customs office. Six officers got out. Just behind them came a command car. In the distance, more sirens.

Two fire engines roared up the hill. Before they stopped rolling their crews were on the ground shooting fire-retardant foam at the inferno.

A crowd gathered, mouths open, staring at the two burning vehicles. The gasoline was soon smothered or gone, and the flames began to die.

Ralph surveyed the crowd and spotted Danny. He was wearing a hat and Turkish clothing, but still he couldn't be mistaken for a Turk.

"There's our old friend," he murmured to Dave, who turned his eyes to Danny. "And there's his old boss."

Spotting Kamanbay, Ralph and Dave walked over to the group of police officers. Ralph flashed his badge wallet, spoke to the commander and mentioned Director Yılmaz. The commander looked toward Kamanbay, then toward Danny, and nodded. He barked an order and the cops moved toward the drug lord and Danny.

Over by the mosque, Dave noticed police officers holding two men whom he had seen running from the fire when everyone else stopped to stare.

Farther down the hill, Devin Halepli's driver saw the flames and Kamanbay's limo, then Kamanbay, then the police moving toward him.

"What do we do?" he asked his boss.

"Get out of the car!" Halepli shouted.

The driver scrambled out. Halepli leapt out of the back seat and ran around to the driver's seat, slamming the door. He gunned the engine, screeched around in a 180-degree turn and shot off down the hill.

At the bottom of the hill, a bus was stopped in the middle of the intersection, blocking his way, as the driver and passengers gaped at the fire. Honking the horn furiously, Halepli finally got the driver to pull ahead.

He had his passport. Bulgaria was only minutes away. His friends there would take care of him. He calculated that he needed only 15 minutes to get across the border.

The bus was gone. As he stepped on the accelerator, Halepli stared across the intersection. A tall blonde woman stood on the far side, perfectly still, looking straight at him, sighting along the barrel of a pistol.

She squeezed the trigger.

59

The New Love Bus

The day following the explosion they were all back at the Customs office for the police report.

Across the street, the burnt-out Love Bus had been towed away. The burnt hulk of the hearse, under police guard, was still parked by the mosque.

A black car with official Turkish government license plates pulled up near the hearse. Two men in dark suits emerged from the back seat. Close behind their car came a grey, late-model Chevrolet panel truck. The men in suits spoke with the policemen guarding the hearse, who then stepped aside. Four men in thick coveralls, helmets and work gloves got out of the Chevy van carrying a variety of tools and a large rectangular metal box. They removed what was left of the charred coffin from the hearse, placed it in the metal box, slid the box into the back of the Chevy and drove away with the Turkish government car following.

Wolfgang was examining Ahmet Kamanbay's limousine which was parked out front. The look on his face was of a man who had dined on gruel for a decade but who was now confronted with a royal banquet at the Château de Versailles.

Dave Coughlin walked over to him.

"Pretty nice, eh?"

"Mercedes-Benz 600 Pullman, 5.5 meters long, single overhead cam, fuel-injected 6.3-liter V-8 engine, 4-speed automatic transmission, and a hydraulic pressure system to power the automatic windows, seats, sun-roof, trunk lid and auto-closing doors," Wolfie said, salivating. "The engine alone is over three times as big and powerful as the one in my Type 2!"

"The ride of kings, princes, presidents, the pope, and the more discerning rock stars," Dave mused.

"Price when new: a hundred thousand Deutsche marks!" Wolfie exclaimed.

They gazed at the gleaming car in admiration.

"Wait, I've got an idea," Dave said.

Dave went into the Customs office, took the director aside and spoke to him in Turkish. He pointed to the pack of Marlboro cigarettes on the director's desk. The director frowned and glared at him. Dave pointed out the window toward the parked cars, the director followed his gesture, and they talked some more. Finally the director scowled, nodded, opened his desk and took out two official forms.

Ricky, Flora, Julien, Denise and Odie were standing and talking quietly outside the Customs office. Denise was wearing a brightly-colored Turkish scarf wrapped around her head like a turban. Flora's T-shirt bore a melted Love Bus and "You can't undo something you couldn't do at first."

They all still looked dazed.

The Customs director got up from his desk with the official forms and walked outside with Dave following.

"This is Director Menemen, Turkish Customs," Dave said to the hippies. "Now that you've given your report, you're free to go."

Dave broke into a broad grin.

"I hope you like your new ride."

"New ride?" Ricky asked.

"Over there," Dave pointed.

"Where?"

"There! That!"

"I don't…"

Dave walked over to Ahmet Kamanbay's limo and thumped his hand on the roof.

"Right here!

"But…what the…?"

"Property confiscated from a drug dealer! Impounded by Turkish Customs!" Dave waved his hand at the director and smiled. "Director Menemen wants this symbol of the pernicious drug trade out of his district and out of the country *now!* He has authorized a disposal auction to be held immediately! Do I hear one lira?"

The hippies stood petrified.

"Ricky! Give him a lira!" Denise shouted.

Ricky stared at her dumbfounded, then fished in his pocket.

"All I have is a two-and-a-half."

"That'll do! Sold! For *iki-buçuk!*"

Ricky gave the coin to Dave. Dave gave the coin to Director Menemen, who smiled wanly and gave the papers to Ricky.

Flora looked at the long, shiny car in wonder.

"It costs the same as a bottle of Guzzle Marmara!"

"Fill in your name and it's yours," Dave told Ricky. "One of the papers is the title, the other is a *Carnet de Passage*. It will get you through borders all the way to Paris, or London, or the Isle of Skye for that matter. Wherever you want. Sell the car when you get there and you'll have plenty of money for plane tickets home—first class! —and lots left over."

"If you ever need a chauffeur, call on me!" Wolfgang said.

"By the way," Dave added smiling, "it's full of gas."

They all looked at Denise.

Epilogue

Two weeks later, Bruce was in Dave's office at the US consulate for a post-mortem.

"Good! You're here," Dave said as Bruce walked in. "Let's have some çay!"

Dave ordered it via the intercom.

The tea was brought in the traditional tulip-shaped glasses. Tinkalinkalinkalink as they stirred sugar in with tiny spoons.

"You recovered from all the excitement yet?" Dave asked.

"You were the one in the worst of it," Bruce answered.

They went through the day's events.

"By the way, the report is in on Halepli's death. He was killed when his car crashed into a stone wall," Dave said. "In Edirne. His driver gave testimony. Apparently Halepli saw the explosion, figured out what was going on, took the wheel and tried to get away to Bulgaria. At the bottom of the hill he hit the wall head-on. It took hours to extract what was left of him from the wreck."

"What about Danny?" Bruce asked. "You had him arrested!"

"Director Yılmaz and I had an agreement," Ralph said. "I don't like to see an American kid go to prison, but Danny knows all about Kamanbay's organization. He can—he *has*—provided Director Yılmaz with most of the information they need to put Kamanbay and his pals away forever. Danny may get a light sentence and a nicer prison because of his cooperation. Maybe they'll even let him out on appeal knowing he'll head straight for the Posta train and Greece. Then he's out of their hair, and ours, and good riddance."

Bruce thought of Marina, the last time he had seen her, and the terrified expression on her face.

"I hope Marina's not in trouble," Bruce said.

"The person you know as Marina is one of us," Dave said, "and did excellent work here."

He gave Bruce a look.

"We won't see that person here again. Promotion, new identity, new post. That person will be fine. You will now forget, forever, that you two ever met."

Bruce thought of that night at Heaven's Garden, now so poignant.

"'That person?'" Bruce said. "Why are you saying…"

They stared at one another.

December 20th. The Consul-General's holiday party. Bruce walked through the dark, chill, wet streets of Istanbul redolent with the sweet-acrid smell of burning lignite coal. The streets were busier than normal with people rushing here and there, carrying shopping bags. Shopkeepers were festooning their shops with lights and decorations.

Christmas? In a Muslim country?

Inside the brightly-lit consular mansion Bruce removed his raincoat, showed his invitation to the Marine guard, and made his way into the grand salon.

"Welcome, Bruce!" the Consul-General greeted him. "Jane, this is the young man I mentioned to you. Bruce Harmone, my wife Jane."

"A pleasure to meet you!" Jane said.

After the greetings, Bruce spotted Dave Coughlin and made his way through the crowd to his side.

"Ready for the holiday?" Dave asked.

"Sure, but do they celebrate Christmas in a Muslim county?"

"I'm not talking about Christmas. I'm talking about *Şeker Bayramı,* the three-day holiday after Ramadan. It starts tonight. Big celebrations."

"Oh, yeah, I remember. End of Ramadan. Tonight?"

"We're getting a head start on the celebration," Dave smiled.

Over Dave's shoulder, Bruce saw Wolfgang. Seeing Bruce, Wolfgang strolled over.

"Wolfgang! How are you? What are you doing here?"

"Our friend Wolfie was a big help," Dave said. "He and that race-car microbus of his. We owe him."

"Glad to help!" Wolfgang said.

Interviewing him after the incident in Edirne, Dave discovered that Wolfgang had suspected there was a nuclear weapon involved. He was told never to mention his suspicion again.

"We've been in touch with friends in West Germany. Told them about Wolfie. They're eager to buy his carpets in quantity. He could open his own shop."

"It's a big opportunity for me," Wolfgang said smiling. "It could make my carpet business ten times bigger…but with such a load, my Type 2 won't be able to outrun the cops!"

They all laughed.

"Look," Dave said to Bruce, "here come some friends of yours."

Bruce turned in the direction of Dave's gaze and saw Ralph Graves and Astrid Hugsted walking toward them.

"Astrid!"

"Hi, Bruce!"

She walked up to Bruce and gave him a kiss on the cheek. Ralph shook Bruce's hand and smiled broadly.

"Thanks again for your help, Bruce," Ralph said. "Close call, but good results."

Bruce looked at Astrid, gorgeous as ever. She smiled at him but said nothing. She had a twinkle in her eye. Something was up.

She held up her left hand. A diamond sparkled on her ring finger. She gave him a goofy look of comical surprise.

"Thought I'd never get hooked," Ralph said. "Then I met her."

He winked at Bruce.

"We're kind of in the same line of work."

Christmas morning. The sun was rising over Asia, casting a streak of gold across the dark, rustling waters of the Bosphorus.

Sarah and Bruce were in their bathrobes, sipping tea and nibbling pastries from the Park Hotel's renowned pastry shop, gazing at the Bosphorus. It was chill and damp outside, but warm and cozy in Bruce's tiny apartment.

It had been a wonderful night.

"School is out for winter break in two weeks," Sarah said.

"And after that?"

"After that? Before that! I don't have to live in Kadıköy for exams. I can commute. But I don't know what the Peace Corps will say—an unmarried female Volunteer living with a male non-Volunteer. I'm not sure it's in the rule book one way or another."

She sipped her tea.

Bruce smiled at her.

"Who says 'unmarried'?"

The Immigration officer stared at Flora's T-shirt: a caricature self-portrait and "Artsy! Even on Mondays!"

He shrugged his shoulders and handed them back their passports. They got in the car.

"We made it!" Denise said. "Back in France!"

"Home to Paris!" Julien cheered.

"But wait,—we're not going to Paris, are we?" Flora wondered.

"Not going to Paris?" Odie asked, confused.

"Of course we're going to Paris!" Julien said. "Why not?"

"But..." Flora said, "Isn't Paris the capital?"

"Flora, you're wonderful!" Ricky shouted.

He tromped on the gas pedal and the huge car surged forward, tires squealing, roaring westward down the highway toward the City of Light.

Acknowledgements

Here it is, short, sweet, and what a treat: **Jane**.

Thanks also to the Concord Free Public Library and its genial staff for providing a comfortable atmosphere for research and writing.

Istanbul 1968

In June 1968 I moved from Izmir to Istanbul—the Istanbul described in these pages, the city so well portrayed by Orhan Pamuk in his wonderful memoir *Istanbul, Memories and the City*. I had been teaching English near Izmir, but my new Peace Corps project was to write a travel guide, *Turkey on $5 a Day*.

At that time, the *Orient Express* was still the thriftiest way to travel from Western Europe to the Bosphorus, though few tourists did so; the US Consulate-General was still housed in the opulent Palazzo Corpi in Beyoğlu (now an exclusive club-hotel); the famous author James Baldwin still spent time writing and communing with friends (including some of mine) in Istanbul; the *Cennet Bahçesi* (Heaven's Garden) was a real restaurant and tea garden—a favorite of Baldwin's (it's now a private club); and one could live fairly well in the city for US$100 a month.

The telephones were unreliable, the electricity (120 volts in Beyoğlu, 240 volts in the rest of Turkey) went off from time to time, the water was rationed in the summer months so one learned to fill pots—or the bathtub—for use until it began to flow again.

There was no TV, let alone mobile phones or the Internet.

But the people were friendly, the fish was always fresh (and cheap!), and it was virtually impossible to encounter a bad meal even in the simplest eateries.

Since then, Turkey has changed greatly, mostly for the better, with improved communication, transportation, education, and health care. Its monumental buildings have been preserved and restored, and tourist services have developed to excellent world-class standards, making it one of the top travel destinations in the world. The Ipek Palas Oteli, which was drab in 1968, now glitters.

But I miss the dear old men sitting in the warm sun by the mosque, chatting with one another or sharing silence because they already know what their lifelong friends are thinking; the taxi drivers who would share their philosophy of life with you on any journey over 10 minutes long; the little charcoal grills set out on the sidewalk in front of köfte shops, heating for the lunchtime crowds, and then, later, the wonderful scent of lamb sizzling on those grills; the ferryboat cruise across the Bosphorus to Haydarpaşa Station, the friendly old-time atmosphere of the station restaurant, and then the comfort of the Ankara Ekspresi sleeper train; how, when you opened a bottle of Tekel beer or Güzel Marmara wine, you never knew if you would savor every sip or pour it down the drain; the way a friend would knock on your door—because no one had phones—and suggest an evening out, and you'd drop everything and go; the way the lira notes were so old and worn—a one-lira note held together by two liras' worth of cellophane tape—and how merchants giving you change would choose the newer, cleaner notes for a foreigner out of Turkish hospitality.

We all change, countries as well as the people in them. It's the memory of the good times that endures.

About the Author

Born and raised in Pennsylvania, Tom joined the US Peace Corps in 1967 to teach English. During his Peace Corps service in Turkey he discovered a fascinating land virtually unknown to most travelers. Tom wrote his first travel guidebook, *Turkey on $5 a Day*, (Frommer's, 1971) as a Peace Corps project.

After graduate school and historical research in the archives of the

Ottoman Empire, Tom devoted himself to writing and photography. His 40 travel guidebooks for Lonely Planet, Frommer's and Berlitz, translated into a dozen languages, covered Belize, Canada, Egypt, England, France, Guatemala, Israel, Mexico, Morocco, New England, Tunisia and Turkey. He now writes and photographs travel websites for his company, Travel Info Exchange, Inc., including TurkeyTravelPlanner.com, FranceTravelPlanner.com, NewEnglandTravelPlanner.com and others, which receive up to seven million annual visitors from 230+ countries.

Tom has served as a Contributing Editor to Budget Travel magazine, has had many articles and photographs published, and has appeared on ABC's Good Morning America, NPR's Talk of the Nation, the Travel Channel and Public Radio International's The Connection. He has given lectures at the American Turkish Council, the Smithsonian Institution, the Cooper-Hewitt National Museum of Design, and other organizations.

If You Enjoyed This Book...

Look for more on tombrosnahan.com. Likes, dislikes, suggestions and corrections are welcome: tom@tombrosnahan.com, or on Facebook (www.facebook.com/tom.brosnahan.77).

Also by Tom Brosnahan

Paris Girls Secret Society, a novel

Three American girls from very different backgrounds arrive in Paris in the autumn of 1967 for a college year abroad: shy but brainy little Charity, from a Boston Brahmin family; gorgeous Amaleen, West Virginia nouveau riche man-killer; politically-committed Josie, from a prominent African-American family near Chicago. Unlikely roommates, their prejudices fall away as they grow into friendship, but May 1968 shatters their cozy world: the Sorbonne explodes in riots as millions of students and workers revolt and France hurtles toward chaos. The girls flee their Latin Quarter apartment, one to explore—and risk death—in the Dordogne's prehistoric caves; one to a lavish life in a Loire chateau where hidden terror lurks; one to dangerous exhilaration on the barricades. Along the way they stumble into love: tender, lustful, perverse, and sublime. In only a month they learn far more about who they are and who they want to be. For the Paris Girls Secret Society, life and love will never be the same. *More at ParisGirlsSecretSociety.com.*

Turkey: Bright Sun, Strong Tea, humorous memoir

So what's it like to be a travel writer? Best job in the world? How do you become one? Does it answer the question of what we are all doing on this planet anyway? *Turkey: Bright Sun, Strong Tea* has the answers.

Tom Brosnahan went to Turkey in 1967 as a US Peace Corps Volunteer, taught English for a year, then had an idea: why not write a guidebook? Turkey was beautiful, friendly, inexpensive and undiscovered. *Turkey on $5 a Day* (Frommer's, 1971) soon became the most popular guide to the country. Later, his *Lonely Planet Turkey* (1985) was its all-time best-seller, and his guidebooks to a dozen other countries sold over four million copies in 10 languages. His TurkeyTravelPlanner.com website has advised many millions of travelers from 230+ countries.

Along the way, Brosnahan starred in a movie, sipped champagne with "fat capitalists" in the sultan's gilded palace, fell in love at a circumcision party, almost got eaten by wolves on the Iranian border, drank endless glasses of strong tea...and discovered the meaning of life. *More at BrightSunStrongTea.com.*

100 Travel Words: Turkish, travelers' language guide

You've seen those silly ads: "Learn a foreign language in 10 days!" Possible? Of course not! It takes *months* or *years* to learn a foreign language. But **anyone can learn 100 words™**—the most useful **100 Travel Words™**. Words like *hello, money, how much, hotel room, hot water, laundry, metro station, ticket, Wifi password,* especially if the 100 words are presented in the best possible way for quick and easy learning.

* * *

I've divided the 100 most useful words for travelers into 10 lessons of about 10 words each. Study one lesson per day in the morning, review it in the evening, and at the end of 10 days you'll have a **100-word vocabulary** of the most useful words a short-trip traveler needs in Turkey. I include a **Pronunciation Guide** and simple lessons on **basic grammar**, if you're interested, and a few other points to help you to cruise through your foreign adventure. *More at 100TravelWords.com.*

The author returning from a Boston-to-Guatemala road trip, 1980.

www.ingramcontent.com/pod-product-compliance
Lightning Source LLC
Chambersburg PA
CBHW021414110726
47901CB00008B/2168